CW01624792

Celebrity SOS: Love Survives

Helen Buckley

Book 2 – Spotlight Series

Books in series:

Strictly on Ice
Celebrity SOS: Love Survives

Choc Lit

Where heroes are like chocolate – irresistible!

Published 2021 by Choc Lit Limited
Penrose House, Crawley Drive, Camberley, Surrey GU15 2AB, UK
www.choc-lit.com

EPUB ISBN: 978-1-78189-494-1
PRINT ISBN: 978-1-78189-495-8

For my boys.

Acknowledgements

A huge thank you first of all to everyone at Choc Lit and Ruby Fiction, for bringing *Celebrity SOS: Love Survives* to publication. Special thanks to the Tasting Panel readers: Deborah Warren, Alan Roberton, Alma Hough, Amy Nordon, Bee Master, Carol Orpwood, Carole Rowsell, Carolina Castro, Donna Morgan, Fran Stevens, Gill Leivers, Hilary Brown, Honor Gilbert, Michele Rollins, Sharon Walsh and Yvonne Greene.

Thank you to my wonderful friends and family who offer their unswerving support and who receive my drafts with both kind words and astute criticism: Mum, Helen Bowen, Amanda Gee, Rachel Raine, Danielle Desanges, and Sarah Duke. Thank you to David Mansfield who patiently corrects my grammar.

I'm delighted to have worked with an excellent Choc Lit editor. Thanks to her comments and those of the Tasting Panel, *Celebrity SOS: Love Survives* is a better and more powerful story, and I'm so grateful for their input.

I'd like to extend a special thank you to Amanda Ward, Wendy Tomsett, and Pip Miller, whose reflections on their personal experiences of meningitis were extremely helpful in writing about Chris' illness.

Finally, thank you to my husband David, for all his suggestions, patience, and support.

Prologue

Katerina stumbled into the force of the wind, leaning almost horizontally into the raging Arctic blizzard. The thick snow slapped her relentlessly across the face, filling her eyes, ears and nose, till she was completely blinded. All she could see were shades of white and grey, all she could hear was the roar of the storm surrounding her. She was completely unprepared for the chilling cold and was unprotected from the storm's onslaught. She had run outside without her gloves or her hat, grabbing only her coat in her desperation to get away.

She couldn't stay a moment longer in that cabin, with the cameras capturing everything, her fellow celebrities gawking and gossiping, and most of all, Finn Drayson's gaze burning into her heart. Even being outside in this unexpected blizzard was better than their stares, their whispers, and having to face the secrets and the lies that had been dredged up and displayed to the world.

Even the rage of an Arctic storm was no match for the turmoil she felt at what had just happened between her and Finn. She would rather be out here, buffeted by the cruel winds, than spend a moment longer in his presence.

She staggered forward, thinking that she heard a shout behind her.

'Kat! Come back!' It was Finn's voice, full of fear and urgency, crying out for her.

She felt the solidity of one of the sheds beneath her hands and leaned against it, the snow still pelting at her. She covered her head with her hands, at a complete loss as to what to do.

She wished she had never come to Alaska, and never seen Finn again.

Chapter One

Eight days earlier

Katerina

'Hold on tight folks – it's going to be a bumpy landing.'

Katerina's fingers tightened around her lap belt as the pilot's voice crackled over her headset. She tried to ignore her stomach lurching and looked out of the window of the helicopter, focusing on the expanse that unfolded beneath her. She wasn't sure if it was the bucking of the helicopter that took her breath away, or if it was the impressive view. She gazed in wonder at the gaunt mountain peaks, swathed in snow and clawing at the leaden sky, towering over the vast ground that spread out below them. Alaska. Endless, wild, compelling.

She was a city girl, a born-and-bred Londoner, usually enchanted by rising spires of steel and glass that never went dark, proud of the frantic bustle of the city and the multitude of people it served, but Alaska was something else. If London made her feel small, a tiny dot in a sea of humanity, Alaska made her feel minuscule. Here, it didn't matter about her fame, her fortune, or her fans. In this wilderness, everyone was vulnerable.

'It's so beautiful, isn't it?' A voice on the headset disturbed her thoughts and the man next to her leaned over, a smile on his face as he gazed out over the dramatic scenery below, his eyes tracing the winding creeks that carved up the ground. It was so strange to be sitting next to a man she had never met but who was so familiar he seemed like an old friend. She had watched Michael Waters on the news almost every evening with her family when she was growing up, and now they were thrown together as Alaskan wilderness castaways.

'They call it the Gates of the Arctic,' he said. 'Vast, untamed, no roads, no trails, no people.'

'Except for us,' Katerina murmured, then gasped in shock as the helicopter jolted violently. She squeezed her eyes shut and her fingers kneaded the lap belt as the helicopter battled the elements to reach their landing zone.

She could hear Michael chuckling over the headset, but she ignored him, keeping her eyes closed as the helicopter was buffeted by the wind.

'What's happening?!' The stunning blonde next to Michael shrieked in fear, and Katerina shot her a glance, opening her eyes for just a second. Cressida grabbed at Michael's knee with her tanned, manicured hand, her voice shrill and reedy with panic. Katerina tried to ignore the waves of hysteria she could feel emanating from the young reality TV star, who somehow still managed to look gorgeous even in the midst of this doomed ride, her blonde hair artfully teased into a flattering high ponytail, her lips carefully glossed. Camera-ready, even in Alaska.

Katerina focused so hard on her breathing, and blocking out Cressida's frightened cries, that she didn't realise they had landed until the roar of the blades ceased and all was quiet. She tentatively opened one eye.

Their survival adventure had begun.

Finn

'Darryl, slow down!' Finn called out hoarsely into the cold air, his breath puffing out in a steady stream as he tried to propel himself forward.

'Hurry up!' Darryl gestured wildly at the horizon, turning his head to look behind at Finn and Carmen. 'We need to get there first to win the prize!' He shrugged his backpack higher onto his shoulders and gripped the straps firmly, turning to continue marching without waiting for a response.

Finn looked across at Carmen. The light was pale but pervasive, and he squinted against it, shielding his eyes with his hand.

'He needs to chill out,' he said, with a grin. Carmen raised an eyebrow, unimpressed at his attempt at humour. A stray curl, dyed honey blonde, peeped out from under her hat, a vibrant contrast against her dark brown eyes, which she shielded with her gloved hand.

'He's right, we should hurry up,' she said, casting a worried glance at Darryl as he moved further away from them. 'I want us to be the first group to the house so we can get the prize.'

Finn nodded, chastened. 'Is he sure he knows where we are going?'

Carmen shrugged. 'Unless you want to map-read, we'd better follow him. He seems pretty confident,' she said, turning to carry on after Darryl.

Finn paused for a moment. He watched Carmen move ahead of him, while Darryl used his Olympic training to quickly become a distant figure silhouetted against the sky. Finn looked around, still hardly able to believe he was in Alaska. There was no horizon, and the land and the sky extended endlessly, merging together into one boundless distance. The stinging cold permeated every fibre of his skin. He shivered, feeling numb despite the exertions of the trek. Carmen, Darryl and he had been dropped at their arrival point and sent on their way to find the wilderness house, the place where they and the other celebrity survivalists would spend two weeks. He was pretty sure they were nowhere near the cabin, and nowhere near anything or anyone.

The air was so clean he felt that every breath was a shot of pure oxygen, its icy freshness hurting his lungs. He hurried on, aware of the cameraman behind them, who was trying to be discreet whilst capturing their every move as they made their way across the frozen, forbidding kilometres.

Katerina

Katerina's chest was so tight her lungs ached as she tried hard to draw in the freezing air to power her exhausted muscles. Her legs burning and feet numb, she barely registered Cressida's excited shout as their cabin came into view.

Katerina paused and looked up to see their wooden refuge standing alone in the midst of the trees on a hillside above them. While she was glad to see it, her heart sank to think of the climb that awaited them. She didn't have much left in the tank.

She felt a gentle hand on her arm. 'Are you okay?' Michael asked her, looking out of puff himself. His voice was muffled by the scarf across his mouth, but she could see the concern in his face by the crease of his brow.

She nodded. 'I'm just out of shape,' she said, forcing a smile. She was aware of the cameraman hovering nearby and didn't want to complain. She didn't want to be seen as a whinger and a moaner.

Michael looked up at the cabin, steadfast and isolated with only the Arctic winds for company. 'Not far now,' he said faintly, rubbing a gloved hand across his face.

'Let's press on,' she said, forcing her legs to propel her forwards. The incline started and her muscles protested but she lowered her head and breathed out with every step, refusing to look at the refuge they were aiming for, lest she be disappointed by how far she still had to go.

She and Michael were largely silent except for their heavy breathing, but Cressida groaned dramatically with every step. 'My feet,' she wailed. 'I'm sure I have frostbite! How am I going to wear Louboutins again if I lose a toe or two?'

Katerina caught Michael's eye and bit her lip to suppress a smile. 'You can do it, Cressida,' Michael called out encouragingly.

Katerina felt relief flood her entire body as they approached the cabin. The trees cleared and the house stood before them, rustic but welcoming. It was two storeys high, and made of wood, roughened and warped in places by exposure to the elements. It wasn't the kind of welcoming refuge Katerina had imagined would be waiting for them: a cute little cabin with glowing windows and a smoking chimney, the likes of which might be seen on a Christmas card. No, it was a simple, squat and functional building, the windows dark and gloomy, and no glimmer of light could be seen inside.

'Maybe no one else is here yet?' Katerina wondered out loud, remembering the promise of a prize for the group that arrived first.

Cressida marched up to the front door and pushed on it hopefully. It swung open with a sigh, as though it were reluctant for its solitude to be disturbed.

'Hello?!' Cressida bellowed, entering the cabin. She pulled off her hat, her blonde ponytail barely ruffled. Katerina followed, blinking against the gloom inside.

'I think we're the only ones here so far,' Cressida said, glancing around.

The ground floor of the cabin was one open space, with a living area and a kitchen. Three large sofas, their cushions sunken and tired, huddled together as though they themselves were weary survivalists, waiting for rescue. Katerina ran her hand over the back of one, feeling the slight rasp of the worn fabric under her fingers. She looked around at the wooden walls and the beam-covered ceiling; she could see the tiny red lights studded throughout the beams, indicating that the cameras were already running. Katerina stared at them, then looked away quickly. They had been told to ignore the cameras and the cameramen, to make the show seem as authentic as possible. It should be easy for her, she thought. After all, she was used to working in front of cameras. Still, there was something about those watchful red lights that she found disturbing, as though the eyes of hundreds of small creatures were looking down on her, waiting to pounce.

She focused on the empty fireplace, the grate blackened and cold. Couldn't there have been something a little more welcoming? She wandered over to it and peered in to see a few sparse ashes gathered at the bottom. There was no wood pile, and she couldn't see any matches either, as she glanced around.

Michael rummaged in the kitchen cupboards. 'Oh great,' he muttered under his breath, as he opened each cupboard door and slammed it shut.

Katerina walked up to him. 'What's the matter?' she asked.

'There's almost nothing here,' he said, throwing his hands up in despair.

'What?' Cressida yelled. She marched over and threw open the cupboards to confirm what Michael had said was true.

Aside from teabags and one loaf of bread standing on the kitchen counter, the cupboards were empty. Katerina wasn't sure what they had expected. After all, this was supposed to be a survival challenge, but she also couldn't help but feel disappointed at the lack of warmth and food.

'What about milk?' Katerina asked, hopefully.

'Not even a fridge,' Michael said, shaking his head.

'Where's this prize they promised us?' said Cressida, standing with her hands on her hips, swivelling her head around to look at the cameras with a raised eyebrow.

Katerina shrugged. 'Maybe it was a trick?'

'Hello?!' A shout from the doorway interrupted them, and they turned in unison to see four people stumbling into the cabin, breathing heavily.

Michael walked up to them with his hands outstretched. 'Hi!' he said, enthusiastically, with a vigorous handshake for each one.

Katerina approached the new group and a movement outside caught her eye. The cameraman who had been following the four newcomers turned and swiftly departed, merging mysteriously into the tree line. Katerina watched him, wondering where he was going, and turned to meet the new arrivals. She recognised most of them – TV doctor Ashif Ali, gardening programme presenter Gideon Jones, and Scottish punk singer Maz. Katerina didn't recognise the stunning young brunette who accompanied them.

'I'm Katerina,' she said, extending her hand to the girl.

'I know who you are, of course,' she said warmly. 'I'm Willow Harper.' She shook Katerina's hand with a smile, her latte-coloured eyes framed with long dark lashes. Katerina still had no idea who she was, but smiled and nodded as if she did, not wanting to be rude.

Cressida swooped over and gave Willow a kiss on the cheek. 'Willow, darling!' she shrieked delightedly. 'This is wonderful – I'm so excited you're here too!'

'When did you arrive?' asked Ashif, following them to the seating area as they perched on the sofas, rubbing their hands together. The air inside the cabin was just as frigid as outside, though it hung still and silent compared to the cold winds that blew outdoors.

'Just now,' Michael replied. 'There's no food and no fire,' he said apologetically, rubbing the back of his neck.

'What?' Maz snapped. 'That's crazy! Are you sure?' She ruffled her bright orange hair, staring at Katerina.

'Um, I think so, yes,' said Katerina. She was slightly nervous of Maz, who had a reputation as a bit of a firecracker. Her drunken antics and arrests used to make headline news, till the singer had a breakdown and went into rehab for a long time.

'That's disappointing,' said Gideon, wearily. He looked a lot older than he did on TV, thought Katerina; his hair was much greyer, his eyes more lined. She had always thought he looked rather young for his sixty-eight years, but out in here in the wilderness, without make-up and flattering lighting, most of the group looked haggard, worn, and cold. Including me, she thought, self-consciously imagining how she looked to the cameras without the benefit of hair and make-up. Only Willow and Cressida managed to look half-decent, and Willow's natural olive complexion served her well in the pale Alaskan light.

'Did you guys find out what the prize was? You got here first, did you get anything?' Ashif asked. He placed his hands on his knees, small, precise and neat. He was just as Katerina had seen him on TV – quiet and exacting, but gentle.

'No.' Cressida shook her head. 'Can you believe it?' she said to Willow, who was sitting next to her. 'We got here first and there was nothing. No sign of any prize or anything like that.'

'Weird,' said Gideon, scrunching his forehead.

'How many are left to arrive?' asked Willow, looking round at the group.

'I think there are ten of us all together, so I guess one more group is still out there,' said Katerina. She glanced at the windows. The long hours of daylight made it impossible to discern the time, but it was already 7.30 p.m. according to her watch. 'I hope they get here soon,' she said, worried about their fellow castaways out in the open, perhaps lost, where the day was becoming colder as the hours wore on.

Michael nodded. 'I wouldn't want to be out there too late,' he said.

'I wonder who else will be with us,' Cressida said excitedly. 'Hopefully some handsome young men,' she whispered to Willow, who giggled and nodded. Katerina overheard and smiled at their hope of romance out here in this barren land, but she guessed stranger things could happen.

Maz was rummaging in the kitchen. 'Why are you all sitting there gossiping?' she said, sounding exasperated. 'We need to make a fire and we need to make tea,' she said, her hands on her hips.

Gideon nodded and rose. 'I can make a fire if there are matches and wood,' he said, making his way to the fireplace and poking around the grate. 'But I don't see either,' he added in a low voice.

Katerina joined him. 'I don't think there are any.'

He looked at her. 'Ah,' he said, quite calmly, but clearly disappointed.

Ashif had wandered outside and came back in, bringing in a fresh gust of cold air with him. In his hands was an axe, looking out of place in his slender fingers, which were more used to medical equipment than wilderness survival tools. 'Clearly we're meant to get the wood ourselves,' he said. 'But I did find matches though.' He triumphantly waved them around. 'It's only a few so I guess we're meant to keep the fire going all the time.'

Maz ran up to him and grabbed at the box. 'Where did you find these?' she demanded.

Ashif looked irritated at her haste to take the matches from him. 'There's a shed around the back of the cabin with all sorts of tools, weapons, everything we might need,' he said, coolly.

'Weapons?' Willow asked nervously. 'What sort of weapons?'

'Guns, traps, axes, knives – for hunting presumably.'

'Who is best placed to chop me some wood?' Gideon asked politely with a hopeful glance around the room. There was a moment of awkward silence. Katerina knew they had all had some preparation for the show but clearly everyone was exhausted after their long trek, and possibly, like her, lacking confidence in being the first to demonstrate their survival aptitude.

Ashif spoke first, looking grimly at the axe in his hands. 'I'll try my best,' he said, with a determined nod, and disappeared once again out the front door.

Michael stood up and followed him. 'I'll lend a hand,' he said. Katerina watched them go and hoped the others would soon arrive.

Finn

'We're lost!' Carmen wailed. '*No quiero morir aqui!* I don't want to die out here!' she cried out mournfully into the unsympathetic evening, her voice disappearing amongst the trees.

'Stay calm, I'm sure we're nearly there,' Darryl said, flapping the map, turning it around and around in his hands. It fluttered in the wind, which swirled around their legs and bit into their backs. Finn shivered and hunched his shoulders.

'Seriously, do you know where we are?' Finn asked, not wanting to sound exasperated, but starting to feel slightly panicky.

'Umm …' Darryl hesitated, and Finn had to stop himself from ripping the map from his hands.

'Yes, here we go,' Darryl said, jabbing at the map excitedly and looking up at Finn and Carmen, a triumphant grin on his face. 'We're about five minutes away.'

'You said that a few hours ago,' sobbed Carmen. 'I can't feel my feet. I'm an ice dancer, I can't injure my feet! My career will be over!' She started to sniff.

‘Hey look, I’m sure it’ll all be okay,’ Finn said, in his most reassuring voice, holding her hands. ‘We’ll be there soon. Right Darryl?’

Darryl nodded. ‘Absolutely,’ he said, confidently, but the sinews on his neck were taut and Finn wondered if he was as confident as he sounded.

They walked on in silence, the only sound that of their breathing and Carmen’s sniffles. The cameraman followed a few metres behind, with a sullen expression on his face. They weren’t supposed to interact with him, but more than once they had tried asking him for directions, out of sheer desperation. He had only sighed and pointed at the map in Darryl’s hands, clearly annoyed at being assigned to follow the hapless group.

They trudged on, beginning a steep incline up a winding path surrounded by trees. Finn was out of breath and nearly out of patience when Darryl cried out triumphantly.

‘I knew it!’ he shouted, the sudden break in the silence startling birds from the trees, cawing in panic at the intrusion.

‘Over there!’ Darryl pointed to the near distance, where the outline of a lodge loomed. The windows glowed bright with a merry welcome and Finn felt his chest swell with relief. Light, warmth and shelter awaited, and of course, the rest of the celebrity survivalists.

Katerina

Katerina watched as the amber flames licked gently at the blackened grate, quivering under Gideon’s patient blowing. Unfortunately the matches had been next to useless, and Gideon had to use three before one would spark, leaving them with only two in the box. Katerina wished she could be more help, but Gideon had taken charge and seemed to know what he was doing as he coaxed the fire into life and fed it with more logs that Ashif had collected. They were damp and hissed slightly at the aggravating heat of the fire, but the flames grew brighter and stronger, staking their claim over the wood.

The air in the cabin still hung unmoving and cold, but tiny slivers of heat began to seep through from the fireplace. Katerina stared at the flames hopefully, willing her body to feel their warmth.

Maz came over to pop a steel kettle onto the fire and managed to make a brew for the group. Katerina clutched at her tin mug, relishing the dark, bitter tea, as if it were a glass of fine wine. She sipped the scalding liquid and winced gratefully as the heat seared down her chest. Her fingers and her feet finally started to thaw as she perched in front of the fire, feeling shuddery from lack of food.

The cabin wasn't too bad, she thought to herself, as she looked around at her fellow survivalists. She feared they would arrive at a shelter that was open to the elements, or tents, or something they would have to construct themselves. At least the cabin was solid wood and protection against wildlife, although it felt spartan and rough and seemed to have no discernible insulation.

The upstairs of the cabin was one large space, divided up by bunk beds hewn out of rough boards, with thin mattresses. Cressida had been unimpressed, wrinkling her nose at the lack of padding on the beds, and Katerina wondered how long she would last out here in the wild. But then her own resolve nearly faltered when they explored the outhouse. Katerina shivered inwardly at the idea of using the shower in that dank little hut, which expelled only a meagre trickle of lukewarm water over the greying tiles.

Katerina had seen other survival programmes before. She knew they were lucky to have shelter provided for them, matches, beds, and a shower. Compared to the poor celebrities on a show she had once watched, abandoned on a tropical island with only ants to eat, this was luxury indeed.

She sipped her tea, nursing her now-scalded tongue, and wondered why her fellow contestants had signed up to this. She was curious about their motivations, especially as several of them were quite high profile, and probably not short of work offers. Like her, they each had to undertake a psychological assessment, and an interview with survivalist Phineas Moreland.

Katerina wondered what the public would think of their group and how much they would really see from the reams of footage. The producers had told her the show would include live footage from the cabin cameras, clips from the participants doing individual interviews, and recorded footage taken by the cameramen when they ventured outside for hunting or fishing. The idea of having so little control over what would be aired made her nervous, but she hoped she would find a way to relax and just be herself.

'I wonder what the other outhouses are for,' Maz said to the group as they sat, overwhelmed and quiet, in front of the steadily growing fire.

'Equipment?' said Katerina.

'Dead bodies?' said Gideon wryly.

'It's a mystery,' sighed Cressida, poking at a loose thread on the rug where she sat.

Three outbuildings were open – one a shed with a variety of survival equipment, another the toilet and shower, the third a small private space with a camera for the participants to give candid chats about their experiences. But the fourth remained closed, for now. They had tried to wrench it open, to no avail. It wasn't something they were meant to see just yet, Katerina guessed.

'Listen, it's getting late, we're all hungry, and we need to decide how to divide up the bread,' Michael said firmly, taking a stand before the fire. 'We don't know if more people are really coming. Perhaps they dropped out or they are getting here another day. In any case, we should eat. We're all starving.'

Maz nodded. 'I'm inclined to agree,' she said, staring moodily into the flames. 'As much as I'd like to wait for the others, as Michael says, we don't know when or even if they are coming.'

'But we were definitely told there would be ten of us,' Katerina said, quietly. 'At least let's divide it between ten and leave enough for the others for when they get here, which could be any minute now.'

'I think Katerina's right,' Ashif said, giving Katerina an approving nod, and she smiled back at him, grateful she wasn't the only one who had voiced an objection.

As Michael opened his mouth to reply, his words were masked by a loud slamming at the front door. Katerina's nerves jangled, and her mind immediately leapt to visions of wolves and bears surrounding their refuge. To her immense relief, three bedraggled people stumbled in rather than any predators.

Gideon threw his hands in the air. 'Finally! We were all getting worried!'

Ashif hurried over to the new arrivals. 'Is everything okay?' he said, going into doctor-mode. The group gathered round the newcomers, and Katerina found herself behind Michael's shoulder, unable to quite see their faces. She peered around him, making out two men and a woman, unravelling their layers and laughing, relieved to have made it, embarrassed to be the final ones to arrive.

One removed his hat, revealing thick blond hair with a slight curl, and pulled off his gloves. The musical notes tattooed on the inside of his wrist were just visible above his sleeve. Katerina stared at the notes as they danced before her, her heart starting to pound. How many people had a tattoo like that? Blood started to rush to her cheeks and the sound of her heartbeat thudding like a drum filled her ears. She heard his laugh, that unmistakeable throaty chuckle, and as he turned around she saw his eyes sparkling like sapphires even in the dim light of the cabin.

Katerina stepped back in shock. Finn Drayson was here.

Chapter Two

Finn

Finn could already feel the comforting warmth of the cabin seeping into his flesh. It felt like liquid gold spreading through his tired limbs as he stripped off his gloves and hat. Although it was a bit embarrassing to be the last to arrive, his feet were hurting so badly he didn't care. They burned and blistered inside his boots which he was desperate to rip off. A gaggle of people surrounded him, some of whom he recognised, and he tried to greet them with a good-natured smile, despite his tiredness and discomfort. He turned and saw a petite figure on the periphery of the group, partially hidden behind the newsreader. Finn felt as though his heart stopped as her eyes, the colours of rich earth and autumn, met his gaze. It had been years since he had looked into those eyes and lost himself in the empathy and love he found in them.

Katerina stood still, looking back at him solemnly. Her face was inscrutable, but he knew she remembered everything, as he did too. You never forget your first love, he thought. It was ingrained in the fibres of you, the first mark on a virgin heart.

The group was babbling around him, and he was aware of their voices but not their words as he took a second to adjust to the fact that Katerina was actually here with him in Alaska. He had seen her on TV and been so proud of her, and always wished he had the chance to talk to her again. And by some perfect strange twist of unpredictable fate, Alaska had brought them together again today.

Finn forgot about the cameras and the audience, he forgot the wilderness that awaited outside, he even forgot about the burning pain in his feet. With one glance from her he was back in London and fifteen again, full of bravado and foolishness and desperate to be known and loved. His heart was giddy with pleasure at being near her again and he felt his chest could burst with excitement. He hoped she felt the same as he bounded towards her with his hand extended, his pain forgotten, enthusiastic as a puppy.

Katerina felt that she was either going to faint, or vomit, or both. The scalding tea she had been sipping so gratefully just moments before was rising swiftly from her stomach into her throat, and her heart was beating out of time, a shuddering syncopated rhythm that left her light-headed.

She swallowed hard, forcing the tea back down, and steadied herself, remembering the cameras. They had an audience much greater than just the eight other celebrities there with them. She forced a smile onto her face, knowing that it was worse than any smile she put on in her acting jobs, but it was the best she could do in the unexpected circumstances. She tried not to flinch as Finn grabbed her hand and looked into her eyes with all the unwanted eagerness of a storm in summer.

Those eyes – blue as the ocean on a summer's day. She thought she had forgotten them. She certainly had tried to, but as he smiled at her she remembered looking into them and falling in love for the first time. The only time.

'Kat, it's so amazing to see you. It's been …' Finn paused, counting the years back. 'Thirteen years or so, right? Wow.'

He gripped her hand, the tips of his fingers still icy from outside, chilling her flesh where he touched her. She wanted to pull away, but she knew the gazes of the participants, and the people at home, would be watching curiously at this unexpected reunion.

Do the producers know our history? The thought flashed into her mind and she felt fear strain at her gut. She shook the thought away, knowing it was impossible. No, this was just bad luck, pure and simple, that of all the times and places they could have bumped into each other – award shows, TV interviews, fundraisers – it had to be *Alaska*, trapped under the merciless gaze of ever-rolling cameras.

'Hi Finn, yes, about that. Where does the time go?' she said weakly, a smile still forced onto her lips. She could feel her cheeks straining and knew her eyes couldn't possibly be reflecting her fake pleasure.

Act better, she told herself. *After all, that's your job.*

'You two know each other already?' Willow asked curiously, coming alongside them and raising a perfectly-groomed eyebrow.

Finn finally let go of Katerina's hand and ran his through his hair. She used to run her fingers through it, she remembered, and tried not to stare at him as the pleasure and the pain of the memory swept over her.

'Yeah, we, um, well …' Finn started sheepishly, and Katerina knew she had to cut him off before he said too much.

'We went to the same school,' she said quickly to Willow, who nodded in interest.

'What an amazing coincidence that you're both here!' she exclaimed.

Katerina nodded, and tried to look pleased. 'Yes, amazing!'

'Did you two go to a performing arts school? Given that you both wound up doing creative professions?' Gideon asked.

Finn shook his head. 'No, it was an ordinary secondary in London. Of course'—he gestured towards Katerina—'Kat here is the most famous alumni. I'm just, well you know, we had a few hits, but nothing comparable to winning a BAFTA, right Kat?' He smiled at her, self-effacing as always, and chuckled.

Katerina had seen him do that so many times, finding it easier to put himself down than be proud of himself. He was still doing it even all these years later, she thought; and then the tiny wave of sympathy that she felt was swiftly blocked by a smart of indignation at him calling her Kat. It was too familiar for someone she hadn't seen for so long, too personal for an ex-boyfriend, too affectionate for someone who had effectively ripped out her heart and stamped on it.

She knew her smile had faded and was grateful when Michael swooped in to usher the newcomers to tea. She perched tentatively on one of the sofas, far away from Finn, feeling the tension gather in her shoulders and neck from the surprise of seeing him and the knowledge that she was stuck here with him in the wilderness. Her mind raced desperately, from excuses for leaving to unwanted memories crashing in on her, the love and the heartache she had tried to forget. Her confused thoughts were interrupted by Carmen's excited shriek.

'Oh look!' she cried. A wooden panel slid away from over the fireplace, uncovering a large TV screen, that crackled to life as soon as it was revealed.

Finn felt a pang of irritation when the newsreader, Michael Something, bustled in and interrupted his unexpected reunion with Katerina.

I've never forgotten you, he thought, as he sat down on the sofa and studied her features, willing her to look his way. They were both a little older, certainly more weather-beaten on this particular occasion, but she still looked the same to him. She wore her chestnut hair in a French plait, a few loose strands falling around her face, a gentle rosy blush high on her pale cheeks. She sat with a slightly blank expression and he wished he knew what was running through her mind at that moment.

He could have danced with happiness at seeing her again. He felt as though he had been handed an incredible gift of fate; the chance to reconnect with Katerina after so long apart.

He turned his gaze from her as the TV appeared, the group silent and expectant as survival expert, Phineas Moreland, loomed on the screen, his forest-green eyes smiling down at them. Finn liked Phineas; they had got on well during his pre-show interview. He had the air of a kind maths teacher, but in reality he was as hard as nails, used to surviving the harshest environments known to man. Finn was in awe of how the thirty-five year old conquered deserts, mountains and jungles on his popular TV series.

'Hi everyone. Welcome to the first ever series of *Celebrity SOS*! I want to say a big well done for navigating your way to the lodge from where you started, several kilometres away, though of course …' He paused with a grin. 'Some of you got here quicker than others.'

There was an amused murmur across the celebrities, except for Darryl, who crossed his arms and looked mildly peeved.

'Katerina, Michael and Cressida arrived first. Congratulations! Your treat will be waiting for you outside the front door after this message ends.' Phineas smiled beneath his beard.

Cressida clapped her hands together in delight. 'I wonder what it is?' she murmured.

Phineas continued. 'You'll notice that there aren't many matches. We provided you with a few to help you get started, especially as much of the wood here is damp and starting a fire without them would have been extremely difficult. Now the key to your survival and comfort out here is to keep your fire going. Temperatures in the Gates of the Arctic National Park and Preserve never climb above freezing and usually dip to around minus seven degrees in the night in May, but could go lower, so keeping the cabin warm is vital. Remember, the weather is unpredictable here – so always be prepared for freezing conditions and snow, regardless of the time of year. You just never know what you're going to get.'

Gideon nodded sagely. Finn thought of the temperatures outside, and the strength of the Arctic wind whipping away any heat. He shuddered internally and looked at the fire, which glowed reassuringly.

'You'll be responsible for gathering food. In the shed outside you have all the weapons you need for fishing, hunting and preparing animals. Your basic training should have prepared you, if you were paying attention. If you work together as a team, use your combined knowledge and skills, and support each other, you will all be able to survive two weeks in the Alaskan wild. Good luck!' Phineas finished with a flourish, and the TV screen went blank.

Cressida leapt up and ran straight to the front door.

'There's a big package here!' she called out.

'Quick, bring it in and shut the door, you're letting the cold air in,' Ashif said urgently, as the cold breeze snaked in around them and the flames danced in protest.

Michael hefted the box into the kitchen and opened it, fishing out a small card from the inside.

'Black bear stew, our local delicacy,' he said, his eyes widening with longing. He carefully extracted a brown ceramic pot from the box and opened the lid. A cloud of fragrant steam rose into the air, instantly awakening the hunger in Finn's stomach. The stew smelled tantalising, but they could all see how little there was, just enough for three people to have a decent portion.

'Enjoy,' Maz muttered with a downcast expression. 'I guess we'd better divide up this loaf of bread,' she said, turning to the group. The air was scented with the aroma of the stew and thick with tension and hunger.

Katerina entered the kitchen and eyed up the prize. She murmured something to Michael and Cressida that Finn couldn't make out, and turned to the group. 'We'll share this out with everyone,' Katerina announced. 'There will only be a tiny amount for each of us, a spoonful or two, but with the bread it means everyone gets a small meal and some protein.'

Gideon applauded. 'Good show!' he said, and the tension in the room lifted instantly with the relief that everyone would eat something decent. Finn marvelled at how confident Katerina seemed, able to command the room without a shout. Her quietness, which once seemed like timidity, now seemed controlled, measured, and powerful. He never had any doubt that her approach would be to share the portion. He had always remembered her faultless generosity towards him and others; it was one of her best qualities. He was glad to see that her fame hadn't changed that.

He took his plate with his slices of bread to the counter, where Katerina studiously measured out two spoonfuls of stew for him and continued to avoid his gaze. A memory of her, gently offering him half her sandwich, filled his mind so vividly that he almost couldn't breathe. He turned away quickly and took a mouthful of food to force down the lump that knotted his throat and to stop the tears that threatened his eyes.

Katerina

It killed her to give away any of the delicious hot food that she herself was so desperate for, but Katerina knew that she, Michael and Cressida couldn't just tuck into it while everyone else was hungry too. Serving food to a line of famished and bedraggled people reminded her of when she helped at the church soup kitchen with her parents. Katerina knew what a difference a full stomach could make to someone's morale, and she was heartened to see the relief on her fellow participants' faces as they savoured the small but significant meal.

She avoided Finn's gaze when he came over, busying herself with serving, and not wanting to look into his eyes. Time may have robbed them of familiarity and friendship, but her memories remained as powerful as ever, although she didn't know if that were the case for him. Every glance at him brought back too many thoughts that made her feel confused if she allowed them in. So, she kept her head down and served his stew, and was relieved when he turned away quickly, presumably too hungry to remember the many times they had shared food together.

She glanced at him underneath her eyelashes as she finally sat down and ate her own meagre portion at the long wooden table. She savoured each tiny mouthful, chewing as slowly as she could to extend the experience, and watched Finn a few chairs away from her, chatting animatedly to Ashif. She wondered if he was still the same Finn she used to know, all front and no confidence, or if having a few hit singles in a boy band had changed him. She looked at the grains of wood in the table, the rough segments with tiny splinters protruding to pierce careless fingers, and tried not to stare at him.

'We haven't really done proper introductions,' Gideon said, looking around the table, and raising his tin mug with an air of ceremony. 'It's nice to meet you all. I'm Gideon and I present a gardening show.'

The group laughed, knowing who Gideon was already, having been a stalwart of TV for many years.

'I live with my husband and two red setters, called Molly and Moomin,' he said. He looked expectantly at Darryl to his right, who took the cue.

'I'm Darryl, an Olympic cyclist. Britain's first black cyclist to win a medal,' he said proudly, to applause from the table. He leaned back in his chair and looked to Maz.

'I'm Maz. I'm a punk singer, originally from Glasgow. Oh, and I own three snakes,' she said, grinning at the laughter from the others.

'What are their names?' called out Cressida.

'Bono, Ringo, and Sting,' Maz said, much to the amusement of the group.

Michael looked to Maz to make sure she was finished and leaned forward, his arms folded on the table in front of him. 'Well, I don't own any exotic animals, but I'm Michael Waters, a newsreader for the BBC. I've been married thirty years,' he said, with a gleam in his eye, 'and it still only feels like we just met.'

Katerina smiled to see the veteran newsreader's face soften at the mention of his wife, the way his eyes twinkled to think of her. She wondered wistfully what it must be like, to be loved by someone so completely for so long. It wasn't something she had experienced, she thought sadly.

Cressida squeezed Michael's arm. 'That's so nice. I'm Cressida Botham-Gilcrest. I'm twenty-eight and from London. I've mainly been busy filming *Raised in Richmond*, but I'd love to be a singer, and I'm working on some new tunes with a few record producers.' She twirled a strand of blonde hair around her index finger.

'That's amazing,' said Willow admiringly, and Cressida beamed.

Ashif spoke next. 'I'm Ashif Ali, consultant doctor for various TV programmes. I'm from Manchester.'

Katerina had warmed to Ashif as soon as she met him a few hours earlier, though it felt like they had been there much longer. There was something so kind and gentle in his manner, and to her he seemed authentic and trustworthy. She had developed a keen radar for people who were fake – a necessary skill in her line of work.

Ashif looked to his right, where Carmen sat. She pushed back a curl from her cheek. 'Hi, I am Carmen Figueroa, an ice dancer on *Sport Star to Skate Star*. I am originally from Mexico, but I moved to the UK to be with family when I was younger.'

'I wish I could ice skate, that would come in handy out here.' Willow sighed.

Gideon snorted. 'Unless you're planning on doing a performance on the lake to attract fish then I don't think ice-skating skills will be all that handy in this wilderness – no offence Carmen,' he said, holding up a placatory hand.

Carmen shook her head and laughed. 'None taken.'

Willow was next. She glanced around the table. 'I guess I'm the youngest here. I'm Willow Harper, twenty-three years old. I'm an actress, most recently on the soap *Ivy Bridge*,' she said, proudly.

'So, we have two talented actresses here then,' Michael said, with a glance at Katerina. She nodded, although she couldn't say she had ever seen Willow on TV before, but she didn't watch soaps. The younger woman was truly beautiful, with flawless skin, and sleek brown hair expertly highlighted with shades of honey and sunshine. Katerina watched Willow smile across the table at Finn, who was next.

He leaned back in his seat. 'Hi, I'm Finn. I was in the boy band 1Dream …'

'With Zach Morgan!' Cressida interrupted delightedly, with a dreamy expression on her face as she said the pop superstar's name.

Finn's jaw tensed at the mention of his former bandmate, whose decision to go solo had effectively ended the band's career. 'We had some hits and touring was a blast but well, all good things must come to an end,' he said, and Katerina saw that the sparkle in his eyes had dimmed just a little. He was disappointed that things hadn't gone better, she thought. She didn't tend to keep up with pop music, but she had seen a poster a few years ago and had been jolted by the sight of Finn's name. She didn't know why she had been so surprised – he always had ideal boy-band looks. Even now, when they were both nearing thirty, he still looked fresh, boyish and handsome, just as she always remembered him.

'And you two already know each other, right?' Willow turned to Katerina. She felt the eyes of the group rest on her, and squirmed inwardly at their scrutiny of a relationship she thought she had left far behind her.

'Yes, we went to the same school,' she said, and she thought a slight frown crossed Finn's face.

Please don't say anything about us, she pleaded inwardly. It was too private to bring out in front of these strangers, not just the ones in the room but also the thousands watching the show. She didn't want to rake it up at all, let alone in front of an audience.

'Yeah. Classmates,' he said, looking at her, a tiny crease forming between his eyebrows.

'So, anyway, I'm Katerina Murphy,' she said, hurrying on to finish the introductions and move the subject away from how she and Finn knew each other. 'I'm an actress.'

'BAFTA-award winning,' chimed in Gideon, giving her an admiring nod.

She gave a wry smile. 'Yes, well, I've been lucky to star in productions with very high-quality writing and directing,' she said, hoping she didn't come across as boastful. 'I live in London,' she said.

'I just can't believe that two people here went to the same school!' exclaimed Willow. 'Did you keep in touch?'

Katerina thought she had ended the conversation about her and Finn's history, and she felt a flash of annoyance at the way Willow was probing.

'Not really, no,' she said, giving Finn a quick sideways glance.

'Were you mates in school? Did you hang out?' Darryl asked.

Katerina could feel her heart quicken and she knew her cheeks warmed with a creeping blush. *Poker face,* her mind warned her, and she pinched the skin on her hands nervously.

'Not really. We were just classmates and we didn't really run in the same circles. Right, Finn?' she asked, with a wary lilt in her voice that she hoped he would pick up on. It was a thinly disguised plea for him to concur.

'Right,' he said, after a moment's pause. Their eyes met and she thought she could detect hurt glimmering in those ocean-blue depths.

Chapter Three

Finn

Finn sat in front of the camera, hoping he didn't look too rough. The warm meal nestled in his stomach, a comforting source of heat in the freezing cold hut outside of the main cabin. He could hear the wind making the rough planks rattle, and he decided to keep it brief. The participants had been encouraged by the producers to use the private hut to talk freely any time they wanted. The footage would be edited and shown to the audience and he knew it was a good opportunity to connect with the viewers.

He was no fool. His current workload was completely dependent on him staying in the public eye, being popular, and taking what offers he could. He was more comfortable behind a microphone than in front of a camera, but he knew he had to use the tools at his disposal on this programme in order to be offered more work.

He shifted on his seat and tried to relax.

'Well, I'm cold, I'm hungry, and I'm tired, but I'm feeling really good about being here.' He looked into the camera with what he hoped was a winsome smile. 'The group is great and I think we're really going to get along.'

Of course, he didn't really know them that well at all, not after so few hours, but he *hoped* that what he said was true, and that they would pull together.

'It's – um – it's really nice to see an old friend here as well, obviously,' he said, his words flowing a little less easily now as he picked his way carefully through what he wanted to say and what he was really feeling in his heart. 'I'm really pleased to see Katerina again,' he said eventually, trying to keep his voice level.

There was so much more he could say about how he felt upon seeing her, and how he winced inwardly when she refused to meet his gaze, and how he was deeply hurt when she told the group they had just been classmates. He had wanted to shake his head vehemently and shout out that it wasn't at all true, that Katerina was so much more to him than just a casual acquaintance, but what could he do when she told such a blatant lie? It would look bad to correct her, and as hurtful as it was, he didn't fully understand her reasoning and didn't want to think ill of her.

He looked at the camera, widening his faltering smile. 'I have a feeling this is going to be an amazing experience,' he said, hoping so much that it was true.

Katerina

Katerina watched Finn re-enter the cabin, shutting the door carefully against the encroaching cold. She waited until he drifted into the kitchen before she quickly headed out to the private hut.

She was studiously trying to make sure their paths crossed as little as possible. That was her only plan, for now. Apart from that, she had no idea what she was doing.

She closed the door of the hut and sat in front of the camera. She realised it would be the first time she was in front of a camera on her own and entirely unscripted. She had done TV interviews before, but her hosts had always been diligent about providing pre-prepared questions to her agent beforehand, as a courtesy. This time it was just her, with no prompts, no preparation, and no scripts. The thought made her feel exposed and queasy with vulnerability. What if she came across badly? What if she said the wrong thing?

Doubt made her feel fuzzy-headed, and it took her a moment to clear her throat and start speaking.

'Alaska is so beautiful,' she said, finally. 'I can't believe I'm really here. This is such … an adventure, so far out of my comfort zone.' She paused. 'I just hope I can learn something from this experience, about survival, about resilience, and about myself.'

She kneaded her fingers together, wondering if she should mention Finn. She felt it would probably be remiss of her not to, and perhaps the audience would think it strange.

'It's so nice to see Finn here, and it'll be great to catch up with him,' she said, as sincerely as she could, though she felt her tone was about as warm as the wind that blew through the wooden sides of the hut.

'Most of all I'm just looking forward to getting to know everyone and seeing Alaska,' she finished, hoping she'd said enough and at the same time not too much.

She rose to go back to the cabin and tried to focus on the truth of what she had just said. She was here to learn, to grow as a person, and she hoped the awkward past between her and Finn would stay exactly that, in the past, and avoid ruining the present.

Then – Finn

'I'm going to school,' Finn yelled as he shut the front door. He didn't know why he bothered shouting when his mum was enveloped in her bed with her headphones on, her usual position for about two-thirds of the day, but he did it anyway. It seemed like something people did, like his neighbours whom he could easily hear through the egg-shell-thin walls. They trumpeted their comings and their goings to each other, and someone replied, and someone cared, and he wanted to be like them. Normal.

The sky was bright with spring sunshine, and it was unseasonably hot for May. It felt as though the summer holidays should be starting soon, but they were months away. Finn dragged his feet as he walked, hardly feeling the warmth of the sun on his shoulders. He had to face double Drama first thing that morning, and they were announcing the role assignments for the play. He knew he shouldn't have taken GCSE Drama. It wasn't what he wanted at all. He had ticked the box to select Music, but the teacher had shaken her head at him and pointed with a pen to the overlooked detail in brackets – *minimum Grade 5 in any instrument required.* His mum couldn't afford bread, let alone music lessons and exam entry fees. So, he had picked Drama instead, and instantly regretted it.

It wasn't that he couldn't handle the acting. He would even kiss one of the girls if that was what the part required. Even Shauna Edmonson, with her slight hint of a moustache and lack of deodorant. He could act any part, behind closed doors. But the play had to be performed publicly at the end of June, and he knew his mates would take the piss out of him, no matter what role he had. He cringed inwardly as he imagined them in the audience, laughing and catcalling.

Finn checked his watch and realised he was running late. He picked up his speed, crossing the road carelessly and narrowly avoided a cyclist who gestured wildly at him with a shout. He scrabbled in his bag of crisps for any final pieces and wiped his mouth with his hands as he dashed in the main entrance of the school, which looked tired and drab even in the sunlight.

Finn hurried to the hall and clanged open the double doors. The hall smelled vaguely of cleaning fluids, and the sunshine filtering in through the windows seemed to turn pale and insipid as it reached the group of students gathered in the hall. He approached and grabbed a chair to join them. They were an odd mixture. There were the smart students with a flair for the dramatic; anxty kids – pasty-faced and with a love of poetry; and those who just couldn't be bothered to pick anything and were lumped into their group because there was still space. A handful of popular and pretty girls with ambitions beyond their talents joined in, hoping to be the next Keira Knightley, dreaming of stardom. And then there was Finn. He lounged awkwardly beside them as their teacher approached just a moment after Finn had sat down. Jude Maguire was a young man, but for some reason that Finn couldn't fathom he dressed like a pensioner, with bow ties and braces and corduroy trousers.

'Folks.' Jude Maguire rubbed his hands together. 'We've come to this, the most important moment of Year Ten. The play.' He smiled eagerly at the group, who didn't mirror his enthusiasm. Mr Maguire was always trying to be on their side, but to Finn it just came across as creepy. *Definitely a perv,* he thought, with a scornful glance at his latest bow tie.

'We're going to be presenting a play of *Breakfast at Tiffany's*. And I'm delighted to announce …' He paused for effect and his eyes searched the group to find where his star was seated. '… Katerina will be taking the lead role. Our very own Audrey Hepburn.'

Katerina glanced up quickly, a look of shock on her face, her mouth opening in a silent 'Oh'.

Finn glanced at Katerina with surprise. She had moved to their school last year and was one of the quieter students. He couldn't recall talking to her or even seeing her around, either with friends or on her own. She floated in their midst like a spirit, barely there, the mousy and timid new girl. He couldn't imagine her being the lead in a play.

'Hey Finn, how exciting.' One of the other girls grabbed his arm. He shook it off.

'What?' he snapped at her.

'The lead role!' She was nodding at him eagerly and he remembered vaguely kissing her at a drunken house party once, the scent of cheap Charlie perfume and Schnapps clogging his mouth. He flushed both with the memory and the confusion at what she was saying. He hadn't heard Mr Maguire's announcement so had missed the vital information that he, Finn Drayson, was going to be the male lead.

His palms instantly started to sweat and he ignored the congratulations from the others. He signed up for an easy GCSE and to find a way to make music, not to be exposed on stage in front of all his mates. He knew he couldn't do it.

After the class ended, he made his way to Mr Maguire, who was chatting with Katerina. She was looking more animated than usual, gesturing at a worn copy of *Breakfast at Tiffany's* in her hands. Mr Maguire was nodding intently, and Finn lurked awkwardly at the edge of their conversation, standing with his hands in his pockets and wishing they would both shut up for just a minute and let him speak.

'Ah, my two leading lights.' Mr Maguire turned to Finn with a smile and gestured at both him and Katerina.

'Um yeah, so about that …' Finn shuffled from one foot to another, unsure how to begin.

'It's going to be marvellous,' Mr Maguire said, his eyes shining. 'You two are very talented young people – this is going to be a great spotlight for you both. And I've got contacts, people I'm inviting who, well, I can't say too much. But if they are impressed, opportunities could follow …' He winked and tapped his nose with a spindly finger.

Katerina looked delighted. 'Wow, that's brilliant, Mr Maguire!'

Finn raised his eyebrows and the word "opportunity" danced in his mind. 'What do you mean, like, agents? Scouts? Reps?' he said, unsure of the right words to use.

'A few old university contacts of mine are working in various fields relating to acting, music, records etc.,' Mr Maguire said, waving his fingers in the air. 'I'm going to make sure they come to see what talent an ordinary comprehensive school has to offer!'

Katerina nodded eagerly with a wide smile. Finn took a moment to consider his options. He could do the play, and perhaps something could come of it. Or he could do the play and have the piss taken out of him. Forever. But even the tiniest chance of an opportunity was enough to tempt him, as he knew he didn't have many in his path. He couldn't afford to turn this one away.

'How do we get started?' Finn asked, making his mind up. He was in, for better or for worse.

Mr Maguire grinned. 'You two should get to know each other.'

Chapter Four

Katerina

Katerina lay awake, her eyes searching the gloom. The cabin shutters were drawn but the early daylight still seeped in through the gaps, making the room murky but not dark. It felt like she was the only one having trouble sleeping, as she could hear the sounds of slumber radiating from the others, deep breaths and a perfectly even snore drifting through the silence. Katerina turned over carefully on the thin mattress, trying not to shake the wooden frame of the bunk, where Cressida lay beneath her on the lower bunk. She winced as her thigh muscles protested against the move, sore from the strain of the arduous trek the day before. Her stomach gnawed at her, demanding food she didn't have, and her mind danced from thought to thought but always came to rest on one thing: Finn.

She couldn't believe he was in this room with her right now, just a bunk or two away. She lay awake and wondered what he thought when he saw her again, what he remembered, what he regretted, if anything.

Katerina closed her eyes and tried to switch off her brain. She wriggled her toes inside her sleeping bag as she attempted to relax her sore muscles, grateful that the thick woollen blankets added an extra layer of warmth. But her skin still prickled from the cold, which crept through the wooden walls of the cabin and sent chilly tendrils of air around her head.

Even here in the bedroom the pinprick lights of the cameras pierced the darkness, a false starry sky above her head. She counted them and imagined how many people at home were watching, as she told herself that she just had to get through these two weeks. *Keep it together, Katerina. You're an actress, so just act like you're okay and people will think you are. And don't get caught up in conversation with Finn. Steer clear and you'll be just fine.*

She rolled on her side as sleep finally forced her eyes closed.

Finn

Finn could vaguely hear people talking and muttering but he pressed his head further into his sleeping bag. Sleep had a firm hold and he didn't want to let go of the comfortable fogginess just yet. But as his eyes began to close again, Cressida and Carmen's excited chatter broke through his peace, and sleep flitted away. He sighed and poked his head out of his sleeping bag, opening one eye to peer around. Some of the bunks were already empty, including the one below his, which belonged to Darryl. Willow was sitting up in the top bunk next to his, pulling on a thermal vest. She looked refreshed and dewy, her hair slightly ruffled from sleep. It was a nice sight to wake up to, thought Finn.

She saw him looking and smiled over at him. 'Morning Finn, how did you sleep?' she said, leaning forward on the edge of the bunk, her hair falling across her shoulders.

He grinned at her. 'Good. Great, in fact. How about you?'

She started to tease her hair into a high bun on her head. 'Pretty good. Apart from some snoring,' she said, rolling her eyes.

'Your snoring?' Finn joked, and she giggled, flashing a set of perfect white teeth.

'I think it was Gideon.' She shimmied off the bunk and climbed down. 'I'm going downstairs, see you in a bit,' she said, walking away.

Finn wriggled out of the layers of his sleeping bag and woollen blankets that ensconced him, feeling the chill prickle his skin as each limb emerged into the icy air. He pulled on his clothes and padded downstairs, feeling a sudden burst of nerves in his stomach about the unknown that lay ahead that day. What would they do? Would they find food? He hoped he could be helpful, to contribute to the group and look good on camera too.

Carmen and Darryl had busied themselves making tea, and Carmen offered him a cup, smiling at him as he walked into the kitchen. He took the mug from her with a grateful nod, happy to have anything warm, even if it didn't have milk or sugar.

'Thanks, Carmen. How did you sleep?' he asked.

She nodded. 'It was okay. I was just so hungry though.' She grimaced and placed a hand on her stomach.

Finn nodded. 'Tell me about it. Speaking of which, any idea what the plans are for today?'

Carmen shrugged. 'Everyone seems to be in different places, doing different things. I think it would be good if we could all sit down and talk about what needs to be done.'

'Makes sense to me,' Finn agreed. He gulped his tea, missing coffee already, and walked to the living room. Katerina stood by the window, clutching her mug and gazing out. His heart quickened a little and he took a breath to slow it. Bathed in the weak light from the window she seemed like an apparition to him, a welcome ghost from his past. If someone had told him now that he had simply dreamt of her presence here in Alaska he would have believed them, so unlikely did it seem.

He walked up to her as she stared out of the window, seemingly unaware of his presence. 'Morning Kat,' he said, from behind her shoulder.

She turned around with a start. She smiled at him, but there was a tension in her mouth and eyes, he assumed from tiredness or hunger. Her hair was pulled into a high ponytail and the red fleece she was wearing lent a warmth to her face, despite her pallor and the dark circles smudged underneath her eyes.

'Oh, hi Finn,' she said flatly, her tone muted. He had hoped she might seem more pleased to see him, but he guessed she hadn't slept well.

'Wow, what a view,' he said, peering out of the window. The trees soared around the cabin, puncturing a pale grey sky. In places the view over the landscape opened up, where the steep incline to their refuge dropped away and revealed swathes of land rolled out around them, the hills rising towards the skies like billowing waves around a ship.

'Hmm,' she said, sipping from her mug.

'Beats the London skyline, hands down,' he said with a smile, hoping that talking about home might help her to loosen up.

'Well, London has its own particular charm,' she murmured.

They stood in silence for a moment.

'You know, it's been amazing seeing you do so well as an actress,' Finn said, still trying to draw her into conversation. 'Not that I ever doubted you, of course. You made a great Holly Golightly at school.' He was skirting around the memories, not wanting to be too obvious in front of the cameras, but he knew that even the smallest mention of that play would be enough to tell her that he hadn't forgotten what they had shared, that intense, sweet and brief time together.

Her eyes flickered but her expression remained impassive. 'Thank you,' she said, after a pause, and Finn felt slightly exasperated at her coldness, at her reticence to have a conversation with him.

He had been badly hurt when she left, both by the abruptness of her departure and the subsequent agonising silence, but time had dulled the raw edges of his hurt, leaving only fond memories of what they had shared. He was hoping that they could be friends, but perhaps the award-winning actress that stood before him was a far cry from the gentle and shy Katerina he had been so desperately, achingly in love with.

He opened his mouth to speak again, not even sure what to say, but Michael's frantic clapping interrupted him.

'Gather round folks,' Michael said, standing in the centre of the living room, his hands on his hips, a determined look on his face.

The survivalists drifted together into the living room, sitting on the sofas or staying on their feet, looking ready for action.

'I miss coffee so much,' muttered Cressida, as she took a sip of her tea and grimaced. Finn looked across and gave her an understanding nod.

Michael looked around to make sure everyone had made it. 'We have a number of tasks to get done, and we really ought to divide them up so we can achieve things quicker.'

Ashif stood up and dragged over a large chalkboard, propping it up on a frame in the centre of the living room. 'I found this in the shed. We can mark down everything on here.' The surface was grimy with dust and he wiped it clean with his sleeve.

'Thank you, Ashif.' Michael grabbed a small broken piece of chalk from the holder on the board, and began scrawling, covering the black surface in spidery letters.

Maz leaned closer to Finn and muttered in his ear, 'Who made him the boss?'

Finn shrugged in response. He wasn't really bothered by who appeared to be in charge. What did bother him was the dull ache he carried in his stomach from lack of food, and he was sure the others felt it too. They all needed to get stuff done, today, and he didn't care who did what as long as they all did *something*.

'From what we've seen in the shed outside, we've got equipment for fishing, and hunting, and foraging, all good ways to gather edible food,' Michael said. 'We also need to gather loads of wood and keep the fire going. That's quite a lot of work already.'

'Does anyone have any proficiency with fishing or hunting? I know we all did survival skills workshops before we came, but does anyone have any particular experience?' Ashif asked, looking around the group, his expression hopeful.

Gideon nodded. 'I do like a spot of fly-fishing,' he said. 'Lovely way to pass the time.'

'I shot a clay pigeon once,' Carmen said, shrugging her shoulders. 'Not that helpful.'

Darryl raised his hand. 'I reckon I could lay some traps and snares. I remember quite a lot of the prep and I'd like to give it a try at least.'

Michael nodded. 'Excellent.' He turned to Gideon. 'According to the maps we have, the nearest lake is about a five-kilometre trek away. Do you think you can get there and back?'

Gideon looked doubtful. 'I don't want to be a weak link, but I'm not sure.' He twiddled his fingers together with a frown, thinking. 'I could teach people to use the equipment though, and give a lesson to those going.' Gideon brightened at the idea.

'That's a great plan,' Willow said, nodding enthusiastically.

Michael jotted down people's names next to the tasks he had already written, and Finn was surprised by the easy cooperation in the group. He had expected more fractious fights over roles, but desperation for food had made people willing to try anything.

'Finn – you're with Darryl on traps and snares,' Michael read out, and Finn nodded, giving Darryl a small smile. He felt disappointed at being paired with Darryl rather than Katerina. He had hoped they could work together and have a chance to talk, but it would have to wait. At least he had two whole weeks here, he consoled himself, more than enough time to see if he and Katerina could be friends, again.

Chapter Five

Katerina

Katerina marvelled at how the air hung so still and quiet, in contrast to the fierce breeze of the day before. She strained her ears to hear anything other than the slight movement of the tree branches, but there were no sounds: no voices, no traffic, no planes. The trees soared overhead, dripping with moisture. An overnight rain had made everything damp, and fat, slushy drops of semi-melted snow fell onto her hair as she and Carmen walked through the forest.

Katerina was running through the survival workshop in her head, trying to remember what could be foraged from an Alaskan forest. The lesson had been brief, although it had seemed useful at the time to prepare her for some of the realities of wilderness survival. What a shame that she couldn't seem to remember any of it now, when she needed it.

'What's the matter?' Carmen said, her breath puffing out in thin white streams.

'What do you mean?'

'You're frowning.'

'Oh, just thinking deeply, trying to remember survival stuff.' Katerina grinned. 'I didn't mean to frown at you.'

Carmen smiled back. 'If you remember anything useful, let me know. I only did a Zoom call with my survival expert and our connection was bad so I missed half of what he said anyway.'

'That sounds helpful,' Katerina said with a laugh. 'By the way, I've seen you on *Sport Star to Skate Star*. I love that show.'

'Really?' Carmen beamed, and her eyes brightened at the compliment.

'Sure, when I have time my son and I watch it together,' Katerina said.

'Oh, you have a son?' Carmen said. Katerina regretted the way the words had slid out of her mouth so casually into the frozen air, like a warm spoon cutting through ice cream. The hairs on the back of her neck stood up, as if she physically felt the presence of the cameraman who stalked behind them.

'Yes,' she said, unwilling to elaborate and hoping Carmen wouldn't ask for any more details. Privacy, especially for her son Christopher, had become the most precious thing to her since her acting career had taken off. She wanted to put up walls around him to protect him from the glare of the public eye. As much as she loved acting, she never wanted to be famous, and never courted publicity. It was a mere side effect of the career she had chosen. For her, acting was all about discovery, putting on a mask and having the chance to be someone else. She never wanted to make it all about her, or her family, something which her agent found exasperating. This show was the first time she had done anything that required her to be herself and not play a role. That daunted her, but Katerina had pushed those fears to one side when she signed up, keen to challenge herself and experience something totally new, even if it made her uncomfortable.

Katerina stopped suddenly and her anxiety about her privacy flitted away, replaced by the light bulb of recognition flashing in her mind. She gestured towards a plant sprouting between the trees. 'I think I recognise this as something we can use,' she said, shaking off a glove and running her fingers over the leaves. She glanced at Carmen.

'Are you sure?' Carmen asked, sounding doubtful.

Katerina hesitated for a moment, trying to force her tired and starving brain to work. 'Yes, I think so,' she said finally.

Carmen grinned. 'Let's get some then.'

They worked quickly to pull together their small harvest and carried on looking. Katerina kept the conversations short and light, trying to be as pleasant as she could be without being too personal. Carmen, in contrast, seemed happy to reveal all the facts of her life, and Katerina was content to listen to her good-natured chatter without saying much in return.

They began to trudge back to the cabin after several hours of work, feeling worn out and woozy.

'What date is it today?' Carmen asked.

'May third,' Katerina said. She wasn't surprised Carmen didn't know, as she was already struggling to remember too. She felt disorientated without phones and calendars and email reminders telling her what to do and when.

Carmen grinned. 'It's my friend Katie Welsh's due date today. I wish I could message her to see how she is.' She sighed wistfully.

Katerina nodded. She felt a flash of sorrow as she heard the words "due date", and thought about missing her son's birthday in just a few days. 'I hope Katie's doing well. I've actually met her before,' she said.

'How do you know Katie?' Carmen asked in surprise.

'I know her husband's sister-in-law, Harriet Laine. She's advised me on some legal matters,' Katerina said, thinking fondly of Harriet and her stern focus and support, and her brilliant work to protect her privacy against the onslaught of the tabloids.

'Like what?' Carmen asked curiously.

Katerina wished she hadn't mentioned Harriet. 'That's private,' she said, the words snapping out more brusquely than she intended. Carmen narrowed her eyes at her curt tone, and they walked the rest of the way in silence, the distance seeming to stretch on and on. Katerina's legs felt like water, and an empty ache moaned in her stomach. She looked at the results of their foraging. It wasn't enough to feed ten hungry people, and she hoped the others had been more successful.

Finn

Finn shuffled his feet in frustration. He had to bite his lip to stop himself from snapping at Darryl to hurry up. Finn's fingers were numb from helping to set the traps, and he couldn't seem to keep warm, despite his thermals and his trekking gear. His muscles shivered and twanged from overuse and undernourishment.

Darryl had an impressive ability to focus and push through pain and exhaustion in his determination to get the traps laid. His attention to detail was exacting, meaning Finn rarely got anything right and had to keep redoing things.

Finn held his breath and told himself not to complain when Darryl redid the camouflaging he had laid down for the fifth snare.

'I thought it was fine the way it was,' Finn said curtly.

'I want everything to be ... just so,' Darryl said. 'You don't get to Olympic level without being a perfectionist.' He glanced up at Finn with a smug grin.

'Right,' said Finn, too irritated to be impressed. 'How many more traps do you think we should set?'

'Just a few more,' Darryl said, and Finn's heart sank into his feet, which were chilled from the frost-spattered ground. He was desperate for a cup of tea, or anything warm at all, and a chance to rest.

He didn't get it till hours later, when he and Darryl finally returned to the cabin, so exhausted and weak from lack of food they could barely say a word to each other.

He kicked off his boots and walked in, feeling the warmth caress him like a lover's touch. Willow turned from where she stood in the kitchen and ran over excitedly to greet them.

'You guys!' Willow exclaimed, grabbing Finn's arm. 'Ashif and Michael shot a bird! We have meat!' she said, triumphantly.

Finn's stomach leaped with anticipation at the thought of having a hot meal after his arduous day. 'That's brilliant news!' he said, smiling at Willow, his spirits instantly lifted.

'What type of bird?' Darryl asked Willow.

'I can't remember the name.' She shrugged. 'But as long as it's edible I couldn't care less.'

'What about you guys?' Cressida asked hopefully, poking her head up from the sofa.

'We laid all the snares and traps we could, but we haven't caught anything yet, although we'll check again tomorrow,' Darryl said, confidently, and Finn hoped that their hard work wouldn't come to nothing. He felt embarrassed about returning empty-handed, though he knew they couldn't have tried any harder than they did.

Finn walked over to the living room, where Cressida was lying on the sofa. Ashif was crouching beside her, taking her pulse, a frown on his face.

'Hey, are you okay?' Finn asked, concerned to see how pale she looked, even underneath her fake tan.

'I'm just feeling a little faint,' she said, shaking her head. 'It's nothing.'

'Probably low blood sugar,' Ashif said, standing up. 'We've all not had much to eat since arriving and you're fairly slender, so you haven't got much in the way of reserves.'

Cressida looked pleased at the compliment, despite her situation. 'At least we'll have food for tonight,' she said, 'thanks to you and Michael.' She smiled coquettishly at him, and Ashif gave her a sheepish grin in return, with an awkward sideways glance at Finn.

Finn resisted the urge to roll his eyes. He sat opposite Cressida, grateful to take the weight off his feet, trying to ignore the aching pains that were shooting through his calves. He breathed in the aroma from the kitchen, earthy but not unpleasant, and felt his stomach constrict with hunger.

'That smells amazing,' he said to Cressida, who nodded eagerly. Carmen walked by and looked over at him with a smile.

'Katerina and I managed to find a few bits to go with it – edible roots, that sort of thing. Hopefully there'll be enough for everyone to have a decent bowlful.'

'You were with Katerina today?' he asked. He was burning with curiosity, but he tried to sound casual.

Carmen did a swift glance over her shoulder to see who was nearby. 'Yep. I have to say that she is a little reserved, right? Like, kind of a cold fish?' she said, stifling a small laugh behind her hand.

Willow walked over from the kitchen and leaned on the back of the sofa over Cressida. 'She seems really introverted to me,' she said, in a hushed voice. 'And not super friendly either.'

Finn frowned and shook his head. 'She's a really sweet person, and incredibly kind. You just need to take a bit of time to know her,' he said, hopeful that Katerina had kept her best traits, the ones that made him fall so deeply in love with her.

Cressida looked at him curiously, her eyebrows raised.

'She was …' He hesitated for a moment, feeling that it might be too personal, but he wanted them to know that underneath her reserved exterior Katerina had a heart of gold. 'She was really nice to me, especially when I had issues with my mum,' he said, looking down at the rough-hewn floor, feeling a rush of sadness.

He looked up upon hearing a slight creak of the warped boards, to see Katerina standing in the doorway. Her arms were crossed, and she was biting her lip, looking at him with a pained expression. He knew she must have heard the tail-end of their conversation. His cheeks flushed at being caught talking about her, even though he had said only positive things. The look on her face made him wish he had kept his mouth shut.

Then – Katerina

Katerina felt her nerves coil and jangle at the thought of being the lead in a play. She had wanted to be an actress for as long as she could remember, and here was a chance to do it, but she was terrified of making a fool out of herself and ending her dream before it had even begun. Added to her nerves was her uncertainty that Finn would turn up, rehearse, and deliver on stage beside her. She couldn't quite describe it, but she felt as though this play was somehow a pivotal moment in determining her future, for better or for worse.

She tapped her foot, the small sound magnifying around the hall's hard surfaces, as she waited for Finn to arrive for their lunchtime read-through. She could hear a cacophony of bangs and shouts from the cafeteria, where a multitude of crisp packets and sandwiches and pasties were consumed by students enjoying their lunches. She took a bite of her own sandwich and felt relieved when she saw Finn heading through the double doors towards her.

His shirt was untucked and creased, his face reddened and his hairline damp from sweat.

'Sorry,' he said. 'I had PE before lunch and was rushing to get changed.'

She nodded. 'That's okay. Did you want to eat something first?' she asked him.

He took a few large gulps from a water bottle and shook his head. 'Nah. Let's crack on.'

He pulled the script from his bag, where it was slightly dog-eared already. 'From the top?' he said, with a grin.

Katerina smiled back. He smelled of Lynx and perspiration, his tie hanging loose around his collar, a couple of his shirt buttons undone. Finn had always been one of the popular boys, one of the cute ones; he was never alone and always joking around with someone. Katerina watched people like him from the margins, wondering what it must be like to come to school and always know that you'd have someone to hang out with. To know that you wouldn't have to drift around the edges of the building, looking for a quiet corner to eat your lunch, because you didn't want to sit, exposed and alone, in the cafeteria. Katerina hadn't made many friends since starting at the school last year. She was shy and everyone already had their groups and their cliques. Popular people like Finn were lucky, she thought, as she turned to the first page of the script and started the opening lines.

It was a lot of dialogue, and it would take loads of time and effort to commit it all to memory. Katerina felt a quiver of doubt press into her as they read, but she pushed it away. She could do this, she told herself firmly.

She paused at one line of dialogue and Finn's stomach gave a vicious rumble in the seconds between his line and hers. He flinched and muttered, embarrassed. She pretended she hadn't heard, but when it happened a third time, she couldn't ignore it any more.

'Do you want to take a break for something to eat?' she asked, lowering her script.

Finn rubbed the back of his neck and looked sheepish. 'Um, well, I forgot my lunch today,' he said. 'And my money,' he added, looking down and fiddling with a shoelace.

'I have a spare sandwich,' she said, fishing it out from her bag and offering it to him.

He raised his eyebrows. 'A spare?'

She laughed. 'My mum is paranoid I don't eat enough so she always makes me take two. You can have it, really, I don't mind at all.'

He took it hesitantly from her outstretched hand. 'Hey, thanks.' He bit off large mouthfuls and chewed frantically. She pretended to scrutinise her script, but she was completely distracted by the way he was eating, so clearly starving.

He finished rapidly, wiping his mouth and gulping some more water. 'That was really nice.' He shook his head with a smile. 'I can't believe your mum makes you one sandwich, let alone two. My mum doesn't even make dinner, let alone lunch.'

'Oh, that's a shame,' Katerina said, unsure if he was joking.

Finn shrugged. 'She isn't … well.' He brushed crumbs off his legs and a strand of hair fell over his forehead. This wasn't the Finn she had observed from a distance, the popular boy with the jokes and the charming smile. All of a sudden he seemed vulnerable, and she resisted an unexpected urge to gently brush away the hair from his face.

'I'm sorry to hear your mum isn't well,' she said quietly.

He shrugged and turned back to the script to continue reading as if he had never said anything personal at all. His easy smile and confident manner returned instantly, as though he had flicked a switch, hiding any hint of vulnerability that he had revealed just seconds before. She looked on as he read, and wondered what life was really like for Finn Drayson.

Then – Finn

Finn glanced around the street, noting how quiet it seemed, how the trees soothed the air with a gentle hush. The houses they passed had a variety of coloured front doors and welcome mats, tasteful slate and pot plants decorating tidy front gardens. Katerina was a few steps in front of him and he followed her with a growing unease, berating himself for having agreed to go to her house. It felt like a bad idea, and already he was tense at the potential awkwardness of it.

It had been Katerina's idea to watch the film together. Finn had shrivelled with embarrassment to say he didn't have a working DVD player. He decided not to clarify that his mum had sold it when there was no money to pay for electricity. That left Katerina's house as their only option, and he wished he had made up an excuse.

She strode through the May sunshine, her hair catching the glow of the afternoon sun, warming the brown strands with a hint of auburn. Her head was bent slightly forward as she walked quickly towards her house. She opened the wrought-iron gate of a neat Victorian terrace, the red bricks glowing warmly in the sun. Finn followed her up the path, waiting behind her as she opened the door.

'I'm home!' she called out.

Finn stood awkwardly in the doorway, his hands thrust into his pockets. Katerina gestured to him.

'Come in,' she said, kicking off her shoes. Finn copied her and removed his, though he cringed with embarrassment at the holes in his socks. They walked through to the living room and Katerina's mum leaned out of the doorway to the kitchen.

'Hi, Kat.' Her eyes caught sight of Finn and she smiled warmly at him. 'Is this the friend you texted me about?'

Katerina nodded. 'This is Finn.'

'Hi, I'm Pauline, Kat's mum,' Pauline said to Finn. She looked younger than he expected, with dark hair like Katerina's, although her eyes were light green rather than brown. She was petite and slightly overweight, clutching a tea towel with flag motifs, her cheeks warm from cooking.

'Would you like a drink? Water? Juice?' she offered.

Finn nodded, his throat dry from the heat of the afternoon. 'Water would be great thanks,' he said.

'Do you want to sit down while I get the drinks?' Katerina gestured to a sofa and Finn plonked himself down gratefully, wishing the cushions would swallow him whole, and tucking his feet together to hide the holes in his socks. Katerina headed to the kitchen and he sneaked a look around the room, feeling slightly nosy. The room was full but not untidy, every surface was spotless; a delicate scent in the air was pleasant but not cloying. The walls were peppered with framed photographs with no discernible pattern in jumbled sizes and frames, yet somehow coherent: all of Katerina's family and her, with wide smiles and laughter.

A crucifix on the mantlepiece caught his eye, the Jesus figure looking at him mournfully, beside a framed prayer, cross-stitched and proudly displayed, perhaps something Katerina or her mum had made, he thought.

Katerina came back with two glasses of water and saw him looking at the photos on the wall. She laughed. 'Oh no! There are so many awful photos of me. With bad hair and even worse clothes.' She rolled her eyes, but there was a tinge to her cheeks that betrayed her embarrassment.

Finn shrugged. 'I think we all had bad clothes and hair when we were little. I blame the 90s,' he said, with a wry smile. There weren't any framed photos on the walls of his flat to help him remember but he was sure it had been the same for him.

Katerina fiddled with the TV and the DVD player. 'Ready,' she said, pressing "Play". Finn was relieved that he wouldn't have to make any more stilted conversation while they immersed themselves in the film and the characters they would be playing.

Katerina was obviously enchanted, mouthing the words to the dialogue, sighing, but it was doubt that Finn felt creeping over him as he watched George Peppard. Finn knew he was nothing like this confident, sophisticated man. He was just a fifteen-year-old with holes in his socks and an empty stomach, and absolutely no clue how to act.

Katerina's mum brought them a plate of biscuits, leaving it on the sofa between them. Finn ate them furtively, taking one every few minutes till the plate was empty. Katerina didn't remark on it, only eating one herself, and he was hoping she was too wrapped up in the film to notice that he had eaten them all. He would have eaten more if they'd been on offer.

The end titles rolled and he stretched his legs, knowing it would soon be time for him to leave. 'Did you like it?' asked Katerina, looking at him with a smile.

He nodded. 'Yeah, it was good. Not sure how we will do it justice though.' He immediately regretted the negativity in his comment, as her mouth turned down slightly at the corners and a shadow crossed her face. He felt as though he had passed on his doubt to her. 'But I'm sure you'll make a great Holly Golightly,' he said quickly, and was relieved that her expression brightened a little.

He stood up, preparing to go, as Pauline came in from the kitchen.

'Are you leaving?' she asked.

'Um yeah,' Finn said. 'Thank you for the biscuits,' he added, remembering to be polite.

Katerina turned to him. 'You could stay for dinner Finn, if you like?' she asked. There was a note of light hopefulness in her voice, but he couldn't tell if she was asking for her sake or his.

He wanted to refuse and go home where he could relax and be himself, but the smell from the kitchen enticed him, and his stomach pleaded with him to stay. He knew his mum wouldn't notice what time he got home, and at least this way he would arrive home properly fed and not have to conduct his usual fruitless search of the cupboards, where his best option would be the dregs of a cereal box or possibly a bag of crisps.

He glanced from Katerina to her mum and nodded slowly. 'You don't mind?' he asked, feeling the weight of their charity on his shoulders and hating it.

Katerina shook her head. 'Mum always cooks way too much food.'

Pauline laughed. 'Yes, that's true,' she said. 'Do stay and eat something love. There's plenty to go round.'

Finn nodded. 'Thank you.' He sat back down, entwining his fingers together. If Katerina sensed his awkwardness, she didn't show it. She took out her notebook, running through the notes she had been taking during the film. He sat back quietly, glad to simply listen to her and not be put on the spot. Her observations were astute. He glanced at her as she spoke and he wondered where this impassioned and articulate girl had been hiding away for the past year. The Katerina sat before him now was completely different from the girl he saw at school – confident, smart, and without hesitation. Mr Maguire must have seen this side to her as well, and it was no wonder he picked her for the lead role. Not just that she knew about acting, and clearly loved it, but also that she had the same delicate quality as Audrey Hepburn, with her dark hair and elfin features, and eyes that looked both enchanting and wistful.

It struck him, as he sat observing her, that Katerina was prettier than he had originally thought. She was probably one of the prettiest girls in the year, but it wasn't obvious to him till he sat here, looking at the way the afternoon sun shimmered over her, seeing her eyes dance in the golden light.

'Finn? What do you think?' she was asking him a question, looking at him intently, and he realised he hadn't been listening properly at all. He wracked his brain to try to think of the last thing she had said, but he had been sunk into his own thoughts. He shrugged, and she looked disappointed.

'You're not sure?' she said.

'Um, not really, let me think. Ask me again, so I can really, er, give it some thought,' he stammered, wishing he had been paying attention and not just staring at her like a moron.

'What do you think of the scene in the taxi? Do you think we should try to get a real cat?' she repeated the question.

He nodded thoughtfully. 'We could try,' he said, liking the way she smiled and how her eyes lit up, and not wanting to tell her that he actually hated cats.

'Dinner's ready!' Pauline called out from the kitchen, amidst the sound of clattering plates and cutlery.

Katerina walked to the dining table, gesturing for Finn to follow her. The living and dining rooms had been knocked through into one, and the dining table took up most of the space.

'Take a seat Finn,' said Katerina, indicating one of the chairs. He sat down, thinking how proper it seemed to eat at a table together as a family instead of on their laps in front of the TV, or as in his case, not eat at all.

Katerina went to fetch the plates and cutlery, and Pauline came out shortly behind her, holding aloft a large pot.

'I hope you like chicken,' she said to Finn, who nodded eagerly.

'It smells amazing,' he said, his mouth starting to water, eyeing the large saucepan where the condensation on the glass lid was a teasing indication of the hot stew within.

'Dad!' Katerina called up the stairs, and Finn could hear shuffling, then heavy footsteps descending the stairs. Finn hadn't realised Katerina's dad would be here, and he instantly felt a new tension clench like a vice between his shoulders.

Katerina's dad walked in, sat down, and extended his hand to Finn.

'I'm Keith, Kat's dad.'

He was stocky, with eyes darker than Katerina's, nestled beneath unruly eyebrows. Finn shook his hand, feeling the rough rasp of the skin, the thickness of the palm.

'I'm Finn.' He looked away quickly, knowing that Keith was sizing him up.

'Well, nice to meet you, Finn. Do tuck in,' he said, gesturing towards the food.

Katerina was right about the amount of food – there was enough for at least six people. Finn helped himself to the stew, wanting to take double what he put on his plate, but he was trying to hold back. He didn't want to seem greedy in front of Katerina and her parents. He felt sweat seep down his back, from discomfort rather than warmth, and he questioned every move he made with his cutlery, every mouthful he ate, and every word he spoke.

Pauline shook her head at his plate. 'You're a teenage boy, you need more than that.'

Keith nodded. 'Too right, you're a growing lad. Here, have some more.' He took a spoon and dished out more onto Finn's plate, and Finn couldn't help but grin with satisfaction as the gravy spread across the plate.

Keith laughed. 'I was a teenager once too, and I remember I just ate and ate and ate. Now of course, it all seems to stay put,' he said, patting his stomach with a grin.

'Okay Dad,' Katerina said, with a slight roll of her eyes at Finn.

'Our Katerina is going to be an actress,' Keith said, his face glowing with pride.

Finn nodded. 'So I hear.'

Katerina looked down at her plate and swirled her stew around. 'Well, hopefully. It's a very competitive industry,' she murmured. Finn watched her poke a mushroom and wondered if she knew how much potential she had.

'It's all she's ever wanted to do. Ever since she was three years old, such determination,' Keith said, shaking his head with a smile. 'We were very excited to hear she had been given the lead in this play. And it's great there's the potential for some agents to come and watch – what an opportunity.'

'We'll see, Dad,' Katerina said, nodding with a faint smile. Finn got the sense she was excited too, but she was trying to manage her parents' expectations, as well as her own.

Finn listened enviously to their conversations: their in-jokes, the fond memories, the cosy familiarity; all shared over the most delicious stew he had ever eaten. He could only mumble replies to Keith's questions about his family, not wanting to go into detail about the mess and chaos of his own life. He sensed Katerina and Pauline looking at him curiously as he gave one-word answers and shovelled food in his mouth so he didn't have to talk much.

'And what are your aims, Finn? Any particular careers spark your interest?' Pauline asked him, leaning forward with a smile. Katerina had her dad's colouring but it was obvious to Finn that her gentle sweetness was all from Pauline.

'I love music,' Finn said, clanking his fork on the plate, and then wishing he hadn't said it.

'Music? Do you play?' Pauline asked.

'I play guitar. I write my own stuff,' he said hesitantly. He didn't tell many people about his musical ambitions, worried it might get thrown back at him with scorn. Music had always been something that made life a little more liveable. When he had his guitar and he could strum away in the evenings, drowning out the noise of the neighbours, that's when he felt peaceful. It was the *only* time he felt peaceful. The hours would slip by and he wouldn't have to constantly *try,* striving to fit in and say and do the right things. Music came easily; the rest of life didn't. He needed the notes like he needed air.

'Wow, I didn't know you played,' Katerina said, her eyes wide. 'But you're not taking Music at school?' she asked, frowning curiously.

'You need grades to do Music, and I haven't taken the exams,' he said with a shrug. It irked him, the unfairness of it, but he didn't want to show that he was bothered.

'So, you'd like to be a singer-songwriter?' Keith asked, and Finn wondered if there was a note of incredulity in his voice or if he was just imagining it.

Finn chewed a mouthful of stew slowly before answering. 'I guess so.'

'Well, I hope we'll be seeing you in the charts, lad,' Keith said, and again, Finn felt the impossibility of his ambition and how ridiculous it seemed to not have any decent career plan except one he couldn't possibly achieve. Most likely he would end up on the dole, as he wasn't clever and had no talent for anything besides making up songs that he sang to an audience of one.

He pushed his chair back abruptly. 'I should get going. I need to get back to my mum,' he said.

They looked surprised, but Finn knew he had overstayed. 'Thank you so much for the food,' he said politely to Pauline. 'It was really delicious.'

He walked to the hallway to retrieve his shoes and Katerina followed him to the door.

'Hey, Finn.'

He turned around on the doorstep, already on the outside looking in, prickling with envy at Katerina's home, her family, her life. He stood in the early evening air and wished he had eaten more stew before leaving.

'Yeah?' he said.

'It was really nice hanging out with you,' she said shyly. His painful sense of jealousy was tempered by the sweetness of the slight flush on her cheeks.

He smiled back. 'It was great. You have a nice family,' he said, a wistful tone creeping into his voice that he tried to hold back.

She nodded. 'I know. Get home safely, okay?'

'Will do.' He hoisted his bag onto one shoulder and walked away. He glanced back and he could still see her, standing in the doorway, silhouetted against the hallway light. He waved and walked on, leaving her behind, but dragging his feelings of inadequacy and envy with him, weighing heavier than his bag.

Chapter Six

Katerina

Katerina watched Finn savour his Alaskan bird stew, remembering when he visited her house for the first time. His stuttering, mumbling nervousness around her parents was such a contrast to the charming, popular Finn she had seen at school. She thought back to how desperate she was not to allow her small crush the oxygen of hope, so sure was she that he wouldn't like her in return.

She looked down at her bowl, willing the memories away. They may have been pleasant, but they were all tainted by his actions later on. At least she had had the satisfaction of leaving and never letting him know how much he had hurt her.

She was furious to have heard her name on his lips earlier, talking about her behind her back with Carmen, Willow and Cressida. She was riled at the way he spoke about her, acting as though they were still acquainted, and she was tempted to slap him around the head, but she had simply ignored him and the hot indignation that burned in her throat.

They all ate their stew slowly, savouring the meagre portions. A few roots, a few vegetables, and a stringy duck was still a feast for hungry people weary from a day of foraging, hunting, and wood-gathering.

Katerina shifted her feet. It was hard to get warm and they felt icy and cold in her woollen thermal socks. She rubbed them together and thought of the warmth in her home on the outskirts of London. It was a gorgeous Victorian cottage, her haven. She missed the scent of honeysuckle from the garden, the way the sunlight pooled across the flagstones of the patio in the late afternoon. She felt a deep stab of longing to be home with her family, with Chris, where she belonged. She held her breath and tried to shake the thought away.

Katerina didn't want to eavesdrop on Finn's and Willow's conversation, but her ears tuned into his voice, as much as she tried to concentrate on what other people were saying.

Willow giggled, touching Finn's arm. 'I loved you in the "Dare 2 Dream" video,' she said, looking up at him with a brilliant smile.

Finn snorted. 'Oh no, that was so embarrassing. I didn't have a clue what I was doing with the choreography. I was all over the place.'

Willow wound a strand of hair around one finger. 'I thought you were dead sexy,' she murmured, leaning close to him, her eyelashes so long they almost grazed his jaw.

Finn's expression brightened at the attentions of the pretty actress. He glanced across the table and for a fleeting second his eyes caught Katerina's gaze. She looked away quickly, her heart pounding, but she knew he had seen her looking, listening. She was irritated that he thought she might care, and she started up a conversation with Darryl next to her, asking about his recent wedding to his long-term partner. Darryl chatted away happily, and Katerina lost herself in his delight. She made it through dinner without meeting Finn's gaze again.

The group congregated in the living room after they finished eating, and the screen once again flickered to life.

'A message!' Cressida shrieked.

'Shhh everyone!' Gideon hissed urgently, and an expectant hush descended on the room.

Phineas appeared, his voice slightly scratchy with static. He was sitting before a roaring fire, the light from the flames shimmering across his face. His words were punctuated by crackles from the burning wood.

'Well done everyone on your successful day today. You've managed to keep the fire going and find food. You're doing extremely well. It's not easy to find food in the wild, especially if you're not experienced hunter-gatherers …' He paused, with a thoughtful nod, putting a hand to his beard. 'I've been observing and, based on what I've seen from the cameras, one pair really stood out to me today.'

'*Ooooh* maybe there'll be a treat,' Maz said, kneading her fingers together eagerly.

Phineas continued with a generous smile. 'I'm pleased to say that Michael and Ashif impressed me most with their stellar efforts in capturing the duck. As a reward, the locked outhouse will open for a period of one hour, and Michael and Ashif will find a reward inside. Enjoy!' He waved goodbye, then the screen went blank.

Michael jumped up from his seat with a leap, almost knocking Carmen out of the way. 'Right then, I want to see what we've got in store,' he said, striding towards the front door.

Ashif hurried after him. 'I can't believe they chose us!' Katerina heard him exclaim as they threw on their coats and headed outside, closely followed by Willow, Carmen, Cressida, and Darryl. The door had flown open, and now flapped in the wind, letting in a gust of crisp air from the bright evening. Katerina secured the front door behind them before returning to the sofas, taking the seat vacated by Cressida, next to Gideon and as far from Finn as possible.

'You're not going?' Katerina asked Gideon.

'Nope. Whatever it is, I'm not going to be able to partake, so I'd rather stay here in the warm,' he said with a slight smile. There was no bitterness in his voice, but he looked tired and wan.

They sat quietly for a moment, Katerina prickling with awareness of Finn's proximity and wishing he had gone with the group outside. Finn leaned back into the other sofa next to Maz, sinking into the worn cushions, and seemed perfectly content. Katerina deliberately kept her eyes from straying towards him, focusing instead on counting the loose threads of wool on the rug in front of them.

It didn't take long for the door to fling open again, and Katerina turned around to see Michael's boots disappearing up the stairs and Ashif hurrying along after him. The rest of the group clattered noisily into the living area.

'You'll never guess what?!' Willow came in, waving her arms in excitement. 'There's a hot tub in there! Can you believe it? An actual hot tub out here in this wilderness!'

Katerina's mouth dropped open in surprise. She had thought it might be some extra food, but a hot tub? It seemed so out of place for a show like this. Maz must have been thinking the same thing, as she let out a loud snort of laughter.

'Well, that's a bit of a luxury for a survival show,' Maz said, shaking her head.

'I'm so jealous they get to use it,' Cressida wailed as she plopped herself down next to Finn, placing a manicured hand on his knee.

'There are cameras in there so I guess it won't switch on if we're not the ones who won the reward,' Willow said, sadly, heaving a dramatic sigh.

'Maybe you'll get to use it next time,' Katerina said, trying to be sympathetic, and Willow shot her a wide smile that didn't quite meet her eyes.

'Oh yes, maybe,' she trilled.

'How are we all going to amuse ourselves in here while they are soaking in the warmth?' Cressida groaned. 'There's no TV, no Netflix, no Internet.' She looked around at the group. 'Any ideas?' she asked, her wide blue eyes gleaming hopefully.

Willow grinned as she reached into her pocket. 'I have just the thing.' She pulled out a deck of cards with a flourish.

'You brought cards?' Maz asked, incredulously.

Willow nodded. 'Yep. I happen to be extremely good at poker.'

Finn raised his eyebrows. 'I would never have you down as a poker player,' he said, and Katerina heard the admiration in his voice.

'But we haven't got anything to bet,' said Carmen.

'Oh yes, we have,' Willow said, arching an eyebrow and shuffling the pack deftly. 'For each round, you'll bet one secret. The person who wins the hand chooses who shares. Simple.'

Cressida laughed. 'What?! You're like an evil genius,' she said to Willow. 'Getting people to spill their secrets. Have you done this before?'

'It's a great way to get to know each other better,' Willow said, nodding. 'Who's in?'

'Not me, thanks,' Gideon said, politely. 'I'm off to bed.' He stood up slowly, wincing as he did so, and shuffled off, rubbing his lower back.

Carmen, Maz, Darryl, Cressida, Willow and Finn gathered closer together as Willow shuffled. Katerina was about to stand up to leave when Willow started dealing the cards out. 'You'll stay won't you, Katerina?' Willow asked her sweetly, and before Katerina could reply Willow swiftly placed a card in front of her.

Katerina found herself holding a hand of cards and stared blankly at them. She had never been good at poker. She clutched them nervously, not even sure what her hand meant, hoping that Willow was just being amusing for the cameras. Surely, she thought, they wouldn't really want to share personal secrets on air?

She glanced around the room at the players, each solemnly holding their cards close to them. Katerina folded at the first opportunity, at a loss as to what her cards meant, and watched with interest as the game progressed. Eventually only Darryl and Carmen remained and he slapped his cards down delightedly.

'Full house!' he said, flashing a triumphant grin.

Carmen sighed and shook her head. 'I was hoping you were bluffing.' She placed her cards down and shrugged off her loss.

'So, Darryl, who do you pick?' Willow said.

'It has to be Carmen,' he said, gesturing at her with an open-palmed hand. Carmen grimaced. 'Does that mean I have to reveal a secret?' she said, her eyes wide.

Cressida laughed. 'Yes!'

'Maybe I don't have any,' Carmen said boldly, leaning back in her chair and folding her arms with a grin.

'Oh, *everyone* has secrets, Carmen. I'll help you if you can't think of a specific one to share,' Willow said. She thought for a moment. 'What's the worst thing you've ever done?'

Carmen's eyebrows shot up. 'Wow, hardcore. Okay, fine.' She paused. 'I once sabotaged a fellow skater,' she said, eventually.

'What? How?' Darryl said excitedly, leaning forward.

'It was a long time ago and I'm not proud of it. We were auditioning for a show and I was a young skater, and there weren't many opportunities, so I … I messed with her skates. That's all I'll say,' Carmen said, a red blush rising high on her cheeks. She looked down at her hands.

Cressida looked impressed at her candour. 'Oh my goodness Carmen, I wouldn't have pegged you for a saboteur.'

'Shall we carry on?' Willow looked around, and the game continued with a new hand.

Katerina felt a sliver of nerves slide into her stomach. This definitely wasn't what she expected from a game of poker and Carmen had been surprisingly frank. Katerina didn't want to risk being asked anything too personal. She decided that if it was her turn she would offer up something mundane, unremarkable, like cheating on a test. Not that she ever had, but she would make something up to satisfy the group. It felt like a cowardly thing to do, but she wasn't going to share anything real with this room of strangers and the audience at home.

Cressida won the second hand. 'I've never won at cards before!' she yelped happily.

'Who do you pick, Cressida?' Willow asked.

Cressida smiled and looked around with an amused expression. 'Maz,' she said finally.

Maz placed her hands on her chest in mock humility. 'Me? I'm honoured. Why don't you ask away? I have nothing to hide.'

Cressida nodded. 'Okay.' She paused for a moment to think. 'Have you ever cheated on someone?' she asked.

Maz snorted. 'Lame. Yes, I have. I've never been faithful. Why do you think I'm single now?' She laughed brashly, but Katerina thought she saw a glimmer of sadness in her eyes.

There was an uncomfortable silence, broken by Finn. 'Next round,' he said, nodding to Willow to deal.

Katerina shifted in her seat. It was getting too personal and she wanted to leave but Willow dealt the next hand, and she felt obliged to continue. She hoped that no one would want to pick her anyway. She folded again straight away, and Finn gave her an amused glance as she did so.

Willow won the hand. She smiled coolly. 'My turn,' she said, looking around the room. Her eyes came to rest on Katerina, and she shuddered. *Stay cool, you're an actress, you can bluff your way through this,* Katerina reminded herself, and met the younger woman's gaze. There was a glint in her eyes that Katerina didn't like the look of. It reminded her of the popular girls at school who whispered mean comments and gossip behind their hands.

'Katerina, when did you lose your virginity?' Willow asked, without hesitation, with a barely suppressed smile.

Katerina tried to freeze her expression so that her horror at the question wouldn't show on her face. Without meaning to, her eyes flickered across the table and caught Finn's gaze. He bit his lip, a red tinge rising up his neck.

'Um, I, er, fifteen I think,' Katerina stuttered, and Cressida laughed. 'You think? What, you don't remember?' she said teasingly.

'Okay, well, I'm off to bed, enjoy the rest of the game.' Katerina rose up, stumbling slightly as the pricks of pins and needles caught her skin where she had crossed her legs so tightly she had cut off her circulation. She hurried up the stairs, ignoring Cressida's giggling and Finn's burning stare.

Finn watched Katerina scurry away up the stairs, her feet pounding on the rough wood. He tried to steady his expression, hoping the hot flush of embarrassment that had swept over him would subside quickly.

'What is her problem?' Cressida laughed.

'I think I'll join her.' Maz got up from the sofa and headed up the stairs. 'This is a dumb game,' she muttered as she left.

Willow rolled her eyes. 'Finn, you know Katerina, right? Has she always been this uptight?'

Finn stared at the spot where Katerina had been sitting.

'Well, it's a personal question, and we all don't know each other that well. I'm sure she was just a bit embarrassed,' Finn said, with a nonchalant shrug, trying to speak levelly and hoping his voice didn't catch in his throat from where it had seized up with discomfort.

Willow raised an eyebrow and turned her attention to the cards. 'Want to carry on?' she asked the group. Darryl, Carmen and Cressida were keen to continue and turned to Finn, eager for his participation. He was tempted to go upstairs but thought there would be no point in trying to speak to Katerina when Maz and Gideon would both be there, so he nodded, trying to look more enthusiastic than he felt. 'Sure, let's go again.'

Willow dealt the cards. Finn took up his hand, wishing he had a better poker face. Acting was definitely Katerina's strength, not his. He folded and waited for the game to play out. Willow won again and she smiled triumphantly. '*Oooh* who should I pick on next?' she said, teasingly. She looked across at Finn. 'You're the only one who hasn't offered up a secret yet, Finn,' she said, a smile playing on her lips. 'So, tell us about your best kiss ever.'

Finn wished he could answer honestly, but he knew he couldn't tell the truth. Although he didn't actually mind telling people that Katerina's kisses had stayed in his mind all these years, she clearly had an issue with their shared past and didn't want to reveal it. She was probably ashamed of being associated with a former boy-band singer, he thought, with a slight twinge of bitterness. He was hurt by her obvious disdain for, and denial of, their teenage romance, which he remembered with fondness despite the way it ended.

He knew he had to answer as the group waited expectantly. 'I dated a girl when I was a teenager. We had …' He paused, trying to think of the right word. 'A connection. I don't know how to describe it but being with her was like being in a dreamworld where every wrong suddenly felt right. Those were the best kisses.'

Carmen sighed with a wistful smile. 'How romantic.'

Willow narrowed her eyes. 'What happened to this teenage sweetheart?' she said.

Finn shrugged. 'It wasn't meant to be. She's married with kids now, but I'll always remember her.'

Willow nodded, and Finn felt a slackening of the tension in his gut that he didn't even know was there till he had answered the question.

The game moved on, but Finn's mind was elsewhere and he soon excused himself to go to bed. He climbed the stairs and slid inside his sleeping bag underneath the thick woollen blankets on his bunk, relishing their weight, even their slight scratchiness on his cheek. The fibres made him want to sneeze and he rubbed his nose, turning over and looking across the room. The perpetual light outside sneaked in around the shutters and curtains, and in the dimness he could see where Katerina lay. She may have been in the same room as him, but they might as well have been miles apart for the distance that he sensed between them.

Then – Katerina

'Are you sure it's okay for me to come over?' Katerina asked hesitantly as she followed Finn. They walked quickly, the rain dampening her socks inside her shoes, the bottoms of her trousers becoming heavy with moisture. The umbrella she held only kept her hair and her face dry, the rain knew how to find the rest of her. Finn marched on without an umbrella, his hood pulled up, hands in his pockets. She struggled to keep up with his pace and was slightly out of breath as she trotted after him.

'Yeah, it's fine,' he said shortly, and she knew he was annoyed. They had met to rehearse in the park, but the rain began shortly after, a river of fat droplets pouring down on them. Neither of them had any money to go somewhere else, and Katerina's parents had visitors. It was Finn's place or nothing, and Katerina got the sense that he had been reluctant to invite her over.

She hurried alongside him in silence. They wound their way onto an estate from the 1960s, the pale brick marred by graffiti. It was quiet, everyone was tucked away in their flats, sheltering from the rain. Finn pushed open the door to one of the buildings and she followed him inside, their wet feet slapping against the blue plastic flooring. Finn started climbing the stairs rapidly and Katerina was puffing hard by the time they stepped onto the fourth floor. She tried not to breathe too noisily, embarrassed by her lack of fitness.

A pale bulb flickered in the hallway light, and Finn stopped before a doorway, where the cream paint was turning yellow and starting to peel off in limp patches, leaving dark scars underneath.

She tried to fix a neutral expression on her face at the piles of mess that confronted her in the hallway of the flat. Stacks of newspapers were piled up high in precarious towers, a large plastic tub of saucepans with burnt bottoms jostled for space with boxes of shoes. The shelves lining the walls overflowed with a variety of plastic bottles and ceramic jugs. There was only just enough space to squeeze through sideways via a narrow pathway carved out among the debris.

Finn turned to her with a pained expression. 'My mum likes to collect things,' he said, in a low voice.

She nodded, unsure what to say, but she felt saddened by the strained look he wore. He was ashamed, she could see it in his grim smile and the bright flush that marred his face, and now she could understand his reluctance to invite her over.

'Mum,' Finn called out cautiously, as they walked into the living room, keeping their wet shoes on.

'Yes love?' Katerina heard a wavering voice from one of the rooms. A bone-thin woman with bleached blonde hair came into the living room, looking pleased to see Finn. Her eyes alighted on Katerina.

'Oh hello, I'm Jenny,' she said. 'Finn, how nice that you've brought a friend home.' A smile stretched across her pale skin. She wasn't an old woman, but she looked like she had been suffering from a long illness, and her skin reminded Katerina of tissue paper; delicate and vulnerable. Her hair was unevenly cut and unbrushed, with random tufts sticking out and dark roots where the blonde dye had been neglected.

'Yes Mum, we're just here to rehearse the play,' he said, casting an anxious glance at Katerina.

'Play?' Jenny said, looking confused.

'Yeah, I told you about it?' he said, a slight note of irritation in his voice. He frowned, stubbing the toe of his shoe into the thin brown carpet.

'Oh, yes of course, right.' She smiled uncertainly and turned to Katerina. 'It's very nice to meet you …'

'Katerina.' Katerina smiled at her and noted how her eyes were like Finn's – the same shade of cobalt blue – except hers were ringed by dark circles, the whites of her eyes yellowed and shot through with spidery red veins.

'Katerina, lovely name.' She smiled sweetly. 'I'll leave you two to practise,' she said, wandering out of the living room.

Finn sighed. 'Want a drink of water?' he asked.

Katerina nodded. 'Sure, thanks.'

Finn gestured to the sofa. 'Take a seat,' he said, with a wry smile.

The living room wasn't as bad as the hallway, but there were piles of clutter in every corner of the room. An old TV teetered on one pile of papers and magazines, the screen thick with grey dust, and there were stacks of water-damaged puzzle boxes piled haphazardly in one corner. The small grey sofa was a clear space in the midst of the mess, but even that had a pillow and blankets slung over the back. A guitar rested on the floor with a pile of books she recognised as their course books from school. She sat down gingerly on the sofa and wondered if she should have come at all, given Finn's obvious discomfort at her being there.

Finn returned with two glasses of water and handed one to her. As he stretched out his hand to give her the glass she noticed a small tattoo on his wrist.

'Thanks,' she said, resting it between her feet on the floor, as there was no coffee table. 'I like your tattoo,' she said, indicating at it.

'Oh yeah?' he pulled back his shirt sleeve a little more so she could see the musical notes etched onto his skin.

'How did you even get one?' she asked curiously. 'You're only fifteen. I thought you had to be eighteen.'

Finn laughed. 'Fake ID,' he said. 'I usually only use it for buying cider to drink with friends but they dared me one time to get a tattoo and I actually like it, so it's okay I guess.'

'Your mum didn't mind?' Katerina asked.

Finn gave her a small half-smile that was more sad than amused. 'She hasn't noticed it.' He cleared his throat and then gestured to the piles of things in the room. 'Sorry about all the stuff in here,' he said sheepishly. 'It's the living room and my bedroom so it's kind of crowded,' he said.

'You sleep in here?' she said, surprised, and looked round for a bed.

'Yeah,' he patted the back of the sofa, and she realised the pillow and blankets were his. This was where he curled up and slept every night. Finn Drayson, the boy with the best smile in school, lived in a hovel. Katerina's heart broke a little and she felt the weight of the personal information he had just shared with her. He had let her into a part of his life he kept hidden from others. She didn't want her crush on Finn to grow, but it now expanded and took up even more space in her heart.

'Is that your guitar?' she asked, changing the subject.

'Yep,' he said.

'Maybe one day you could play a song for me?' she asked, hopefully.

Finn laughed. 'Maybe, yeah. I don't really play my stuff for anyone though.'

'Don't you want to be a singer?' she asked.

'I'd like to be,' he said with a nod.

'Well then you have to learn to play in front of people,' she said, smiling at him.

He grinned back and grabbed his copy of the script. 'Come on, let's start,' he said. 'We've got that group rehearsal tomorrow and we're not quite ready yet.'

Katerina was impressed that Finn had obviously been practising. She hadn't quite expected him to be so dedicated. At school he seemed to be entirely nonchalant about his work and apathetic about his grades. She was seeing a different side of him here, someone who was really trying.

When they finished the script, he leaned back, stretching his arms behind him. 'It's okay, I suppose. Right?' he said, raising one eyebrow and giving her a lopsided smile.

Katerina felt a new kind of desire sweep through her, a longing both physical and emotional, and so powerful and unexpected it made her legs shake. Finn was sitting so close that she could smell the heady mix of his perspiration, hair gel and Lynx spray. She had been trying so hard to keep her mini-crush under control, but Finn's proximity and his gorgeous carefree smile only stoked it further.

'Yeah, it's fine, I mean, it's good,' she said, trying to force her mind to focus and ignoring the nervous damp patches under her arms.

'Finn.' Jenny came into the room, wringing her hands, her eyes wide. 'Have you seen the china doll? The angel? I can't find it anywhere.' Katerina could see her trembling like a child.

'Oh, no Mum, I haven't,' Finn said. 'Katerina was just going, and then I'll help you look for it,' he said, jumping up from the sofa.

Katerina felt a wave of disappointment sweep through her and drown the butterflies that had been fluttering in her stomach. He clearly wanted her to go. She followed him to the doorway and he stepped outside with her into the corridor. 'Mum, I'll just walk Katerina out and I'll be right back, okay?' he yelled. Jenny mumbled a reply, and he shut the door with a gentle click.

'You don't need …' Katerina started to say, but he held up a hand.

'It's no problem,' he said.

Katerina knew he didn't have to walk her out, and she felt a hopeful burst of pleasure at the thought that perhaps he wanted to spend more time with her.

'I'm sorry about my mum,' he said, as they walked down the stairs.

'That's okay, I hope she finds the angel,' she said.

'It's something she does a lot. She loses something and then we have to spend hours searching for it,' he said. 'She has some problems, anxiety and stuff. She can't really leave the flat any more.' He sighed, shoving his hands into his pockets.

'That must be tough,' Katerina said, placing a hand gently on his upper arm then quickly pulling it away, feeling like it was too forward.

He smiled at her and didn't reply.

They walked slowly through the corridor and out of the doors, where a blast of rain-cleansed air hit Katerina in the face. She shivered even though it wasn't cold. They were dawdling, she thought, both unwilling to end the afternoon.

'Your parents seem so nice,' Finn said suddenly.

He hadn't mentioned them since the dinner at her house, so Katerina had been worried that he didn't like them. She nodded. 'I'm pretty lucky really,' she said, pleased that he had complimented her family. She was fairly close to her parents, and although they often drove her crazy, she also knew that she got on better with them than many teenagers did with their own families. She was proud of her dad for getting a new job, even if it meant moving to a new area and changing schools.

'They think the world of you,' he said, as they walked through the estate, swerving to avoid the puddles that had collected on the uneven ground. 'They're obviously very proud.'

She shrugged. 'It's a lot of pressure sometimes, being an only child on a pedestal. I'm not allowed to make mistakes,' she said with a slight frown.

Finn scuffed his shoe on the pavement. 'What are they like with your boyfriends?' he asked, not looking at her.

'Oh, um, I haven't had any,' she said, feeling her face flush despite the cool air. 'But I imagine, well, my parents are pretty strict Catholics, and I think me dating someone would be … a bit awkward.' She knew her parents would be overprotective and horrified about her dating, and insist on no sex before marriage, and certainly no boyfriends before university. She left it unsaid though. She didn't want to risk putting Finn off.

'Awkward, right, sure,' Finn said, nodding as if he understood.

They left the estate and Finn paused. 'I better get back to my mum,' he said, nodding his head towards his block of flats.

'Of course. Thanks for walking me out,' Katerina said. 'And thanks for the rehearsal space.' She glanced at him, wishing she could read his mind.

'No problem. See you tomorrow?' he asked.

'Sure.'

He turned and walked away, marching across the estate without a backward glance. Katerina watched him for a moment and all she could think about was how he didn't ask her out and how much she longed for him to do so.

Chapter Seven

Finn

The morning air was sharp and cold, like a drink of pure iced-water for his lungs. Finn inhaled till his chest ached, the wind making his cheeks smart. There was a smattering of snow on the ground, a gentle frosting of white over the earth, as though someone had been sifting icing sugar. Finn walked back to the cabin, proud of his ability to withstand the freezing shower for more than ten seconds. He felt chilled all over, but at least he was somewhat clean. His skin still throbbed bright red from the painful slap of the icy water, and he rubbed his arms underneath his fleece, looking forward to the cosy warmth of the cabin. He glanced at the hot-tub shed as he walked by and he thought jealously of the treat that Michael and Ashif enjoyed yesterday. It was certainly an unexpected feature of their retreat, and Finn hoped that he would get to use it soon.

The cabin was filled with the subdued morning murmurings of tired people, yawning and still hungry. Finn headed for the kitchen and took a cup of steaming tea, burning his tongue as he took a large gulp. He glanced around. Maz and Michael were talking in the kitchen, and Gideon was making his way slowly down the stairs. Ashif came in from the front door, followed by Katerina, her cheeks reddened from the cold.

They all drifted together in the living room. There was an air of increased confidence about them, and although they were tired and still hungry, Finn thought everyone looked ready to work, keen to replicate the success of yesterday.

'I really want to go and check the traps I laid yesterday,' Darryl said. 'I'm hoping we caught something overnight.' He looked across at Finn expectantly, and Finn tried not to wince as he thought of spending another day being Darryl's helper. Before he could open his mouth, knowing he had no decent excuse not to go with Darryl, Cressida piped up.

'I'll go with you, Darryl,' she said brightly.

Finn was surprised at her enthusiasm but relieved he didn't have to go with Darryl again. It crossed his mind that Cressida might be offering in the hope that the traps had caught something and she could share in the glory. Even if her offer was motivated by the hope of a reward, Finn was happy to let her go, if it meant not traipsing around after Darryl's perfectionist pursuits all day.

'We need someone to go to the lake,' Gideon said, looking around hopefully. 'No one made it there yesterday but if we could catch some fish it would be excellent nutrition.'

They all fell silent, thinking about the trek there and back. Although Gideon had offered to give a fishing lesson yesterday, there hadn't been any takers and they had all been busy with other tasks. But he was right, Finn thought, it made sense to try at least. He was pondering whether or not he should offer to go, when Katerina spoke up from where she sat, sandwiched between Ashif and Carmen.

'I'll go,' she said. 'My dad and I used to fish a little together. I think I have the energy to get there today and give it a try.'

Finn looked at her determined expression with admiration. He could see that she was tired, her eyes shadowy and her complexion wan, and given her slender build he guessed that her reserves were pretty low. She was probably struggling with the lack of food as much as any of them, but she was willing to go out on a limb to help the group.

'Excellent, good for you!' Michael declared, with an approving nod.

'You can't go on your own, surely?' Gideon said with concern. 'Are there any other volunteers to go with Katerina?'

'I'll go,' Finn said quickly, before anyone else could offer. This was his chance to do something for the group, help Katerina, and hopefully get the opportunity to talk to her that he had been waiting for. He looked at her for her reaction. She glanced at him and nodded stiffly, her lips pressed together. She didn't look too pleased, thought Finn. Still, perhaps she was just being restrained in front of the group and secretly she was excited, like him, at the prospect of spending some time alone together, even if a cameraman followed them.

Katerina

No, no, no, no, no. Katerina wanted to make her objection clear, but instead she stared at the toe of her boot and her mind scrambled for an excuse. She couldn't find one in time, and the discussion moved on. She was happy to help with the fishing, just not with Finn. Anyone but him. There was too much history and too much water under the bridge. She wanted to avoid him and now she would be forced into spending an entire day with him alone. It was like a terrible nightmare and she berated herself for not thinking of this as a possibility before she volunteered to go to the lake.

She tried to breathe slowly and concentrated hard, biting down on her lower lip as she always did when trying to find a solution. She had to have a plan of action to get through the day with her former first love. *Don't get drawn into conversation*, she told herself. *Keep it light. No reminiscing.*

Her stomach knotted as she tied up her boots and Finn bounded over, pulling on his gloves, his dark-green jacket zipped to his chin. He looked at her eagerly and she felt a nudge of guilt at his enthusiasm that she couldn't match.

'Hey, ready to go?' he asked.

'Yes, let's go,' she said, trying to sound neutral. She didn't want to sound too pleased or too dismissive, but Finn didn't seem to notice her measured tone as he grinned at her.

With Gideon's help, Katerina had selected a few items of fishing equipment from the shed – rods, reels, hooks and lures. She knew roughly what she needed, remembering vaguely from her trips with her dad, and Gideon kindly filled in the blanks for her.

She and Finn walked out into the crisp air, the bags of equipment slung on their shoulders. The frost was dissipating, and the straw-coloured sun glimmered in a sky that looked bleached and wrung of colour. Katerina clutched at the map and tried to focus on the landmarks as they trudged up a slight incline. A chill wind blew around them but the marching pace they sustained kept her blood moving.

Occasionally she heard the shuffled steps of the cameraman behind them, reminding her that this was all being observed by their silent partner, and would later be watched by many thousands more.

Finn walked along with her, looking delighted. The breeze ruffled his hair and his eyes seemed even bluer as he squinted against the pale Alaskan light.

'I can't believe the crazy coincidence, us two being here together,' he said. He kept his voice level and low, but Katerina could hear the shiver of expectation in his words. He glanced around at the cameraman and leaned close to her, speaking barely above a whisper, his words almost snatched away by the wind. 'I missed you, Kat.'

She didn't want to hear the same tenderness in his voice that he used to have when he talked to her, reminding her of the boy in the messy flat, the hungry teen who had awakened all her desires. She would prefer to run to the lake and throw herself in rather than experience the pressing and intense sweetness of loving Finn Drayson again. She couldn't allow herself to be reminded of the emotions that stayed with her for years after they parted and had been so hard to smother.

'I can't believe all the amazing things you've done,' he said, a note of admiration in his voice. 'Those TV dramas, that Dickens adaptation, the awards …' He trailed off. 'Not that I ever had any doubt in your talents of course.'

She gave him a slight smile, not wanting his admiration but pleased despite herself that he had been following her career. 'Thank you. It's been a bit of a rollercoaster really. I've been lucky.'

'What brings you here?' he asked curiously. 'I mean, you're clearly not short of work. Why put yourself in the middle of Alaska for two weeks?'

Katerina paused, wondering how open to be. 'I wanted a real challenge,' she said, finally. 'I'm at a bit of a turning point, in many ways,' she added, waving a hand in the air, not wanting to explain. 'I thought doing something like this, outside my comfort zone, would be inspiring.'

Finn nodded. 'I heard about your divorce,' he said. 'That must have been tough. And you have a son, right? I'm sure that was difficult for him too.'

Katerina prickled at the mention of her son by the boy who had broken her heart. The ache she felt when she thought about Chris made it harder to breathe. She felt physically bereft when he wasn't nearby, an intensity of affection she had never known before she became a mother.

'It was very difficult,' she said, in clipped tones that she hoped would warn Finn off asking any more questions about her home life.

She was thankful that he seemed to get the hint and changed the subject.

'How are your parents?' he asked.

'My dad passed away,' Katerina said, remembering the awkwardness between him and Finn, and his insistence that Finn wasn't good enough for her. She had always defended Finn, but her dad had been a better judge of character than her. She had been blinded by hormones, lust and foolish teenage fancies.

‘Oh, I’m sorry,’ Finn said, a look of sympathy on his face. ‘When did he die?’

‘A few years ago. He had pancreatic cancer,’ she said. She had spent so much time googling facts about the illness, looking for potential cures and possible treatments, that she felt like she could give reams of information whenever anyone asked about it, but she didn’t want to elaborate on this occasion.

Finn sucked on his teeth. ‘Nasty. That’s a real shame,’ he said.

She nodded and stopped for a moment to check the map, as much to check their direction as to focus her eyes on something else while she blinked away the tears that gathered. She held her compass against the map, the needle quivering. They were heading in the right direction.

‘Nearly there,’ she said.

‘Great.’

They continued, winding their way through the trees that towered above them. The birds circled and cawed overhead, their calls echoing into the emptiness.

Finn had given up making small talk, she noted gratefully. They were both moving fast, eager to get to their destination. It wasn’t until they were almost at the lake edge that the trees parted and they could actually see it, spread out in front of them. A vast glimmering body of water, hugging the shoreline; a mirror stretched out to reflect the heavens.

‘Wow,’ Finn said, gazing around with a sigh. ‘It’s incredible here.’

Katerina nodded. ‘It’s stunning. So tranquil, so different to London.’ She scanned the water’s edge. The lake was deserted, the waters still and deep, where the reflection of the trees shimmered on the surface so clearly it was like a flattened forest laid out under their feet. Although there was a smattering of ice and snow on the banks, the lake itself was too deep to have frozen over.

She unpacked the bags and clumsily set up the poles, her gloved hands fumbling with the equipment. Her dad had been much more proficient, but she remembered the basic steps that he showed her. She hoped they could catch something, as the group was still desperate for more food, and she felt the weight of their hope and hunger on her shoulders.

Finn followed her instructions quietly, his earlier enthusiasm dampened by the tiring walk and the frozen air blowing at them from across the water.

They sat side by side, looking out over the lake. It felt colder now they weren't moving, and Katerina wrapped her arms tightly around herself, tucking her hands beneath her armpits. She glanced at Finn. 'How is your mum?' she asked, tentatively. She felt guilty for not asking him sooner. As much as she didn't want to reconnect with him, she remembered his mum with fondness and hoped he would be able to tell her something positive about how Jenny was now.

Finn sighed and ran his hands through his hair. 'She died,' he said, looking at Katerina, then turning his gaze back to the lake. 'Well, actually, she killed herself,' he said flatly, his mouth turned down at the corners.

'Oh, Finn, I'm so sorry. That's terrible,' Katerina said with a gasp, shocked at the awfulness of the news. She felt a deep pang of sorrow, for him and for Jenny. 'When did it happen?'

'Years ago, when I was eighteen,' he said. 'I had to fend for myself after that. Fortunately, the audition for the band came along at just the right time, and although it's not necessarily what I wanted, it meant I didn't have to go on the dole or on the streets or anything like that.' He said it nonchalantly, without emotion or self-pity, as if it were normal for someone to have made such choices at such a young age.

Katerina shivered from sadness rather than the cold. She grasped for the right words, unable to imagine how awful it must have been. It had happened not long after she had left. Guilt churned in her stomach at the thought of Finn alone, coping with the devastation of losing his only parent and trying to put a brave face on it, as she knew he would have done.

'Finn, I'm so sorry. That must have been so hard, I can't even imagine.' She allowed herself to weaken for just a moment and put a hand on his arm.

He ran his hand over hers, just briefly. 'It was. You were long gone by that point though, weren't you?' His tone changed, a hard edge of accusation creeping in. His eyes narrowed slightly, but he continued looking out at the water rather than at her.

She ignored him and fiddled with her fishing line, knowing he had a point, and not knowing how to counter it.

'You could have called,' he said, murmuring almost to himself.

Katerina thought about the last text she sent him and cringed at the memory of her teenage inability to be honest and to do the right thing, even if she had been angry at him. She didn't say anything and allowed the gentle lapping of the lake to fill the gap in her ability to respond.

Then – Finn

'You two have great chemistry,' Mr Maguire said, clapping his hands and nodding in approval at their rehearsal. 'I'm very confident that you'll both be brilliant.'

Finn tried not to look too pleased, but it felt good to do well in something, especially as he wasn't brilliant at his other subjects.

Katerina frowned and looked over her script. 'I wanted to ask you about a few things,' she said, waving it at Mr Maguire. 'I wonder if there are some improvements we can make …' She trailed off as Mr Maguire laughed.

'Always a perfectionist,' he said, shaking his head. 'No, we won't tamper with it. You've been rehearsing this for two months. It's perfect the way it is. Perfect for the performances.'

Finn felt a slew of nerves entwine in his stomach at the idea of performing on stage in front of the other students, his friends, and maybe an agent or two.

Mr Maguire checked his watch. 'Okay, time to go,' he announced. It was already past 5 p.m. and the school was closing.

The small group hurried out into the early evening, the sky a pale blue, golden sheaths of late-afternoon sunshine pooling on the pavement. Mr Maguire hurried off, his spindly legs taking him in the direction of the car park that was now emptying. Katerina and Finn lagged behind, shuffling their feet.

Katerina turned to go, the chemistry of their rehearsal gone now they had cast off their characters, their teenage awkwardness returning. 'I'll see you tomorrow,' she said with a faint smile.

Finn grabbed her arm before she walked off. 'I was going to get some chips. Do you wanna come?' he asked, feeling jittery with nerves. He wanted an excuse to avoid going home, and also wanted someone to hang out with who wouldn't take the piss out of him.

Katerina nodded, checking her watch. 'Okay. I'll call my mum to let her know I'll be home a bit later.'

She rummaged in her school bag for her mobile and dialled, turning away from Finn while she talked.

'Hi Mum, the rehearsal is going on later than planned so I'll be a little while longer, okay?' she said, without batting an eyelid and sounding entirely convincing.

That's the problem with girls who are good actresses, thought Finn, watching her. *They're also good liars.*

She turned to him and nodded. 'All good to go,' she said.

They walked together down the road, their footsteps echoing in unison.

'How come you didn't tell her what you were really doing?' he asked.

She shrugged and didn't quite meet his gaze. 'I just didn't think they would like it.'

'What, you hanging out with a boy or you hanging out with me specifically?' he said, the words feeling bitter on his tongue.

'Any boy,' she said, rolling her eyes, and he felt a little mollified.

They turned onto the main road, where the noise of cars filled the air that had felt so still and sleepy just moments ago. They stopped by the fish-and-chip shop, the sharp aroma of vinegar and the scent of hot oil clinging to them even when they walked outside with their chips. Finn had scrounged a small amount of money from his mum that morning, even though usually she didn't have much to spare. He could have bought something for lunch but held out, hoping Katerina would come with him after the rehearsal. It was worth the hunger pangs and the sour taste in his mouth to wait to eat with her, sitting on a park bench where graffiti tags were etched amateurishly into the roughened wood. Katerina smoothed out the paper around her chips and Finn watched her eat, enjoying looking at her as the sunshine cast its warm glow over them.

Katerina caught Finn staring at her and smiled nervously. 'What? Do I have ketchup on my face?' she asked, swiping a self-conscious hand across her cheeks.

'No.' Finn laughed, shaking his head. 'I just like the way you eat.'

'The way I eat?' Katerina said incredulously, raising her eyebrows.

Finn mimicked her delicate, careful eating, so graceful even with a wooden chip fork in hand. Katerina sputtered with laughter. 'I do *not* eat like that,' she said.

Finn nodded. 'You do. Very posh.' He grinned. 'Thank you for gracing me with your presence for chips a la park bench, mademoiselle.'

She grinned at his faux-French accent. 'Best spot in town.'

'Perfect for a hot date,' he said, glancing at her furtively, trying to flirt with her and not really sure how to.

He saw the glow on her cheeks and the way she looked down at her hands with a small smile, and thought that perhaps she liked him too. He had thought about her more and more over the past few weeks. They had been spending a lot of time together, and she was kind to his mum when she came to his flat, which was important to him. Katerina always listened carefully to what he said but he never felt judged by her. When he was with her, he felt less alone with his problems, like he had an ally.

His friends had asked him why he was hanging out with Katerina, laughingly calling her a stuck-up cow. He had fobbed them off, telling them she was just a rehearsal partner. He'd not defended her, and had burned with shame at the flimsy bravado. He knew they wouldn't like her and vice versa, so he preferred to keep his deepening feelings for Katerina hidden. They were too precious to share with such idiots.

'So,' he said casually, discarding the chip papers onto the ground, and leaning back, one hand slung across the back of the bench. He could almost touch her hair or reach across to rest his arm on her shoulder, he thought, his heart beating quickly.

She smiled at him. 'So … what, Finn?' she asked, the sound of his name on her lips thrilling him.

He wanted to say something smooth and clever, but he couldn't think of anything, so he decided to lean in to kiss her anyway. He moved a little too quickly, mouth open, hoping for the best.

Katerina practically jumped away from him, leaning back, her eyes wide with panic.

'What are you doing?' she said, in a horrified whisper.

'Oh, um, sorry, I just thought you …' Finn stammered, wishing the ground would swallow him up. He stared at the chip papers, rustling in the breeze, preparing for flight. *Take me with you*, he wanted to beg them.

'You thought wrong, Finn,' she snapped at him, looking mortified. 'You can't just lean in and kiss me without warning, without saying anything first.'

Finn knew he should have prepared something to say and wanted to kick himself. Embarrassment piqued his annoyance.

'I thought you were interested, that's all,' he muttered. 'What do you want? Flowers? An engagement ring first?'

She pressed her mouth into a line. 'Don't be a dickhead. It doesn't suit you.'

'I'm not good enough for you? Is that it?' he asked, wishing he could stop the words, but they poured out like a vicious waterfall that was beyond his control.

'It's not like that,' she said, shaking her head. 'I just don't want to kiss someone who isn't my actual boyfriend.'

'Really? Well, maybe I'm not smart enough or rich enough to be your boyfriend?' he said, snapping the words at her, almost wanting her to confirm his suspicions so he could stop hoping there was a chance.

'Do you even want to be my boyfriend?' she asked, looking surprised.

'No,' he said curtly. He got up and walked off, feeling hot and stupid and angry, and leaving her behind on the bench.

Then – Katerina

'You are such a moron,' Katerina hissed at Finn, trying to keep her voice low so they wouldn't be overheard by the other students milling around backstage. 'You left me on that bench. So rude.' She was still hurt and annoyed, and his smirk only served to increase her frustration.

'Sorry princess,' Finn said nonchalantly, his hands in his pockets. 'I didn't realise I was supposed to escort you to your limo.'

Katerina rolled her eyes and huffed, her irritation robbing her of anything articulate or useful to say. 'So immature.'

'Everything okay with you two?' Mr Maguire asked, appearing behind them and looking concerned at Katerina's stony expression and Finn's sullen glare.

There was a restless murmur behind the curtains as the audience took their seats. Katerina could hear a rumble of voices, chairs scraping, the programmes rustling in hundreds of hands, all waiting to see her and Finn.

'It's all fine, Mr Maguire,' Katerina said, with a confident smile that was completely fake. 'We're totally prepared and ready to go.'

Mr Maguire looked at them, frowning at Finn's slightly ruffled appearance. 'Finn, get ready please, you haven't got long,' he said, turning to walk away and resolve an issue with the lighting.

Finn shrugged in response and Katerina could have strangled him. 'Don't be a wanker. You know there are agents in the audience that Mr Maguire invited. Don't mess this up just because I wouldn't kiss you on a park bench,' she snapped.

'Whatever you say, madame,' Finn said with a mock bow, and he sauntered off, irritatingly slow.

Katerina kneaded her hands together, feeling anxious and clammy. It wasn't the performance that worried her, as she knew her lines and she didn't get stage fright. It was Finn messing with her head that was the problem. He didn't know that she had been dying to kiss him on the bench that evening, desperate to feel his lips on hers, to stroke a hand in his hair, to feel the weight of his arm around her shoulders. But she was no fool. She wanted her first kiss to be with a boyfriend, and Finn hadn't even tried to ask her out properly. Now she felt hot and fidgety and distracted, all because of him and the fact that she had let him get to her.

Eventually Finn was ready, and they took their starting positions, listening as Mr Maguire gave the welcome and introduction. She took a breath and tried to focus her mind on the lines, not on Finn's unnerving gaze. He stared at her, eyes sparkling in the spotlights, and she looked away as the curtains opened.

She was worried that he might deliberately mess it up, but she had misjudged him; he was just as good as any of their rehearsals, if not better. Her anger and his annoyance gave them a biting, snappy chemistry, an added fire to their exchanges that the audience loved. They didn't actually kiss in any of the scenes, although there were moments when they held each other close, hands and heads strategically placed so it looked as though they were. Katerina both hated and loved the proximity to him, wishing she didn't want him as much as she did.

They finished to enthusiastic applause and Katerina closed her eyes for a second and allowed herself to think of this on a larger scale. This was a triumph, and perhaps she had a real chance to do this for a living. She looked across at Finn and she knew he was lapping it up too. They held hands and bowed, then let go quickly as the curtain dropped and Mr Maguire hurried over in delight.

He dragged Katerina away to meet his agent friend, and they left Finn behind, watching them go. Katerina glanced over her shoulder and wanted to tell the agent, *look over there, he's got talent too*. But she allowed herself to be swept along and lost herself in the conversation and the praise over her performance.

It was late when she finally made it backstage to collect her bag. The hall was emptying out and her parents were waiting in the car park to take her home. She rummaged through costumes and coats, finally finding her bag, readying herself to leave.

'How did it go with the agent?' Finn asked, approaching her from the shadows.

She jumped with surprise. 'You scared me,' she said, a hand on her chest. 'Um, it went well. Something might come of it, but perhaps he was just being polite and friendly for Mr Maguire's sake,' she said.

Finn shook his head. 'You're too modest – I'm sure there are so many opportunities for you. The world is your oyster, Kat,' he said, gesturing widely.

'You were really good as well,' she said, looking at the floor. 'You deserve opportunities too.'

He gave a tight smile. 'You're the talented one. I'm just …' He shrugged. 'A kid from an estate with a mad mum. Who would be interested?'

Katerina dropped her bag and walked up to him, standing directly before him. She gently touched his face, lifting it so his eyes met hers. 'I would be,' she said, hardly knowing what she was doing, but entirely swept away with the evening and her emotions.

It was just the slightest lean forward, a shifting of his gravity towards her, but the distance between them was so small that it was enough for their lips to meet. Katerina forgot to breathe for a long moment while they kissed. Her heart was pounding and she kept picturing the kisses she had seen on films and wondering if she was doing it right, confused about which way to tilt her head, and where to put her hands. Her brain wouldn't stop, every synapse firing, and when Finn pulled away she breathed out suddenly, like a sigh of relief.

He grinned at her. 'Are you okay?'

She smiled. 'Yeah. You just … you took my breath away.' And Finn laughed and leaned in to do it again.

Finn

'Any luck?' he asked Katerina, nodding at the fishing line and breaking the silence that had settled between them.

She shook her head. 'None so far. Keep still and keep waiting though. My dad always taught me to give it time.'

He nodded, opened his mouth to speak, and thought better of it. His mind was churning with so many memories of falling in love with the girl, now woman, sitting next to him. He didn't trust himself to speak any more.

The breeze stirred the strands of hair that escaped her neat French braid. They danced gently over her forehead and he was tempted to lean in and brush them away. She was as still as the rocks that studded the ground around the lake, and he wished he could say something to change the stony apathy with which she now treated him, to try to bring back the heartfelt love she used to show him.

'My mum really liked the adaptation you were in,' he said, clearing his throat. 'The one with the sailor … what was it called?'

'*Persuasion*?' she asked, furrowing her forehead at his vague description.

'That's the one.'

'I'm glad she liked it,' Katerina murmured.

'She didn't have that many pleasures in life,' he said, sadly.

'Apart from you, and your music,' Katerina remarked. 'She loved to hear you sing.'

He nodded, his throat tightening at the image of his mum listening to his crappy songs on the guitar, nodding along with a peaceful expression, the anxiety that normally marked her features momentarily soothed by his childish lyrics.

'I'm not sure she would have liked 1Dream all that much though,' he said, shaking his head.

Katerina gave him a wry smile. 'You had a few hits.'

'Ah, so you know,' he said, with a grin. 'Did you buy our album? Put up my poster?'

Katerina laughed and he loved that he made her smile. 'Um, no. But I did see you in the magazines and papers. You were pretty big for a time,' she said.

'For just a little while,' Finn added. 'All good things must come to an end, especially in this fickle game of fame,' he said.

'Too true,' she agreed.

His line shifted and tugged. He felt the pressure and it took a moment for his mind to click into gear. 'A bite!' he said excitedly, looking at Katerina for instructions.

Katerina sprang into action, leaning across to help him extract a large, flailing fish, flashing silver in the pale sunlight.

'Wow!' she shrieked. 'This is amazing!'

They both looked at the fish flopping helplessly on the ground, its mouth gaping. Eventually it stopped convulsing, and Katerina covered it in ice. 'At least we know it'll stay fairly fresh,' she said. 'Let's see if we can get lucky and catch some more.'

'Imagine how pleased the group will be,' Finn said, delighted they wouldn't be returning empty-handed.

Katerina smiled. 'Good job, Finn,' she said, her tone genuine.

'Did you ever doubt me and my rod?' he said with an impish grin, and she sputtered with laughter at his silly joke.

Katerina

Katerina didn't want to laugh and joke with Finn, but she couldn't help giggling at his cheesy remark. She could feel the ice between them thawing, drop by drop, and she felt powerless to stop it. She didn't want to feel that likeable familiarity, that spark of attraction, again. Her teenage self didn't know any better and couldn't fight it, but she was a grown woman, nearly thirty, and she could. She had to.

He looked over the lake and the breeze ruffled his hair, the summery hue of his eyes contrasting with the insipid sky. Although Katerina didn't want to feel anything for Finn, she couldn't help but experience a deep unsettling sadness when she thought about his mum. She knew how devastating the loss of a parent could be, and she and her mum had each other to see them through the grief. They had helped each other through her dad's funeral, had packed boxes together, had made decisions, had signed papers. There had been no one for Finn. Katerina could bet that his mum hadn't had any documents or finances organised for him. Her heart hurt to think of him alone and grieving and trying to cope, and she felt a stab of guilt drive into her guts. In another life, where she was braver and more honest, she would have been there by his side. Maybe she still would have been now. She shook her head, trying to dislodge the what-ifs.

'Why did you sign up to come to Alaska?' she asked him, as they sat quiet and still, waiting for more fish.

He glanced over at her. 'I heard you would be here,' he said. He flashed her a grin and she knew he was joking. They hadn't been told who else would be participating, an unusual rule for a show like this.

'The real reason?'

He shrugged. 'It sounded like a good challenge. I hadn't been offered *I'm a Celebrity*, or *Strictly*, so I took this. Gotta take the opportunities when you can,' he said.

'Did you enjoy being in a boy band?' she asked curiously. 'I was kind of surprised when I saw you in one, as I didn't think that was your thing.'

'Yes, well, I wasn't exactly drowning in offers. Not like you,' he said. 'Able to up and leave all of a sudden and pursue your big dreams.' She knew what he was alluding to and she tried to ignore it, just like she was trying to block out the presence of the cameraman who lurked nearby, rustling every now and then in the bushes, a predator looking for meaty gossip.

She was saved from having to reply when her line twitched. She grabbed it, pulling hard to reel it in. A fish exploded from the surface, sending silver flecks of water streaming from it as she hauled it towards her.

'Brilliant!' Finn high-fived her, his momentary dig at her forgotten, as they stared down at their catch.

'Reckon we can get some more?' he said, his eyes bright with excitement.

She nodded with a grin, as fired up by their success as he was. 'No reason why not!'

Their enthusiasm powered them through the day, but was waning by the time they caught their fifth fish. It was a great haul, but they were both cold and exhausted, weak from several days of meagre food, unable to keep warm while sitting still in the chill breeze. Packing up, Katerina's knees ached from the morning trek, and her muscles were beginning to tremble with fatigue. She was relieved that the day was nearly over, apart from the long walk home.

As she squatted down to inspect their haul, her shaking knees gave way and she tumbled forward, feeling a swooping acceleration take hold of her. She tried to pinion her arms and legs to the ground, flailing as the earth slipped from her grasp, and she tumbled straight into the water.

The cold slapped her into shock, and she was instantly frozen, unable to draw breath. The sides of the bank dropped away steeply and she floundered, her feet unable to find any traction in the mud and silt.

'Katerina! Kat!' She could hear Finn's panicked voice and swung towards him, her mouth agape and her eyes wide. Her lungs were growing tighter and tighter like over-filled balloons. Finn knelt down and extended his hands towards her. She finally connected to the part of her brain that controlled her breathing and told herself to inhale. She reached out to him, dragging air into her lungs with ragged gasps.

He grabbed her hands and hauled her onto the bank. She felt inexplicably confused about where she was, why she was there, why was Finn there? A grey fog descended on her brain and she could hear Finn's voice telling her she would be okay, grabbing at her sodden fleece, pulling it off, replacing it with his own. His arms encased her, wrapping her in a foil blanket. *Like a chicken in an oven*, she thought, fingering the shiny material. Finn was looking into her eyes, speaking frantically.

'Are you okay? Talk to me, Kat!' he said, his hands on her shoulders.

She stared blankly at him. 'I need to get back,' she said, her lips trembling. Her brain fired facts at her, but they were just jumbled words about body temperature and hypothermia; she couldn't make sense of it, couldn't make sense of anything except red alarms flashing in her brain and her body.

She felt Finn haul her to her feet and put his arm round her waist, pulling her close to him and moving her feet, leaden and slow. They proceeded awkwardly, lumbering, and her limbs started to judder out of her control. She was aware of being scooped off the floor, and a movement propelling her forward, much faster now, the trees above her sliding away.

With every shaking breath she drew she could hear Finn's answering exhale, harder and harder, as he pushed through the forest and towards the cabin.

She didn't know how long it took as her mind clouded over, aware of only fog and motion, but then heat enveloped her. Ashif was there, how did he get there? She gazed up at him, confused, as he barked orders at people milling around with concerned faces. Her hands were wet and warm, her body weighed down with blankets, hot tea was spooned into her mouth, Finn was there, always there, hovering fearfully in her periphery.

Ashif's face loomed into her vision again. 'Katerina, talk to me. Tell me how you feel,' he said, gently demanding.

She blinked, the cloud in her brain starting to lift. 'Okay, but … confused,' she mumbled through lips that felt uncoordinated.

Ashif nodded gravely. 'You fell in the water at the lake,' he said.

She nodded her understanding – she remembered the lake and the sharp attack of its cold waters.

'You were very close to hypothermia when you got here,' Ashif continued.

'Hypothermia,' she repeated, forcing her brain to focus.

'Yes. It was only Finn's quick work to wrap you in the emergency blanket and get you back here that saved you,' he said.

She looked across at Finn, who was standing watchfully nearby. 'Thank you,' she mouthed to him.

He grinned, relief breaking the concern on his expression. 'No problem. Just don't do it again,' he said.

Willow fluttered near him. 'Wow, Finn, you're a hero. You saved her life,' she said, a dreamy expression on her face, her hand on his arm, a small gesture that irked Katerina, but she couldn't think why.

'A hero indeed,' Michael proclaimed.

Finn looked nonplussed. 'Catch fish, save friend,' he mimed ticking off an imaginary list. 'I've been productive today,' he said, to laughter from the group. Katerina could see they were warming to his relaxed, funny, self-deprecating nature. He really hadn't changed that much from when she knew and loved him, she thought, as she looked on from where she lay on the living room floor.

She let herself lie back, with her eyes closed. She still felt slightly cloudy, but the rough boards of the floor underneath her blanket kept her anchored and awake. She listened to the bustle of the preparations for dinner, the sharing of successes for the day, and tried not to sink into daydreams about her rescuer.

Finn

Although Finn would never admit it, he felt a little puffed with pride from the day's exertions. Not only had they returned with fish, but he had also dragged Katerina from the water, had done what he remembered from the survival training, and had got her back to the cabin. It felt pretty good to be the one who was lauded and appreciated that evening, over a delicious dinner of grilled fish.

He was so thankful that she was okay. Her pale, expressionless face while he was half-walking, half-running back to the cabin had scared him deeply, more than he would admit to anyone. It was like she had been slipping into the afterlife before his eyes and he would have given anything to help her. He would have run a thousand times that distance in the frozen cold if that would have saved her.

He was grateful for Ashif's calm efficiency, and for how Katerina had recovered enough to sit at the table and eat, looking wan and exhausted, staying quiet but seeming well. He stole more than one glance at her over dinner, when he could look away from Willow's admiring gaze and eager chatter about awards parties.

'It was such a crazy night!' Willow exclaimed. 'All those soap actors letting their hair down – some of the things I saw you just wouldn't believe.'

'Hmm, sounds like fun,' he said, not entirely interested by the gossip.

Willow looked a bit put out by his unenthusiastic response. 'You should come to the next one,' she said in a low voice, placing a finger on his thigh under the table, and circling it gently. Finn smiled politely and shifted his position so her hand left his leg. 'Maybe,' he said, and Willow's beautiful eyes looked disappointed.

He was relieved to find himself sitting next to Maz and Gideon on the sofas after dinner, neither of whom were particularly interested in making extensive conversation. He relaxed and sipped his tea, watching Katerina across the room. Her eyes met his and he flashed her a smile, but she looked away. He was trying, he really was, but even saving her life didn't seem to make her behaviour change towards him. He clenched his jaw with frustration. What more could he possibly do?

The screen on the wall turned on, and the group hushed. It was the same time as yesterday's announcement, and they had come to expect it, assuming there would be one every day. Phineas appeared, standing in front of a wooden wall.

'Well done on surviving another day out here in the wilderness,' declared Phineas. He was in a cabin somewhere, dressed in trekking gear. Finn wondered if he had any normal clothes or just wore survival gear all the time as part of his personal brand. 'By now you must be feeling hungry as you've been burning way more calories than you've been consuming. If it weren't for the fish caught by Katerina and Finn you would be starving. Also, Finn showed great presence of mind and quick thinking to help Katerina today, undoubtedly saving her life.'

Finn beamed as the eyes of the group turned to him, except Katerina's, whose gaze remained fixed on Phineas.

'For that reason, Finn and Katerina, you today have won a reward,' Phineas continued. 'You know where to go. Enjoy!' He grinned at the camera and the screen went blank.

'You're so lucky,' wailed Cressida. 'All day I was busting a gut to help Darryl and we've still caught nothing in those traps, and I'm desperate to go in the hot tub.'

'Sorry, Cressida,' Finn said, consolingly, delighted that he and Katerina had something so nice to look forward to. He stood up. 'Maybe you'll win tomorrow.'

'Well deserved, Finn,' Maz said, nodding in approval.

'Go and enjoy you two – it's bloody brilliant,' said Michael, who had been raving about his hot tub experience a little too much and infuriating the others.

Finn turned to Katerina. 'Are you coming?'

Chapter Eight

Katerina

Katerina had been hoping to get some distance between herself and Finn when the day was over, but now there was even more opportunity to be near him. Proximity to Finn felt dangerous, and alarm bells were ringing in her head, but she couldn't pass up the chance to be in the warm water for an hour, even if it was with Finn. She shuddered at the thought of the cold shower hut where the wind howled through cracks in the walls, and there was no question of turning down their treat.

She nodded to Finn. 'I'll go and get my swim suit,' she said.

She had wondered why they were told to bring swimming things with them for the trip. She had assumed it was something to do with diving or fishing, but now it made more sense.

After gathering her things, she headed out to the largest outbuilding where Finn was already waiting for her. She noted the camera lights at various angles on the ceiling. The room was heated and the warmth wrapped around her like a cosy blanket. A large wooden-panelled hot tub awaited, which fired into action as soon as she shut the door behind her. Steam misted the air and she practically tore off her clothes with trembling hands, her swim suit underneath, and stepped into the tub, her legs shaking. The water enveloped her and sent a shot of endorphins through her entire body. Looking over she could see Finn felt the same, a rapturous look on his face as he sank into the bubbles, the jets gently massaging away the knots and aches of the day.

'It's funny how after just a few days hot water seems like such a luxury,' he said.

'It feels amazing,' she said, leaning her head back, relishing the sense of weightlessness, feeling the pain in her muscles start to ease.

She kept her eyes closed but the image of Finn's semi-naked body was already burned into her mind. He had been thinner when she knew him as a teen, probably from the lack of food. Now he was clearly a gym user, a defined six-pack nestling just under the water line. A pale line ran across his right pectoral, a scar he had from a childhood accident, and she remembered running her fingers over it, brushing her lips over it … She mentally shook herself and tried to focus her mind on something else, anything else, anything other than Finn and the jumble of feelings he awakened in her, a mixture of anger, and lust, and guilt.

She opened her eyes and caught Finn staring at her. He grinned, unembarrassed. Her cheeks were hot, but she told herself it was just the steam. Finn didn't, shouldn't, have the power to fluster her any more, she thought firmly. She wouldn't let him.

'I can't believe we're both nearly thirty,' he said with a shake of the head.

'I know,' she murmured. 'Life goes by in a blink,' she said, thinking of how quickly the last thirteen years had slid by.

'At least you've been married and have a kid,' he said. 'I've never quite made it down the aisle yet.' He looked amused rather than chagrined.

She nodded without saying anything.

'So, how long were you married for?' Finn asked, and she winced at the personal nature of the question.

She cleared her throat but still mumbled. 'About six years.' After a pause, she asked, 'I thought you were engaged recently?'

'I was engaged for a little while, to Sierra, from the girl group Femme Fatale. We weren't well suited,' he said, rolling his eyes.

'That's a shame,' Katerina said, wracking her brains to see if it she could remember who Sierra was. She had a feeling she was blonde. She put a hand unconsciously to her own dark hair, damp from steam and slightly curled in the humidity. 'What do you think went wrong?'

'She was just a bit too high maintenance for me,' he said, with a smile. 'You know my type. I like quiet brunettes with big dreams.'

Katerina stared back at him. *Please don't flirt with me*, she thought desperately. Instead, she laced her hands together under the water in a silent prayer and stayed quiet.

'What happened with your husband?' Finn asked curiously.

Katerina sighed, remembering back over the loveless, lifeless marriage of convenience to Wyatt, the man she picked to provide stability and career help, a man like her dad, kind and deserving of so much better than she gave him. After years of dutiful sex and unpassionate date nights, her acting skills failed her, and she couldn't convince him that she really loved him. It was a hard role to play if you weren't truly committed to the part.

'It just wasn't meant to be,' she said. 'It wasn't his fault, it was mine. My mistake,' she added, looking at Finn.

He nodded sagely, as if he understood.

'At least he didn't break my heart though,' she added, wondering if Finn knew what she was referring to.

If he did, he didn't give her any sign of their mutual understanding.

'That's a blessing,' he said. 'Broken hearts are hard to recover from.' He looked at her sadly.

She wondered if she would ever tell him the truth about why she left, why she sent that final text message, but she wasn't sure she had the courage.

Katerina Murphy, you are a coward, she thought, staring at the ceiling and wishing she were anywhere but there.

Then – Finn

Katerina had kissed him.

Finn repeated the scene again and again in his head as he walked home, his footsteps buoyant with triumph. Okay, so it hadn't been the most coordinated, experienced kiss in the world. It had been a bit confusing and he hadn't known what he was doing, but they had kissed, not once, but twice. His mind was full of the sensations of her as he walked back through the park, where just a few days ago she had pushed him away.

'Hey, Drayson.' A voice cut through his thoughts, and he turned to see some of his mates, clustered by a bench, swigging from cans of cider.

He walked over to them, feeling full of bravado. 'Hey,' he said, accepting a can of cider with a nod.

'We saw you tonight,' Bradley said, a stupid, tipsy grin spread wide on his face. 'Oh, Ms Golightly,' he mimicked, with a sneer, to laughter from the others.

'Piss off,' Finn said, scowling at him. He took several long gulps of cider. 'I was forced into it to get a pass.'

'Yeah right,' Rowan said, his eyes slightly unfocused. 'So, are you fucking the frigid cow then? That Karen girl? 'Cos it certainly looked like you wanted to.'

'It's called acting. And she's called Katerina,' Finn snapped back, their idiocy taking the glow off his evening. He wished he hadn't bumped into them; he knew he should have taken a different route home.

'*Oooh,* sorry,' Rowan said, holding his hands up in a mock apology.

'I will if you won't,' Daniel said, throwing his empty can on the floor. 'I love having a pop at a virgin.'

Bradley laughed, the manic unhinged laughter of a teenager drunk on alcohol and idiotic behaviour. Finn felt a cold hard anger tighten his chest, but he clasped his can and shrugged, unwilling to let them see that he was bothered. 'Whatever. I'm not interested in her. Boring as fuck,' he said.

Finn hated the words even as he said them, but what he and Katerina had was separate from everything else, and he wanted to keep it unsullied, private. No one else needed to know, and certainly not these morons. He set the can down after draining it. 'Thanks guys, but I better get back,' he said.

Bradley rolled his eyes. 'Fine. See you tomorrow for football.'

Finn nodded and walked off. His simple happiness from earlier now felt soiled by his denial of Katerina's importance to him and his casual dismissal of her in front of his friends. She deserved better than that, he knew it.

His phone buzzed in his pocket and he pulled it out, keeping one eye on the screen while walking, trying to avoid tripping over the kerb. It was Katerina. He grinned, feeling his spirits rise again.

Hope you get home okay. See you tomorrow?

It's a date, he replied.

Then – Katerina

Katerina was buzzing like a firefly, alight with excitement. Her first kiss. It hadn't been perfect, but … she sunk into bed and grabbed a pillow to squeeze, closing her eyes blissfully. He liked her. Handsome, popular, fun Finn Drayson liked her. Katerina felt like life was just slotting into place beautifully.

Her mum had looked at her strangely that evening but hadn't said anything. Katerina wondered if she somehow knew what had happened. She couldn't possibly, but she'd always had an eerie mother's intuition that Katerina found hard to fool. She could probably tell by the flush high on her cheeks and the smile on her lips that something was up, although Katerina made out that it was just meeting the agent that she was excited about.

Of course she was excited about that as well, but it was Finn who filled her thoughts right now.

He'd texted her back. *It's a date.*

She smiled and replayed the kiss again and again in her mind. She knew sleep was going to be impossible when she was this happy.

Chapter Nine

Finn

The day dawned cold and bright, and Finn woke up feeling pumped and raring to go. He was surprisingly ready for more hard graft. He knew that his burst of energy was partly due to eating a decent dinner, but mainly motivated by his delight at how yesterday had worked out.

He had spent the entire day with Katerina, and the evening too, and he was so relieved that she was safe and well after the accident. He couldn't help the feelings of attraction that surged in him whenever he saw her, and especially seeing her in the hot tub. In her plain black one-piece she looked more attractive to him than his ex-fiancée had in any number of skimpy bikinis.

The others were stirring already as he swung his legs out of his bed, his sore muscles protesting. As tired and hungry as they all were, everyone knew they had to continue to get the firewood and find food, or their situation would worsen quickly. They were only ever a few hours away from not eating or from the fire going out.

He was intensely grateful for the bread that was delivered each morning, one small loaf on the doorstop, one and a half slices each, basic sustenance for the day until they could get enough to make dinner. The producers had been surprisingly generous. Finn had seen other survival programmes, where celebrities like them were marooned on desert islands or in unforgiving jungles, and this one, while tough and exhausting, had been manageable so far. No one had gone mad from hunger or needed to leave because of illness or injury. Yet.

He traipsed downstairs, finding Carmen already preparing the tea by the fire. 'Morning,' he said, running a hand over the stubble that was fast springing up on his chin. 'Do you need help?' he asked, noticing Carmen's hands shaking.

'Yes, please,' she said, shoving the kettle towards him. Her eyes were glimmering with tears.

'Hey, are you okay? What's wrong?' he asked, concerned to see her so distressed.

'I just couldn't get warm last night, and I feel so tired,' she whispered. She put a hand to her forehead. 'My head hurts badly too.'

Finn took her hand and led her to the sofa to sit down. 'Sit here,' he said. 'I'll make you some hot tea and get your bread for you, and I'm sure you'll feel better.' He was trying to sound in control and reassuring, like Ashif.

He grabbed one of the woollen blankets from the back of the sofa and threw it over her, and she nodded miserably. 'Thank you.'

He had brought the boiling water back to the kitchen to pour tea when he heard Ashif come in the front door. He quickly took over in the living room, asking Carmen questions in concerned tones. Cressida came downstairs and drifted over to see what was happening, and she took Carmen's hand in hers, a worried expression on her face.

Finn brought Carmen her tea and she took it gratefully, gingerly wrapping her fingers around the hot metal cup.

'Thank you, Finn,' Ashif said, standing up. 'I think we all need to have a chat this morning. Can you gather everyone together?'

Finn nodded and walked around to find everyone. A few he had to nudge awake, others were already roaming around outside in the fresh air. Katerina was one of them, chatting quietly with Darryl. They looked up as he approached and Finn ushered them inside. He would have liked to speak to Katerina but felt that Ashif's request had a note of urgency and he didn't want to delay.

They came together in the living room. Ashif stood in their midst, rubbing his eyes, which were marred by dark circles.

'We're all suffering from the cold and lack of food,' he said. 'We've had very little sustenance since we arrived and some of us are getting problems like low blood sugar, which can cause headaches, fatigue and dizziness. If anyone feels like this or doesn't feel well, you must say so,' he said, insistently. He paused, looking around.

'I'm feeling pretty ropey,' Michael admitted with a grim expression. 'I keep getting woozy spells.'

Ashif nodded. 'I'll take your blood pressure, Michael, and we'll see what the problem might be, but I suspect it'll be the same thing.'

Gideon stood up. 'As great as that fish was yesterday, it wasn't much, and we need more food.'

'Stating the obvious,' muttered Maz.

Gideon ignored her. 'Who feels up to working today?' he said.

'I think Carmen and Michael should take some time out,' Ashif said. 'I'd like to keep them indoors if they're both feeling unwell.'

'They can watch the fire then,' Gideon said, with a nod.

Ashif looked across at Katerina. 'How are you feeling today?'

'I'm fine,' Katerina said, softly but firmly. 'I'd like to do something today. I'd like to keep busy.' A shadow of concern crossed Ashif's face but Katerina crossed her arms, her mouth set in a resolute line, and he didn't argue with her.

Finn was feeling weaker than usual, his head starting to function slower with tiredness, but he had slept well and felt like he could carry on. 'I'm happy to do anything,' he volunteered optimistically.

'Maybe chopping wood for the fire?' Gideon asked him.

Finn nodded. 'Sure.'

'I'll go with him,' Willow piped up eagerly, and Finn was a little disappointed that Katerina wouldn't be with him that day. He could see her sitting across from him, studiously avoiding looking in his direction. He felt as though they had made some connection yesterday, but there was something that held her back from him that he just couldn't work out.

Willow hurried to his side. 'We'll have a great time,' she said, brightly.

Finn nodded stiffly. He wanted to glance back at Katerina but decided not to. He had to focus on the task at hand.

The jobs were agreed and the groups set out into the morning. Only a spattering of snow remained on the cold, hard earth, and the stillness in the air offered some respite from the chill wind of yesterday. Birds cawed into the endless sky, their mournful calls accompanying the celebrities as they trudged through the frozen forest.

Willow walked beside Finn, trying to make conversation. He didn't want to be rude to her, but he was trying to conserve his energy for cutting wood, which was made a lot harder given Willow was an eight-stone weakling who seemed content to watch him rather than actually help.

He bit back his annoyance and set to work on a spruce tree, using one of the saws from the shed. It gnawed slowly back and forth into the bark, and Finn panted with the exertion. His muscles felt weak, but at least he was warm from the effort. Willow watched with an admiring smile.

'Strong arms,' she remarked, and he shrugged, wishing she would help rather than pay compliments. 'I do my best.'

The day passed like that on repeat, cutting tree after tree, with Willow trimming what she could, and regular trips back to the cabin to dump the logs. It was exhausting work and Finn began to feel like he was breathing through soup. He sat down for a moment on the tree he had just cut and Willow perched next to him.

She looked around. 'It's so beautiful out here, isn't it? All this silence.'

He nodded, thinking it was ironic that she liked silence yet wouldn't stop talking to him.

'Are you feeling homesick yet? Do you miss your family?' she asked.

He shook his head. 'I don't have any family.'

'Oh Finn, I'm sorry,' she said, rubbing his arm with a thickly gloved hand. She let her hand rest on him and didn't try to move it. 'What about your girlfriend, sorry, fiancée? Sarah? Saskia?' She wrinkled her nose, trying to remember the name.

'Sierra. No, we're not together any more,' he said shortly, not wanting to talk about his failed engagement and how no woman had been able to replace Kat in his heart.

'What a shame,' Willow murmured.

'What about you? Any family you're missing right now?' he asked.

'My parents and my sisters,' she said. 'No boyfriend though,' she said with a sigh.

'I'm surprised that you're single,' he said, and he wasn't just trying to pay her an empty compliment. His surprise was genuine – Willow was clearly stunning and seemed like a nice girl.

She flashed him a brilliant smile. 'You're so sweet, Finn. I was dating someone recently, but he definitely wasn't the right man. But I believe I'll find the right one eventually, even somewhere unexpected.'

'I'm sure you will,' Finn said, standing up and forcing himself to carry on. He couldn't say that Willow's pointed flirting with him was entirely unwelcome. The attentions of the gorgeous young actress made him feel good. But frustratingly she wasn't the one he wanted to share cosy conversations with. It was Katerina and her coldness towards him that haunted him, and Willow's flirting was only a momentary distraction from Katerina's inexplicable grip over his heart.

Katerina's stomach was tight with hunger and her mouth tasted sour as she and Cressida trudged back to the cabin. They walked in silence, disappointed at the meagre bag of roots they had foraged from a day of exertion, using energy neither of them really had. Katerina's insides felt hollow and she hoped that someone had fared better than them.

Katerina wanted to keep busy to try to keep her mind off the fact that it was Chris's birthday. Despite her best efforts, her mind returned again and again to thoughts of Chris and her mum and what they would be doing today. It killed her not to be able to see him and give him his presents. The day of his birth had been hard and awful, but his premature arrival was one of her most cherished memories, the moment her tiny infant son was handed to her, changing the world and her in an instant. From that moment on, no one had been more important to her than Chris, and here she was, thousands of miles away and unable to celebrate his special day with him.

But she was here and she determined to try her best to stay positive and to focus on the tasks that had to be done – they could celebrate his birthday again, together, when she returned home.

When she entered the cabin she could instantly sense the deflated air in the living room. Ashif was shaking his head, apologising, and Carmen's eyes were shining with tears. Finn was seated on the sofa and rested his head in his hands, looking utterly worn out. Katerina resisted the urge to go and put a comforting hand on his shoulder.

'What are we going to eat tonight?' Carmen said, mournfully.

Ashif looked across at them and Katerina hated seeing the flicker of hope on their faces that she would quickly extinguish.

'I'm sorry guys,' she said, her voice low. 'We only have a small amount of roots to go around. I guess we looked in the wrong places today,' she said, apologetically.

'That's okay, Katerina, we can do something with that,' Maz said, her mouth a grim line. She had become the unofficial chef of the group and no one quite dared to take her place. She looked through the bag Katerina gave to her, and set off to the kitchen, Cressida trotting after her to help with what she could.

'Is he okay?' Katerina nodded towards Finn.

He raised his head wearily as he heard her voice. 'Just a bit worn out,' he said, roughly. Willow looped her arm around his shoulders and gave him a squeeze.

'He worked so hard today,' she said.

Katerina couldn't help but notice how comfortable Willow looked with him, her legs pressed against his even though there was no need to sit that close. A tiny niggle of jealousy threatened but she pushed it away.

The group sat in taciturn silence, without the energy or desire to chat. As they sat absorbed by hunger and exhaustion, the screen flickered, and Phineas appeared.

'Guys, we have a message!' Darryl called out to Cressida and Maz, who hurried back.

Phineas gave them a grim smile. 'It's been a tough day, right, guys? Wilderness survival is all about having fortitude and resilience to make it through the days when there isn't any food and you feel like quitting. If you truly want to be a survivor, you have to power through and try again tomorrow.'

He looked down on them sympathetically, as though he were there in the room and could read the anxiety and demotivation written across their faces.

'To cheer you up, all of you may use the hot tub tonight between seven and eight,' Phineas said.

His words had the desired effect. Immediately the atmosphere lifted at the thought of the treat that awaited them all that evening.

'*Wooooo*!' Cressida yelled out, and even Carmen looked perkier at the thought of the reward.

Dinner was a disappointing affair as they picked at the meagre soup, which mainly consisted of water. Katerina swirled hers around the bowl, wishing she and Cressida had found something else to put into it. She forced it down, trying to pretend it was enough, and focused instead on the promise of the hot tub.

When 7 p.m. came around, they all gathered eagerly at the outbuilding, tugging on the doors till the lock switched off.

It was a squeeze to fit them all into the hot tub, but no one cared about the lack of personal space. Katerina felt the heat of the water reviving her, easing her muscles and she finally felt warm, for the first time that day.

It struck her as mildly amusing that the first time she had felt comfortable all day was when she was crowded into a hot tub with people she didn't know very well, her legs pressed up against Darryl's.

Cressida and Willow had somehow decided that bikinis were suitable for the Alaskan wilderness. Katerina felt frumpy in her plain one piece, and tried not to stare enviously as Willow splashed and giggled next to Finn, her impressive cleavage flatteringly wrapped in a crimson bandeau top, the low cut bottoms revealing acres of smooth, naturally-tanned skin and seemingly endless legs.

Finn seemed to enjoy being squeezed next to the soap star, she noted, as he joked around and made Willow laugh. Of course, Finn could charm anyone, she thought, closing her eyes and trying to ignore the flirting that was ramping up a notch. It was none of her business, and she didn't want to be around Finn anyway, she told herself. Willow was welcome to him.

Katerina was walking briskly back to the cabin, hurrying through the cold evening air which caught at the dampness in her hair, when Finn followed after her. She was surprised as she had left slightly before their time was up.

'Hey Kat, wait!' he called out.

She stopped and shivered as he caught up with her.

'How are you feeling today?' he asked, as they walked quickly together.

'I'm all right.' She sighed. 'I'm just gutted we didn't find more food. I'm a bit worried about tomorrow.'

'Tell me about it,' he said, as they entered the cabin. 'Do you want to hang out for a bit in front of the fire?' he asked, hopefully.

'I'm exhausted,' she said with a slight shake of her head. 'I'm going up to bed.' She didn't know why he looked disappointed when he could easily have Willow there instead of her, and she walked up the stairs, wondering if he was watching her go, and telling herself it didn't matter even if he did.

Finn

Finn dragged himself from sleep, scarcely able to open his eyes. His energy levels were dangerously low and his muscles felt watery and insubstantial. He wasn't sure if he was up for another day's work, but he knew he had to try. He gritted his teeth and got out of bed, following Darryl down the stairs.

Despite everyone's delight at the hot tub treat last night, the reality of waking up hungry this morning was clearly hitting home as the group sat round morosely, sipping their black tea.

'Hey, everyone.' Maz's voice trembled as she walked from the front door where she went to retrieve their daily bread. 'They've only given us half a loaf this time,' she said, holding up the tiny portion.

'What?! Do they want us to die out here?' wailed Cressida.

Darryl, who had become quieter and quieter in the past twenty-four hours, thumped his fist on the table. 'Damn them!' he yelled.

Carmen put her head in her hands. 'What are we going to do?' she said, her voice just above a whisper.

Maz counted the slices. 'If we all want some, there is enough for just about half a slice each.' She started to portion them out. Finn awaited his eagerly, anything for sustenance, anything to fill the burning emptiness in his stomach.

Gideon held up his hand. 'Wait a minute!' he barked. They all looked at him. 'Don't you think we should give more to those who are actually going to go out today to find food? Surely they need more energy and should have more bread?' he said, looking around to see who agreed with him.

'Give bread to some and not others?' Maz cried. 'You can't do that! We all deserve to eat!'

'I see what he's getting at,' Darryl piped up. 'If some people aren't going out today then perhaps those that are going to do the work need more food than them.' He didn't name any names, but the implication that some people were not pulling their weight hung heavy in the air.

Michael, his eyes red and his hair uncombed, slammed his palm on the table, making Willow jump where she sat next to Finn. 'What are you saying? That I'm not pulling my weight and I don't deserve food? I got that duck on the first day, don't forget! What have you brought home from your snares and traps that you keep checking over and over? Nothing!'

The sniping and arguments rose in volume and vitriol. Finn opened his mouth to say something but couldn't get a word in edgeways, with Carmen and Cressida near hysterics, Maz involved in a three-way shouting match with Darryl and Michael, and Gideon trying to impose order. Finn looked at Katerina and shrugged helplessly. She held up her hands and mouthed to him: 'What do we do?'

Carmen stood up, weeping. 'I will not be accused of being lazy. I have done my bit here and now you want to deny me food! I am leaving!' she shrieked. She looked around at the cameras. 'Do you hear me? Get me out, I want to leave!' she yelled.

'Carmen, no!' Willow jumped up and tried to grab her hands, but Carmen shook her away.

'There's no need for this,' Gideon said, trying to calm everyone.

'I want to go!' Carmen shouted.

The screen in the living room turned on, with a message written in stark white letters on the black screen.

Carmen, if you want to leave, wait outside the cabin in thirty minutes and transport will be provided for you.

'Good!' she shrieked and ran upstairs to grab her bag. Willow and Cressida hurried after her, pleading with her to change her mind.

The group sat tersely around the table, hearing Carmen flinging her things into her bag, then storming down the stairs. She came over to the group and gave Finn and Michael a rushed hug each, and tight sobbing embraces for the girls.

'I'm sorry, but I can't do this any more,' she said to them all, heading for the front door, weeping into her hands.

Finn, Katerina and Ashif rushed to the windows to see her getting onto the back of a quad bike that was, with its driver, waiting for her outside. She clambered on and they sped away, disappearing among the trees in an instant.

The group sat in shocked silence at her sudden departure. They each ate half a slice of bread, all thoughts of unevenly distributing the provisions gone along with Carmen and her dramatic exit.

Finn swallowed his last chunk of bread, desperately wishing for more and wondering what the producers were playing at by halving their daily amount. He guessed they felt the team was getting on a bit too well and wanted to stoke some drama. Their plan had certainly succeeded. He rested his hands on the table. 'What do we need to do today?' he said, breaking the silence. 'We still have to crack on, no matter how rough we feel, no matter how sad we are that Carmen chose to leave. We've got to carry on.'

Gideon nodded, and Katerina turned to look at him. He thought he detected a look of admiration on her face, but it was hard to tell. Either way, it didn't matter right now. His concern was that there were tasks to be done and they wouldn't get any easier the longer they sat there nursing their teas.

'I wonder if the cameramen have food,' muttered Maz.

'Maybe we could stage a heist?' Darryl suggested, jokingly, but his humour only raised weak smiles.

They sat and assigned the tasks. Michael agreed to stay and watch the fire, but the rest of the group agreed to go out.

Finn was apprehensive about being assigned to go hunting with Ashif. He had never hunted before. He thought back to his survival-skills workshop with the lessons on gun safety and hunting tips. He could barely remember them and hoped he wouldn't injure himself or Ashif. He followed Ashif outside to the shed, gritting his teeth and forcing his legs to move, trying to ignore the pounding headache in his left temple. He gulped some water from his bottle and felt it stream down into his empty stomach. His hands were shaky around the bottle and he felt a wave of doubt, coupled with a lingering sense of nauseous apprehension, that he could do anything useful that day.

'You'll have to show me what you did to get that bird on the first day,' Finn said to Ashif, swallowing hard against his nausea and trying to be positive. 'Maybe we can get another one.'

Ashif pressed his mouth into a thin line. 'To be honest with you, Finn, I am beginning to think that it was a plant by the producers just to make sure we at least got something on those first days.'

'What do you mean?' Finn asked.

'Well, it was just standing there looking dozy. It was like …' Ashif paused, '… like it had been drugged or something.' He hung his head. 'Michael and I acted like we'd done something amazing, but I haven't been able to get anything since.'

Finn's heart sank. He hoped Ashif was wrong, or failing that, that the producers would take pity on them and release something edible and drowsy in their direction. He and Ashif stocked up on ammunition and Finn held his gun in trembling hands, wishing he knew what he was doing.

Katerina's arms shuddered as she tried to strip the tree of leaves and thin branches. She gripped the shears, forcing herself to focus despite how woozy she felt. She was feeling awful. She could feel her body crying out for food, and she had nothing to give it. She had always been slender and tried to put on weight for this show but had only managed to put on a few pounds, all of which had now melted away. She wished she had more reserves.

She gritted her teeth, determined not to complain. She had come here for a challenge, and she was getting what she came for.

Darryl paused beside her, wiping a bead of sweat from his head. 'Phew,' he said, straightening up. 'This is tough on my back.'

She nodded. They were both breathing heavily and had hardly made any progress, but the wood was vital. Failure wasn't an option. They pressed on, side by side, Darryl cutting the trees down, Katerina stripping the branches and leaves.

She looked at her hands, numb and weak, and made a fist a few times, trying to summon the power and energy she needed. She hung her head, working on tree after tree, until she couldn't see or hear anything except her own exertions.

They traipsed back to the cabin, fatigued and shivering, even Darryl's Olympic fitness failing him. He looked at Katerina as they approached the cabin, dragging their last load of logs with them. 'I hope this is enough,' he said quietly.

'I'm sure it is,' she said, looking at the pile they had accumulated.

'I don't think I can do much more without food,' Darryl said, pausing before they entered the front door. He looked at her and she could see he was desperate not to be a quitter, but his resolve, like hers, was being eaten away by hunger.

She reached over and gave him a hug. 'You can do this, we both can,' she said, trying to reassure him as much as herself.

Katerina knew almost as soon as she entered that there would be very little to eat again that night. Most of the others were already back, and she could read the situation from the downturned corners of their mouths, from the tension in their jaws. When Gideon and Maz came back from foraging, the last two to return, they all knew from their faces that a watery stew would be their only sustenance tonight.

Katerina felt her throat constrict with longing for something else, anything more substantial, but she knew it wouldn't be forthcoming.

'Guys, I can't do this. I'm done.' Gideon stood up sadly. Katerina looked up at him in surprise. 'I'm physically wrecked and I can't get warm. I spoke to Ashif yesterday and we agreed I shouldn't carry on if there was another day like this.' He shook his head. 'I did my best today in the hope things would get better, but I'm going to have to leave.'

'If that's what you have to do for your health, then it's the right decision,' Darryl said, standing up and shaking his hand.

Katerina patted him on the arm. 'We'll miss you,' she said, feeling genuinely sad at the thought of the group diminishing yet again.

Cressida gave Gideon a hug, wiping away a few tears, and he looked up at one of the cameras. 'I need to leave now please,' he said. They waited in tense silence for a few moments, wondering if anyone had heard.

Finally, the screen flashed the expected message.

Gideon, your transport will be outside in thirty minutes.

Gideon went upstairs to pack. His goodbyes were short and muted, in contrast to Carmen's emotional departure that morning.

He left on a quad bike, waving, and Katerina envied what food might be waiting for him wherever it was they took him. Finn joined her as she watched from the window, long after Gideon's silhouette had roared away into the distance.

'How are you doing today?' he asked her gently. 'You don't look very well.'

She looked up at him. 'I'm feeling pretty bad,' she admitted, in a hushed voice, not wanting to be overheard. 'I'm cold, my head hurts, I'm dizzy. I'm sure you must be feeling the same.'

He nodded grimly. 'Ashif and I were so close. We saw some kind of bird and I almost had it in my aim, but I missed it.' He looked crushed. 'I feel so guilty I couldn't bring anything back.'

She squeezed his shoulder and left her hand there. 'Please, Finn. We're all doing our best. I know I should go back to the lake and fish, but I'm not sure I'm up for the journey now. I don't think anyone is.'

He shook his head. 'It's too far, feeling like this. It could be dangerous.'

The lack of food made her head swim, and her wariness of Finn's closeness was lessened. Without thinking, she reached up and gently touched his cheek where the beginnings of a beard were coming through. She smiled. 'It suits you,' she said. 'You look like a caveman boy-band singer,' she said laughing.

He grinned at her, about to say something, but Willow came over. 'What are you both staring at?' she said, standing directly behind them so they had to part to be polite.

'We were just watching Gideon leave,' Finn said.

Willow inserted herself between them with a smile. 'What was that I heard about a caveman boy-band?' she said, giggling. 'Sounds like my kind of thing.'

Katerina was amazed she had the energy to flirt with Finn when they were all starving, but maybe she really liked him, she thought as she watched them chat amicably. As the conversation no longer included her, she drifted away from them and sat in front of the fire, feeling the heat of the flames soothing some of the pain in her head.

Dinner was as expected, and Katerina stirred her stew around the bowl. It was basically hot water with a few leaves floating in it. It wasn't enough to fill her up even for ten minutes, and she thought longingly of the well-stocked fridge in her home. She felt a deep stab of homesickness as she wondered what Chris was doing right now, and she had to look down at the table so no one would see the tears gathering in the corners of her eyes.

The group huddled together before the fire that evening, the mood low, and their energy entirely spent.

Phineas appeared on the TV screen for his nightly message. Katerina barely had the power to lift her head up to watch him. 'Hi guys, you've done really well to make it this far. I know you're all exhausted, and health complications can arise when you are this hungry. We'll see how you get on tomorrow, but I have a few tips for you.'

He ran through a list of things to help them, clues and pointers about where to hunt, what mistakes they might have made with their snares, what might be nearby for better foraging. It felt a little bit like a cheat sheet, but Katerina knew none of them would spurn the advice they so desperately needed. They were starving and shattered, and in those conditions, no one was too proud to admit they needed help.

Darryl looked around after the message finished. 'Tomorrow will be a better day,' he said, but his smile was faint and he convinced no one.

The group drifted upstairs one by one, until only Katerina was left by the fire. She was too tired to move. She hadn't wanted to say how bad she felt. She didn't want to be a weakling or a complainer, but the feeling of faintness that enveloped her wouldn't go away. She tried to warm herself as close as possible to the fire, feeling nauseous, the ground beneath her swaying slightly.

She was startled when Finn sat down beside her. 'Are you okay?' he said, frowning with concern.

She shook her head, staring blankly at the flames. 'I'm all right.'

'Do you even have the energy to get upstairs?'

She shrugged. 'I'll go in a minute or two.'

'Have you spoken to Ashif?'

She looked at him. 'It's okay, Finn, really. I don't want to complain.'

'It's not complaining if you need help,' he insisted.

He looked around furtively, then put his hand in his pocket. 'I saved this,' he said, drawing out a small square of bread. 'You know, for emergencies.' He offered it to her. 'Please take it.'

'Finn, no, I can't possibly! You need to eat just as much as I do,' Katerina said, horrified at the thought of taking the emergency portion he'd saved. She tried to push his hand away but didn't quite have the energy. Instead, her fingers rested on his wrist, over his tattoo, where his pulse beat against her fingers.

He took her hand, turned it palm up, and gently placed the bread into it, curling her fingers over and pushing her hand back to her. 'Eat it,' he said.

Katerina could feel the bread nestling against her skin and her mouth burned for it. Aching with guilt, she chewed on it slowly, relishing every tiny morsel, as Finn looked on.

'Thank you,' she said, leaning against his arm, which he put round her. She was too tired and hungry to protest, too weak to care about the cameras. All she wanted was to feel better.

'It's okay. After all, you gave me food more times than I can count,' he muttered into her hair, and as she stared into the flames she was powerless to stop the memories from flooding her mind.

Then – Finn

Finn's shirt felt damp with sweat as he hurried to meet Katerina in the park. The July heat radiated off the pavement, waves of smoggy air drifting over him from passing cars. The streets hadn't cooled for days and his flat felt airless and parched. He was glad to be outside, glad to have a chance to spend some stolen moments with his girl.

She was standing by their bench, her pale, tightless legs almost reflecting the sunlight. Her shirt was loosely tucked into her skirt, her school tie removed, her hair hurriedly tied back without care. It took his breath away to see her standing in the sunshine, waiting for him. He bounded up to her with a grin, kissing her on the lips, relishing the taste of her cherry lip balm.

He sat down on the bench, pulling her to sit next to him. Their bench was one overshadowed by a large oak tree, the shadow of the branches partially shielding them from view. Finn felt slightly on edge as he knew the warm weather would entice his mates out to the park. He and Katerina got together at the end of June after the play and his mates still didn't know he was dating her. Although dating didn't seem like quite the right word to him given that he couldn't actually take her on any dates. He never had any money to take her anywhere, and his spirit felt a little crushed every time he asked her to meet him in the park after school and she readily agreed, when he knew she deserved more than that.

She rummaged in her bag and clasped a packet of salt and vinegar crisps. 'Want to share?' she said, dangling the bag out towards him. It took most of his self-control not to grab it and tear into its contents straight away.

'Great, yeah,' he said, eyeing the bag between them that she carefully parted and opened down the middle. He grabbed a crisp, forced himself to chew it slowly, watching her take another, then taking two more for himself. The crisps only served to arouse even more the hunger in his stomach that he had carried with him all day. There had been no food in the flat for breakfast, and all he had had for lunch was half a bag of chips that one of his mates had given him. He hated the charitable gestures from any of them, but most especially from her.

She casually shoved the bag towards him. 'Actually, I don't really want any more. Have the rest Finn,' she said, and he nodded, finishing them off in seconds. She eyed him carefully and asked, tentatively, 'Are you still hungry?'

'Maybe just a little,' he said, sheepishly. He was ashamed, but he knew Katerina was the one person he could be honest with about how things were with his mum. Being open with her was easier than with friends he had known since primary school. But he didn't want her pity. He wanted her.

'I have this sandwich left over from lunch if you'd like it?' she offered, fishing a small Tupperware box out of her bag. 'It's just peanut butter – it lasts better in the heat.'

He smiled. 'If it was a cheese sandwich it would be a toasty by now.'

She laughed. 'Take it.' She handed him the box and he took it gratefully, dispatching the sandwich in moments.

'You know you can always come to my house for dinner,' she said, avoiding his gaze, and picking at a whorl on the wooden bench. 'We could just tell my parents we're doing some more work together for drama. I'm sure they won't mind,' she said.

But Finn knew she was wrong. They did mind. He had gone to her house a few weeks ago and the atmosphere had been very different from when he had first been welcomed there. Katerina's dad had looked at him with suspicious eyes, and Finn knew that he knew. They couldn't hide the way they felt about each other, it was too obvious. Katerina's blushes, the way she bit her lip with shy happiness every time Finn looked her way, the way their hands brushed under the table. Finn was surprised her dad didn't just ask him to leave there and then, but he was a polite man. He saved his obvious displeasure for when Katerina had gone to the bathroom, and he had looked at Finn coldly, and suggested that perhaps Katerina was being unnecessarily distracted by acquaintances that she would be better off without.

Finn knew that he couldn't go back there and had avoided every invitation from her to return there since. She was always welcome at his flat, but he felt ashamed of its squalor compared with her parents' house and didn't like to invite her round too often. He felt a grain of fear in his stomach that every time she saw how crappy it was she might change her mind about him.

'I'm okay, Kat,' he said, taking her hand off the bench and holding it in his own, his palm slightly sweaty against hers. He rubbed his thumb over her knuckles, staring at her inexpertly-applied pink nail varnish that had smudged onto the skin.

'Are you though?' she asked, raising her eyebrows. 'What have you eaten today?'

'Not a lot,' he said. 'But it's okay, really. I'm used to it.' He loved that she was concerned about him. His own mother wasn't, she was too wrapped up in her own mental muddle, but Katerina, she cared about him. He felt lucky, despite the hunger.

She nodded and leaned her head on his shoulder. He wound his fingers in her hair, dark and hot from the sun, and kissed the top of her head. He sang softly to her about the way she lit up his life like sunshine, and she giggled.

'Anything you need, Finn,' she said. 'I've got your back.'

Perhaps it was naivety, his desperate need to be cared for, or his wholehearted infatuation, but he believed her.

Then – Katerina

Katerina put her key in the lock and quietly pushed open the door. She removed her shoes, which were still damp from the unexpected rainstorm earlier that afternoon. She and Finn had been forced to take shelter at his flat, and she had stayed longer than intended. She knew her parents would be annoyed, and tried to make as little sound as possible, hoping they might not even notice her return.

Her cheeks were still flushed with the warmth of Finn's embrace, her hair untidy from where he had run his fingers through it. She knew she should have left earlier but she was hooked on his presence, addicted to pressing him close and smelling his scent on herself even hours later. Her head was dizzy with infatuation, and all she could think about was Finn. Other considerations just faded into insignificance compared to the intoxication of being with him.

'Katerina,' Keith called, and Katerina winced. She could tell from the flat tone of her dad's voice that he wasn't pleased. She traipsed into the living room, quickly running a hand through her hair and self-consciously over her mouth, where her lips and chin were slightly sore from Finn's kisses. She hoped her parents wouldn't be able to tell where she had been and what she had been doing.

'Sorry I'm late,' she said to her parents, who were sitting on the sofa, *Emmerdale* playing on the TV. 'I was at drama club again …'

'We know you weren't at the drama class, we're not born yesterday,' Keith snapped, stabbing at the remote to put the TV on mute. He folded his arms and gave Katerina a stern stare.

Pauline nodded. 'I saw Mr Maguire in Tesco and he told me there was no after-school drama club. So, all these afternoons out recently, where have you really been?' Her tone was gentler, but Katerina could tell she too was angry.

'Do we even need to ask?' Keith said.

Katerina bit her lip, still tender from where Finn's had pressed against it. 'I'm sorry for lying,' she said, eventually. 'I just knew you wouldn't be okay with me seeing a boy.' She figured it was better not to attempt more lies and get herself in a muddle.

'Finn?' Pauline asked, her eyebrows raised.

Katerina nodded, her blood rising to her cheeks even at the mention of his name.

Keith stood up and she could tell he was trying to be calm. 'Katerina, listen to me, you're only fifteen—'

'Sixteen in September,' Katerina said, interrupting her dad.

'Yes, but you need to focus on school, not dating. You'll be in Year 11 soon, you'll have exams. Plus you might have some opportunities coming your way and you don't want to be tied into some foolish romance with a boy who, with all due respect, hasn't really got anything to offer you.' He folded his arms, his mouth pressed into a thin line.

'But Finn is really important to me,' she said, feeling a knot forming in her throat, stunting her usual ability to be articulate and explain her point of view. Instead she swallowed hard, stuttering, feeling frustrated that they couldn't – wouldn't – try to understand.

Keith shook his head. 'He may be now, but in the future he'll just be a memory you'd rather forget. Don't go cultivating regrets, Katerina – just focus on the important things for now. You've got so much going for you.'

Katerina knew there was no point in arguing with her parents so she nodded, her eyes prickling with tears. 'Okay.' She turned to go upstairs to her room, her hands clenched, seething that her cover story was blown. She would just have to find another way to be with Finn.

Fortunately, thought Katerina, she was very good at acting. If she had to lie, at least she could do it convincingly.

Chapter Ten

Finn

'Kat!' Finn yelled, his voice echoing off the trees. He felt his lagging energy rejuvenated by a surge of excitement. 'We've got one!'

Katerina hurried up to him, her breath puffing out in small clouds. 'What? Where?' she said urgently.

She stood next to him and looked down at where he indicated, where one of the traps had caught a squat furry animal.

'Wow!' she shrieked in delight and grabbed his arm. 'We'll all be able to eat something tonight! This is amazing!'

She was practically bouncing with joy, a welcome contrast to her quiet and muted mood earlier in the day. Finn grinned at her, delighted that they had been partnered together today, grateful they would have something to bring to the group. The thought that he and Katerina might be rewarded with some more time in the hot tub, alone, also crossed his mind.

Win-win, he thought, and bent down to undo the trap, his hands trembling slightly.

'Do you need some help?' She knelt down beside him. 'What is it?' she asked, as they stared at it curiously.

Finn shrugged. 'Looks like a big fat squirrel,' he said, unsure of the name. The body lay limp on the ground, and Finn couldn't even feel sorry for it, so desperate was he to eat proper food again.

'Let's check the other snare,' he said, and scooped up the body to carry with them. The brown fur felt velvety-soft under his fingers, and he looked at its face. 'I'm sorry, little guy,' he muttered, tucking it under his arm.

Katerina smiled at his words, and they both walked on, their steps lighter at the promise of food at the end of the day's work.

'Everyone is going to be so pleased,' Katerina said.

Finn nodded. 'It's bloody brilliant.'

It was beyond their expectations to have caught a second animal in the other trap. They both whooped with excitement to see it, their loud exuberance scaring several birds from the trees, which flew away, squawking with panic.

'I know what this is,' Katerina said. 'I think it's a weasel, or something like that.'

Katerina removed it from the trap, and Finn slung both animals over his shoulder.

'Finn the Hunter, from Ealing.' She laughed. 'Who would have thought?'

He smiled, running a hand self-consciously over his chin where his beard was growing. He knew he looked mangled and rough after over a week in the wild. Katerina, on the other hand, was pale and tired but she still looked beautiful to him. He was proud to think that her natural beauty was something he had recognised and treasured first, long before she appeared on TV.

They headed back after resetting the traps, and walked companionably side by side.

Since he had given her the extra bread, Finn felt some of the distance between them beginning to close. She was behaving more like the girl he used to know, the warm and friendly Kat who, for a short time at least, was his closest friend. Perhaps it had just taken her time to adjust to being on camera in a reality TV situation, he thought. Or maybe she had genuinely felt awkward about their shared history. Either way, he was glad that the frost between them was starting to dissipate.

Katerina stopped suddenly. 'Finn,' she hissed urgently, her entire body still, the sinews in her neck stretched taut, her eyes wide.

'Woah, what? Are you okay? You look really weird,' he said, alarmed by her strange expression.

'*Shhh!*' she said, pointing with a shaking finger towards the trees.

He shook his head, confused, and looked at where she was pointing. His stomach constricted as he saw what she saw. A bear was lurking close by, giant and looming and looking right at them.

'Oh no,' Katerina whispered, her voice trembling.

'Shit, shit, shit,' Finn whispered, wracking his brains to try to remember what to do in this situation. He couldn't think straight. Run? Don't run? Play dead?

'Bear attacks are rare,' said Katerina in a low voice. 'Maybe it'll leave us alone.'

The bear lurched towards them, looking ungainly and slow, and Finn reckoned they could outrun it. He looked at Katerina and mouthed "run" but she put a hand out to stop him, shaking her head, her breath coming in tight narrow gasps.

'No, Finn, don't run!' she begged.

The bear moved closer and began to growl. It was squat and heavy, rippling with thick black fur. Finn felt his stomach loosen with fear and hoped he wouldn't wet himself on camera, although that was the least of his worries.

'I think it can smell the meat,' she said, glancing at their haul over Finn's shoulder.

'He isn't going to get this without a fight,' he murmured. It was half-bravado, half-serious. He knew they were in danger, but hunger had made him desperate.

'Perhaps you should throw it at him?' she said, her voice high with tension.

'No, we need it!' he hissed back.

The bear paced agitatedly, then made a sudden start towards him, springing forwards with a deafening growl. Finn froze and he felt blinded by fear, unable to breathe and his pulse racing. The bear was just yards away when it shuddered and lurched upwards with a grunt, a powerful stream of vapour shooting straight towards it from Katerina's outstretched hand. She stood stock still, clasping an orange can, aiming the jet steadily towards the bear. It stopped in its tracks, as if dazed, and staggered backwards.

'*Now* we should run,' she yelled.

Move, Finn ordered his legs, and thankfully they obeyed. He and Katerina fled, casting frantic glances behind them as they ran towards the cabin. They didn't wait to see what the cameraman did and assumed that he had also fled to safety.

Finn threw open the cabin door and pushed Katerina inside before leaping in himself, slamming the door shut and landing on her with a thump. They lay entangled on the floor, panting with fear, with the carcases lolling next to them. Katerina looked at Finn and started to giggle, from sheer relief, and he laid his head on her shoulder and gasped with laughter, unable to calm himself because of the sheer amount of adrenaline coursing through his body. It took them a few moments to quieten down, breathing hard.

'You saved my life,' he said finally, pushing himself up to look at her face. He was quite enjoying the nearness of her, and wasn't ready to move just yet.

She reached up to ruffle his hair, a loving gesture that sent a shiver down his back. 'You owe me big time,' she said. 'You definitely would have died out there.'

'Absolutely,' he agreed.

He could have stayed there for ages, but Maz approached, interrupting them.

'What's going on here then?' Maz asked, looking baffled at the scene.

Katerina wriggled her way out from underneath him, looking slightly sheepish, and Finn wished their unexpected clinch didn't have to end, even if it had been brought on by a bear attack, of all things.

Katerina

'Wow, how brave,' Darryl said, as Finn relayed the bear attack story yet again at the dinner table.

Katerina blushed while he told it, as he looked over at her admiringly, relating how she had saved his life.

'It's no big deal,' she said with a modest shrug. 'I just followed the instructions and used the bear spray.'

'No big deal? You faced a bear and saved Finn's life!' Cressida exclaimed. 'I could never have done that!'

'He looked pretty thankful when I found you two on the floor by the front door,' Maz said, with a wink.

Katerina looked down and focused on her plate while Willow shot her a curious glance. 'What were you both doing on the floor?'

'Oh, we just fell in the doorway, we were running so fast,' Katerina said, not really liking the flicker of tension that darted across Willow's pretty features.

'Yeah, sure,' Maz said incredulously, and the group tittered.

The meat from the weasel and what Katerina later found out was a marten, was delicious, hearty and warming. Even the small portions felt filling to their shrunken stomachs. Katerina relished the feeling of being even slightly full. It was so easy to forget, she thought, that just a week ago she was living in the lap of luxury, with hot water and a full stomach every day. Now, that life seemed so far away. She felt a pang in her heart at the thought of Chris, thousands of miles away. She missed him every second of every minute, even with all the hardships and distractions here.

A slight gloom settled on her, an uneasy melancholy that was unexpected after the triumphs of the day. She carried the feeling with her for the rest of dinner and while they gathered in the living room afterwards.

Phineas came onto the screen, as expected, with his usual warm smile. 'You've all done brilliantly today, and particularly Katerina for braving that bear. Katerina, you kept a cool head and knew what to do, and that's a key way to survive in the wilderness. I couldn't have done better myself,' he lauded her. Katerina felt pleased at the compliment, though she was still hardly able to believe the events of a few hours ago were even real. She felt a swell of pride at doing something she never thought she would have to do.

'I have an extra special treat for you,' Phineas continued. 'You get to choose what you receive tonight, Katerina. An hour in the hot tub or …' He paused. 'You can choose a treat for the whole group, if you prefer.'

Katerina raised her eyebrows. As much as she liked the hot tub, she would much rather they all have a treat. It was an easy choice. 'I choose something for all of us please,' she said, out loud and without hesitation, looking to the nearest camera.

Cressida reached across and squeezed her arm in gratitude, and Michael nodded his thanks.

'Very well, you'll find your group reward outside the front door in thirty minutes.' Phineas ended his message with a nod.

Thirty minutes passed like an ice age. Darryl tapped his feet impatiently and Maz frowned at him, while Michael was practically glued to his watch. Eventually he looked up. 'It's time,' he announced, looking to Katerina.

Katerina got up and tentatively opened the front door a crack, trying not to let too much cold air swirl in. A small brown box lay before her feet. She scooped it up and carried it back to the group, setting it gently on the worn table before the fire.

'What is it?' Michael craned his neck to see.

Katerina opened it up and removed the items. They were only simple pleasures, but they seemed like the finest luxury items for people who'd been living on almost nothing for a week. Butter, milk, jam, a new loaf of bread, and coffee.

'Oh my gosh,' Cressida said, reaching out and holding the coffee aloft like a trophy. 'Coffee! Hurrah!'

She threw her arms around Katerina, who was caught off guard by the strength of her embrace. 'Thank you, darling!' Cressida exclaimed, and Katerina couldn't help but laugh at her delight.

Ashif looked at the bread and jam. 'Who would have thought that bread and jam could make us all so happy?' he said with an amused smile.

'Wait, there's something else,' Katerina said, her fingers grazing something cold and hard at the bottom of the box. She drew out a bottle of whisky.

'Wow wee!' said Michael, taking it from her and looking at the label. 'This'll warm us right up.'

'I'll get the mugs.' Maz hurried to the kitchen, the fastest Katerina had ever seen her move.

Sipping whiskey in front of the fire, Katerina felt the lush sensation of fuzzy warmth envelop her, the most comfortable she had been since she arrived. She knew the others felt the same and they were soon looking flushed and dozy.

One by one they went to bed, leaving her, Willow, Cressida, and Finn before the fire. Cressida stood up with a stretch. 'I'm exhausted,' she said, giggling slightly at the head rush from standing too quickly. 'I've got to get some sleep.' She headed upstairs, humming gently to herself and swaying slightly from side to side.

Willow was curled up on the sofa, close to Finn. 'I'm so sleepy,' she said, smiling up at him, leaning her head onto his chest with a sigh.

Finn, who had his hands behind his head, made no attempt to move, and Katerina thought that he looked rather pleased as Willow nestled into him.

Katerina drifted towards the kitchen to wash her mug, listening to them murmur on the sofa. A hard, angry jealousy goaded her and she squeezed her eyes shut against the intrusive emotion. She was not supposed to be feeling like this. Not about Finn, or anyone, ever again. For some reason, the sight of him curled up with Willow bothered her immensely. She knew it shouldn't – Finn wasn't hers, hadn't been for a long time and never would be again. But she felt usurped by the younger actress; Willow's head where hers used to lie.

She saw their heads move closer together, and quickly went upstairs. She was in no mood to witness their hook up, although she knew the world would see it on camera.

Finn

Finn woke early and couldn't get back to sleep. His head was slightly blurry from the whisky, but he felt better than he had done for days – the type of comfort that only came from being full.

He quietly pushed back the covers and padded softly downstairs. He pulled on his boots and his jacket and opened the front door, bracing himself for the cold blast of early morning air. He headed for the toilet block, and was surprised to see Katerina outside the cabin, standing with her back to him, looking out at the forest and the endless sky, which glowed with a dusky pink hue.

'Morning,' he said, walking up behind her.

She jumped. 'Oh hey,' she said, putting a hand on her heart. 'You scared me!'

'Sorry,' he said. 'It's gorgeous isn't it?' He looked at the sky.

'I've never seen anything quite like it,' she said, nodding. 'It's so strange here, so quiet compared to London. It's disorienting.'

'Tell me about it,' he said. 'You get so used to being surrounded by buildings, traffic, people that silence actually feels surprising.'

Katerina nodded, poking the ground with the tip of her boot.

'Anyway,' he said, hands deep in his pockets to avoid the chill. 'I hope we get partnered again today. I might need another bear bodyguard.' He nudged her with his shoulder.

She looked surprised, raising an eyebrow. 'Really? I would have thought you'd like to be paired with Willow.' Her tone was slightly brittle and he saw a red flush briefly burn on each cheek, though he wasn't sure if it was from embarrassment or some other emotion.

'What do you mean?' he asked quietly. He wasn't sure if the cameramen were around but there were cameras on the outside of the cabin and it was almost certain they could pick up their conversation and zoom in.

'Nothing, just that you two looked pretty cosy last night,' she said, her face impassive.

'There's nothing going on with me and Willow,' Finn said, incredulously, although he knew it probably looked that way. Willow was certainly keen to get close to him, but he felt nothing for her other than friendship. He just didn't want to be rude by pushing her away last night when she was clearly cold and needed some comfort.

Katerina looked unconvinced.

'Seriously Kat, I'm not interested in Willow,' he said, bemused as to why they were even having this conversation.

'I think she's very interested in you,' Katerina replied, her gaze turned away from the sky and staring at him instead.

'She might be, but I'm pretty sure I've shown her nothing but friendship,' he insisted, hoping she would believe him. They both stood in silence for a moment, and he wondered why he was trying to convince Katerina that nothing was going on between him and Willow. What did it matter to her? Why was she so interested? A hopeful thought blossomed in his mind that perhaps she was jealous. Finn wasn't up for playing games but provoking Katerina's jealousy might be a good thing, he thought, as it might make her realise that they still had something to offer each other.

'Okay, well, I think you would make a nice couple,' Katerina said brusquely.

'That won't happen,' Finn said. 'But thanks for the interest in my love life.' He looked at her with a sideways glance, but he still couldn't read her face.

The silence rested between them and he realised he still needed the loo. 'I'm going to use the delightful facilities,' he said, gesturing towards the outhouse.

'See you later,' Katerina said, and walked back towards the cabin without a glance back at him.

Finn felt a stab of irritation at her coldness and walked to the toilet, feeling confused and slightly mad at her. One minute they were getting on, the next minute she was like this. He just couldn't work her out. She was, as always, a mystery to him.

Katerina sipped her tea, the chipped edges of the stained mug rough against her lips. She set it down on the patchy carpet in front of the sofa that also served as Finn's bed.

'It sucks that your parents are being more vigilant,' Finn said. Katerina reached out a hand and brushed a hair away from his forehead. Even when he was downcast he was still cute, she thought. She was worried about her parents' insistence that she stop dating him, but she was happy just to be in his presence for that moment so she pushed her concerns away.

She and Finn skipped the afternoon at school, she with a "headache" and he with the "flu", so they could spend time together. It felt daring and illicit and she knew she shouldn't be missing school, but she needed to be with Finn.

They couldn't go to Katerina's house so they were at Finn's flat. His mum was having a bad day and was locked in her bedroom in the gloom, her favourite music playing on repeat. She would usually be there until the evening, so Finn and Katerina had some time and space to themselves.

Katerina knew she shouldn't lie to her parents, or to the school, and she should be spending more time doing school work, but Finn was all she wanted. She was hopelessly in love with him. He was the first boy she had loved, kissed, and wanted to be with him so desperately it threw all her good senses to the wind. There were no future considerations that seemed more important than Finn, today, here and now.

'At least we have this afternoon,' she said. 'And when GCSEs are finished next year, I think my parents might relax a bit.' She made her voice sound confident, although she wasn't sure that it was true. They would be horrified at how deeply in love she was with Finn, especially as they were stalwart Catholics who had always taught her about the importance of waiting for marriage. Not that her and Finn had slept together, yet. They had come close, but Katerina wanted to wait until she was sixteen. It wasn't that she wanted to turn her back on everything her parents had taught her, but they couldn't possibly understand how she felt. No one could, so their love was their beautiful secret.

She picked up Finn's guitar from beside the sofa, and gently brushed her fingers against the strings, feeling the tension in them, the pressure on her fingertips. The noise sounded hollow and tuneless in the silence of the flat.

'You should sing for me,' she said, looking at Finn.

'You always say that, and I always say no.' Finn laughed.

'Come on, please, I want to hear you sing,' she said pleadingly, handing him the guitar.

He looked embarrassed. 'What if it's no good?' he said, a flicker of anxiety crossing his face. 'That'll just embarrass us both. It's better that I don't,' he said, shaking his head.

'You should have more confidence in yourself,' she said encouragingly. 'Have a little self-belief.'

'Actually I – er – I'm writing a song for you,' he half-said it, half-mumbled it, so Katerina wasn't sure that she had heard correctly.

'What?'

'I'm writing a song for you,' he said, and Katerina felt delight blossom in her chest. She had always thought of herself as quite a plain and unremarkable person, one who was only comfortable pretending to be someone else, and she never thought a boy would write a song for her. She beamed. 'Please let me hear it,' she begged.

'It's not quite finished yet, it needs some work,' Finn warned.

'I don't care. I want to hear it.' She leaned back expectantly, and Finn looked down at his guitar. She wasn't sure if he would actually do it, but after a moment he began to play, and then he sang for her. It was a song about unexpected love, about their love, and she adored it from the first chord. She closed her eyes, enraptured. This was *her* song.

Finn finished. 'What do you think?' he asked nervously.

Katerina opened her eyes. 'Oh, Finn that was gorgeous,' she said with a sigh.

'Really?' he replied, and she could see the relief in his eyes.

'Really.' She nodded. 'I loved it. What's the song called?'

'"Never Lose Our Love",' he said.

'It's perfect.' She smiled. 'You've got so much talent. Imagine what you could do!'

He grinned, a shy, uncertain smile that made her love him all the more for not being big-headed about his talent. 'Maybe when I'm a famous singer and you're a famous actress we can travel around on our private plane together,' he said.

'Just try and stop me,' she said, dizzy with thoughts of their shared future and how many possibilities lay before them.

Then – Finn

Finn was buzzing that Katerina had liked his song. She looked genuine too, not like she was trying to put on an act to save his feelings. It was a big moment, he realised, to sing for her. He hadn't sung for anyone except his mum before and he now let Katerina into that private place with him. There wasn't much else now that they didn't share. Almost everything was out in the open, transparent and uncomplicated, and he loved her even more deeply for it.

He was washing up the mugs in the kitchen, when he heard his mum talking to Katerina in the living room.

'Great.' He wiped his hands on a towel and hurried back, anxious to stop whatever mad prattle his mum might be saying.

'You have to be careful, lady,' Jenny said. She stood at the window, her hand on a curtain, peering behind it tremulously. 'People watch. And when they watch, they know. They know your name, your number, your address. You can be followed. You can be taken,' she said, her hand trembling.

Katerina was nodding politely, humouring her, and Finn burned with embarrassment at his girlfriend having to deal with his mum's ramblings. She often became less lucid after one of her gloomy days, and he was ashamed of her. Ashamed of her torn dressing gown with the tea stains on it, of her ratty blonde hair, lank from lack of washing, of her waxy grey skin and sallow eyes, that aged her and made her look so much older than the other mums. And he was ashamed of their crummy flat and their shabby life.

'Mum,' he said, sharply. 'Kat doesn't want to hear about it, okay?'

His mum looked at him blankly. 'Oh, hi love. You gave me a fright. For a moment I thought your father was standing there,' she said, putting a hand to her head. 'I think I'll go back to my room.' She shuffled away in her slippers, looking thin and stooped.

Katerina watched her go with pity written on her face and Finn wanted to tell her, *No, don't pity us. I want your love, your pride, your passion, but not your pity. Anything but that.*

She looked up at him when his mum had left the room. 'Sorry about her,' he said, sitting back on the sofa. 'She's having a weird day. She has better ones,' he said, although he knew they were few and far between.

Katerina took his hand. 'She mentioned your dad, but you've never spoken about him to me,' she said.

Finn withdrew his hand and rubbed his own together, kneading his knuckles. 'There's nothing to say.'

'Well, where is he?' Katerina asked.

Finn considered making up something that sounded cool, like his dad worked abroad, but he was a rubbish liar. He took a breath. 'He left. When I was two. I've never seen him since.'

'That's awful,' Katerina murmured, stroking his hair, the gentle gesture almost making Finn want to cry. She was the only one who actually tried to nurture him.

'It is what it is,' he mumbled, leaning into her shoulder, enveloping his face in her hair, smelling the scent of fabric softener and shampoo, the scents of a girl who was well provided for, who came from a home where shampoo was readily available, laundry was done, and milk wasn't always on the turn.

'If I ever get to be a dad, I will never leave my kids,' he said, a determined edge in his voice. 'I will always be there for them.'

Katerina nodded and continued to stroke his hair, kissing his head. Finn wrapped his arms around her. She was his world and he didn't need anyone else.

Chapter Eleven

Katerina

Katerina carefully chopped some roots, wondering what the meal would turn out like. She had never been a brilliant cook, unlike her mum, but Maz was suffering from a high temperature and sore throat, so Katerina had volunteered to make the dinner that evening. She was starting to wish she hadn't, as Maz kept giving her garbled instructions from where she lay on the sofa, despite Ashif's best efforts to tell her to be quiet and rest.

She gutted the fish, teasing apart the silver scales and the flesh. She had another successful trip to the lake, but this time with Darryl. Katerina knew Finn might have volunteered to go with her, so she had turned to Darryl and asked him to go with her before Finn had the chance to speak. Darryl had been surprised but pleased to be asked, as Katerina flattered him and told him he was the fittest one and the most capable of making it there and back. Finn had looked hurt, but she ignored it. Being with him was almost physically painful, so intense were the emotions he aroused in her, and every time she was near him she felt her resolve crumbling. She needed to be more careful.

Willow sidled over to the kitchen and grabbed a knife. 'I'll help,' she said, and took some of the roots to chop.

'Oh okay, sure, thank you,' Katerina said hesitantly, as there wasn't much left to do.

'It's great you managed to catch these,' Willow said, nodding her head at the fish. 'A good meal for us tonight.'

Katerina nodded. 'Glad I could help.' She paused. 'How was your day?'

'Finn and I chopped wood,' she said, looking down at her board, her fingers carefully and slowly slicing the roots. 'You know, I really like Finn,' she said, in a low voice, her gaze fixed on the chopping board. 'But it's funny, he doesn't seem interested at all.'

'Oh,' Katerina said, feeling increasingly uncomfortable at the turn of the conversation. She stirred the pot that was beginning to bubble on the small stove, and wished she could walk away, but she had duties to fulfil.

'In fact, he keeps pushing me away. Not literally,' she said, with a slight laugh. 'But he definitely is trying to ignore the obvious chemistry we have. And I just can't figure out why.'

She paused, laying her knife down, and put a hand on her hip, looking directly at Katerina. 'I keep thinking that perhaps he likes someone else.'

Katerina added the roots to the stew, and stirred them in. 'I wouldn't know,' she said coolly.

'I thought it might be someone from his past, you know, that keeps him dangling.' A hard edge crept into Willow's voice. The expression on her face was pleasant, a gentle smile on her lips, but her eyes glittered like glass. 'And I thought, wouldn't that be unfair, you know, if that person doesn't like Finn, to do that? Like, maybe they should be upfront with him and honest, and just say, nope, not interested. Then he can turn his attention to people who are.' Willow began tapping her fingers on the chopping board.

Katerina felt her stomach swirl with anxiety, unsure what to say. Could Finn really be snubbing Willow because he still had feelings for her? Surely not after all this time? Her chest tightened with confusion. She didn't want him to want her but there was a small nugget of satisfaction she took from the thought, even though she knew it was wrong.

'Perhaps you should mind your own business,' Katerina said, amazed at the bluntness of her words. She wasn't normally so forthright and had been intending to say something much more placatory, but the words slipped out before she could stop them. 'Finn is a grown man. He can make his own choices.'

Willow's mouth pressed into a thin line. 'Right,' she said. She folded her arms across her chest and walked off to the living room, her back rigid with tension.

Katerina sighed. This was getting absurd and complicated. She hadn't planned to get caught in any dramas – she saved that sort of thing for her acting roles. This wasn't what she wanted. She looked desperately around at the cameras, wishing they weren't there.

Katerina tried her best to ignore Willow's icy stare as she served up the fish and vegetables, to congratulations from the group. Even Maz croaked out a thank you from the sofa where she ate, curled up under a blanket.

'I did my best,' said Katerina, modestly.

'It's perfect,' Ashif said, nodding in approval.

They waited in the living room for their usual after-dinner message and without fail, the screen came on and Phineas reappeared. Not for the first time Katerina wondered where Phineas was staying, and whether he was close by in case of emergencies.

'Hi everyone, another day where Katerina used her fishing skills and some great work from all of you joining together to keep warm and stay fed. I know you're all feeling run down and that the wilderness can take its toll on your health. Right now, you're probably suffering from bad backs, aches and pains, bruises, headaches, tiredness, sore throats, and colds.'

Maz nodded and coughed from the sofa. Michael leaned over to Katerina. 'My back is killing me,' he said softly.

Katerina nodded. She was spent from the day and desperate for sleep. There wasn't much energy for anything else other than the basics.

Phineas continued. 'We have a little treat for you all. When you signed up for the programme you were asked to pick one luxury item that you would love to have with you. We've decided to deliver those items to you tonight. You'll find them outside the front door. Enjoy!'

'Oh yay!' Willow cried out joyfully as Cressida, Darryl and Finn hurried to the door to fetch the items.

'I can't remember what I asked for, but it better be good,' Maz rasped. 'Although right now I would settle for a Lemsip above all else.'

Willow patted her on the arm. 'You poor thing,' she said, sympathetically. Katerina caught her eye and looked away quickly, feeling awkward about the tension that remained between them.

'Make way folks,' Darryl announced triumphantly, as they lugged a large box to the centre of the room.

Cressida wrenched it open eagerly and began reading out the labels and dispatching the items to the right people.

Maz was delighted to have her gin and hugged the bottle joyfully to herself while the others laughed. 'I feel better already,' she said, waving the full-sized bottle around.

Katerina took her parcel gratefully. She remembered exactly what it was. It was a large bar of dark chocolate, her favourite. She knew she wouldn't get much as she would share it with the group, but even the thought of one or two squares made her mouth water.

'Finn, wow! This is super!' Cressida lifted Finn's guitar out of the box with an excited smile.

Finn grabbed it happily. 'Hello old girl,' he said, patting it fondly, as if it were a cherished family pet. Katerina stared as he unzipped the worn black case with the fraying straps and took out the guitar she had seen so many times. It was exactly the same as she remembered, the wood slightly tarnished and chipped in places, and an old Foo Fighters sticker that wouldn't come off on the back. She looked away and busied herself with opening her chocolate and sharing it round. She didn't want to look at Finn with that guitar. It reminded her too much of being hopelessly in love with him and the strength of those memories made her want to run away from the cabin and away from him.

'Are you going to sing for us?' Willow asked dreamily, leaning forward and smiling up at Finn.

'If you like,' he said, entirely relaxed about the request, and Katerina recalled a time when he used to be so shy about his singing.

'You must!' Cressida insisted, nibbling with joy on the chocolate Katerina gave her.

Ashif poured everyone a cup of Maz's gin, at her request, and they sat down to listen to Finn.

He strummed a few opening chords, warming up, and without saying anything went straight into a song.

That melody. Those lyrics. Katerina wanted to put her hands over her ears and beg him to stop. It was her song. Why, of all the songs in the world, was he singing that song now? She screwed on her poker face as tightly as she could, her mouth trembling. Finn wasn't looking at her as he sang, but when he finished he stared across at her and her throat was so tight with unshed tears that she could barely breathe and hardly speak.

He went on to sing other songs, but she remained in turmoil, her body in the present but her heart reliving the past.

Finn

Katerina had a great poker face, Finn knew that. He had seen it often enough. But he knew he had sent her a message, loud and clear, by singing her song for her that evening. And no matter how hard she tried to hide it, he had seen on her face that she had been affected by it. It was the tension in her jaw, and the tiny glimmer in her eye, that gave it away.

He had tried to be clear with Willow that day. She had become increasingly tactile with him, and he gently hinted to her that he wasn't interested, that there was someone in his life already. He wasn't sure she had really understood or taken the hint, but he hoped she would. He didn't want anything getting in the way of him and Katerina. If there were any barriers he wanted them gone. He felt like fate had handed him an opportunity to see her again, and he didn't want to squander it. Just like the song that he wrote for her said, he had never lost his love for her.

The group clapped when he finished his impromptu gig, and he smiled with pleasure, both from their applause and from the joy he got from being able to hold his guitar and sing again.

'Good stuff,' Michael said. 'Did you write that yourself?'

Finn nodded, delighted to have the chance to show that he wasn't just a boy-band reject. He genuinely loved music, loved playing and writing his own songs. He was hoping the audience at home would like it as well, and a record company or two might be interested after the show aired. That's why he had chosen his guitar for his luxury item. He had no idea he would be using it to once again serenade the one that got away, thirteen years after he first performed for her, but fortunately that track had never left his mind, just like the girl he wrote it for.

'Yeah. I have lots of songs that I've written,' he said. 'Loads of material.' He mentally crossed his fingers that this performance would get him far more than he originally hoped for.

'You're so talented,' Willow said. 'Those were beautiful lyrics.'

'Thanks,' he said, gratefully taking his mug of gin.

Katerina didn't say anything to him when she passed him his square of chocolate from her luxury item, and though the praise from everyone was warm enough, it was hers that he wanted. But she went to bed early and he didn't get a chance to speak to her properly for the rest of the evening.

Chapter Twelve

Katerina

Katerina's thigh pressed uncomfortably close to Finn's. She wished she could move away, hating the thrill that she got from being so close to him, but there wasn't much room in the dog sled to sit further apart.

They whooshed through the trees, going at an incredible pace, the chilly air whipping past their faces, making their cheeks burn. Katerina could hear the excited whoops and shrieks of the others as their own sleds careened through the forest.

'This is amazing!' Finn yelled, the force of the wind stealing away his words so even though he was right next to her he sounded far away.

She gripped the handles in front of her and tried to focus on the adrenalin rush from the eager racing of the dogs rather than the heart-pounding nearness of Finn.

This show was full of ups and downs. She had been as excited as the others when Phineas announced that they would be getting a dog-sledding session. But her heart sank when the producers paired Finn and her together. Ashif and Darryl first, then Finn and her, then Cressida and Maz, then Michael and Willow. Willow had looked displeased, and Katerina thought about offering to swap partners, but Finn had grabbed her arm and dragged her to their sled before she had a chance. After a few hours' practice, led by a local expert, they were allowed to go it alone.

The pace slackened slightly, and Katerina realised they were slowing down. 'What's the matter?' she said to Finn, who was holding the reins.

'Nothing,' he said, grinning. 'I just thought it was a shame to be racing along and miss all the scenery.'

'Finn, there's nothing here but trees,' she said incredulously, looking around her.

'Well, I wanted to make the most of your company then,' he said.

She wished his smile didn't still churn up the butterflies in her stomach, but it did. Her gut reaction when it came to Finn was both attraction and the urge to flee. She wasn't sure which one was shouting loudest at her right now and she felt like her emotions were tearing her in two.

'Did you enjoy the music last night?' he asked her, his words light. She knew what he really wanted to ask her, about whether or not she remembered the song he wrote for her.

She thought for a moment. 'Yes. I've always said you're very talented. I hope that the people at home notice that too.'

He looked shyly down at the reins. 'Did you recognise any of the songs?'

'You know I did,' she said. 'But why play it here, now? It's not relevant any more.' She looked away into the trees, but before she did she saw his face fall a little. She could sense his disappointment. Katerina knew from the moment he had started to play the song last night that Finn must still harbour some feelings for her. She couldn't ignore the way he looked at her, a mixture of hope and happiness, the same expression she had seen on his face before when they were younger. She thought she had left Finn behind in the past and had tried so hard to move on, but here he was, making her feel emotions just as strongly as he had done when they were teens, emotions she had only ever felt when she was with him.

The dogs walked slowly, panting, steam from their fur rising in the air. Finn ignored where they were going and turned to face her.

She glanced around – no cameraman. There was only the small hand-held camera attached to the front of the sled. Finn saw her glance nervously at it and he swiped at it, knocking it to the hard ground, where it bounced and the back popped off. For the first time in Alaska, they were alone with no cameras.

'Listen.' He took one gloved hand and held hers, squeezing her fingers tightly. 'I always regretted not telling you how much I was in love with you,' he said. 'I always wondered if things could have been different. Every time I saw you on TV, I thought about the future we could have shared together.'

She made to interrupt but he wouldn't let her. She wanted to pull her hand away, but he held it so tightly that her fingers were going slightly numb.

'I know that you've got loads going for you, you always have, and I will probably always be just a throwback memory to a teenage mistake, but I'd love to see you again after this programme, love to take you out properly. Not just, you know, sitting in a park sharing a bag of crisps,' he said, earnestly.

She could see the sincerity shining in his eyes, and she was torn between a desperation to experience actual love again, and the desire to run screaming from the sled. Finn was no good for her, he never had been, she knew that, her dad certainly did. There was too much water under the bridge, too much that had happened for them to reclaim anything they thought they once had.

She removed her hand from under his, not wanting to see the disappointment in his eyes, but knowing what it would look like all the same.

'I'm sorry, but I can't.'

'Why not?' he pressed her. 'Give me a reason so I can understand. Otherwise I just don't know why you're not willing to give us another chance, especially when what we had was so good.'

Katerina snorted derisively, a small flame of anger stoked by his words. 'Really? You know what? The reason I don't want to go on a date with you and try to rekindle some long-lost romance is because we were a mistake, a mistake that I'll never be able to get away from, and you, Finn, you broke my heart.' Her words ended in a sob.

He raised his eyebrows and shook his head gently. 'No, Katerina. You broke mine.'

Then – Finn

Finn's phone buzzed noisily, the vibration sounding like an angry muffled bee against the thin carpet.

The flat was boiling even though it was October. An Indian summer defied the onset of autumn, sending golden streams of sunshine through the living room window, where his curtains had fallen down a while ago.

Finn rubbed his eyes and blinked lazily. He was a bit hung-over from hanging out with his friends last night, but he couldn't wait to spend Sunday with Katerina. The summer had passed in a haze of heat and lovemaking, tender kisses on sunburned skin. He had never been so happy as those few months they had been together. Now that they were back at school for Year 11, they were still trying to hide their relationship from her parents, still trying to cover it up from his mates. When he was with her all else faded into the background and all he could see, smell, hear, or think about was her and her eyes looking into his as she lay semi-naked on his sofa.

He had never pressured her into sleeping with him, but a few days after her sixteenth birthday she had asked him if he wanted to, and of course, he had said yes, himself having turned sixteen just before her. They say you never forget your first, and Finn knew he would never forget Katerina and the way she had looked and felt that afternoon when they clumsily made love for the first time, giggling with nerves, fumbling with their clothes, fearful her parents would return from their day trip early and discover them in her bedroom.

Finn had no doubt that Katerina was his soulmate. He couldn't explain it, but he was sure she was the person he was meant to be with. It physically hurt him to be apart from her, and he begrudged every slow second that ticked by without her in his arms.

He scrabbled for his phone and found it, half hidden behind a cushion that had fallen on the floor. It was a message from Katerina. He grinned and clicked on it, eager to see her words.

I'm moving away. Today. I won't see you again.

He squinted, confused, and rechecked the sender. The message definitely came from her phone. He sat up quickly, rubbing his temples where a dull headache threatened.

He typed a reply with shaking fingers, frowning. She must have made a mistake. Or maybe it was some kind of weird joke?

What do you mean? Are you okay? he typed, and pressed "Send".

He waited expectantly for a response, but none came. He tapped his knees. Walked around the living room. Got a glass of water. Checked his phone three times to make sure it was working. Nothing from Katerina.

He dialled her number and held the phone to his ear, and it went straight to voicemail. He sat down, rereading the message, his heart starting to pound with anxiety. Surely this couldn't be real?

He had only seen her two days ago, when they had spent a few hours in the park after school. She had seemed completely fine, laughing and joking and kissing him. He wracked his brains to think of an explanation for the text, to analyse the last time he saw her, to try to work out if he had done something wrong. He sat on the sofa and waited, stuck in his confusion and fear. The daylight began to fade and darkness finally took over, and her phone still went to voicemail and his texts remained unanswered. By the time night arrived, he knew this was no mistake, knew that he should go and find her, but it was too late to go knocking on her parents' door.

It was an agony of waiting for the day to dawn. He lay restless and awake, clutching his phone, his tears soaking into the sofa. Eventually the sun rose, and he got up, showered and dressed. He had to go to Kat's house to find out what was going on.

He hurried down the street, the air humid from a storm last night that he hadn't even heard. He walked the familiar route to her house, each step taking him both closer and further away from hope. He knocked on the door with a shuddering hand, holding every muscle as still as he could to avoid trembling with nerves and anxiety and lack of sleep. He didn't want to go to her house, as he knew he wouldn't be welcome, but what choice did he have? He couldn't wait any longer for an answer.

Keith opened the door and stared at him coolly. Finn opened his mouth to speak but Keith beat him to it.

'She's gone. I won't tell you where. Don't try to contact her,' he said shortly, before moving to shut the door. Finn stepped forward and shoved his foot in between the door and the frame, wincing as Keith trapped it there, but he refused to budge.

'Would you mind?' Keith said politely, but his tone had turned dark and his skin was reddening.

'Please, I don't understand. Why has she gone? What's happened? Is she okay?' Finn asked pleadingly.

Keith shook his head and gave Finn a look that made him feel about three inches tall. 'I'm sorry lad, but Katerina's got opportunities she just can't turn down right now. You want her to be happy right?'

Finn nodded slowly.

'Then leave her be. She's going to make something of herself. Without you dragging her down.' Keith nudged Finn's unprotesting foot out of the doorway and shut it with a decisive click.

Finn made it two houses down the road before he had to stop to sit on the kerb, his head reeling. He thought he was going to be sick and swallowed hard, clutching his hair with both hands, his stomach lurching into his throat.

He couldn't believe Katerina would do this. He couldn't believe she would just up and leave and treat him like something to throw away. He loved her and she loved him, there was no faking that. Finn took a shuddering breath when he thought of the days stretching ahead without her, without her smile and her laughter, and all he was left with was a flat like a hovel and a mum who was surely going insane.

Katerina

Katerina bit her lip in shame when she heard Finn recount how he had felt when she left. She could tell the hurt still resonated, even all these years later, yet he still had her on a pedestal, was forgiving in his nature, and wanted to try to rekindle their romance despite what she had done. She burned with guilt about how she had hurt him and lied to him. She had her reasons. But now she heard the distress in his voice, she remembered the lost lonely boy she loved and knew she had wounded him more than anyone else could have.

'Listen, to me, it's water under the bridge, okay?' he said, staring at her intently. 'Yes, my heart was broken but we were young. I still think that you are the only girl, woman, I have ever loved like that, and regardless of how it ended, I'd still love to give it another shot.'

She stared at the ground, tears forming in her eyes.

'I just – I want to know why, Kat, why you left the way you did?' he asked her, a question he had clearly been saving up for a long time.

She looked up. 'I am sorry. I know that must have been rough.' She paused. 'Do you remember what you were doing the night before you got that text message?' she asked him.

A look of confusion crossed his face at her question, which seemed so irrelevant to answering his. He frowned. 'Not really, no.'

'Let me help you remember,' she said.

Then – Katerina

Katerina hurried to the park, her footsteps echoing on the pavement. Her heart pounded as she walked fast, sweat seeping down her back. She was desperate to see Finn. She needed to talk to him right away.

She knew where he was as she had texted him earlier in the day to ask what he was up to. She didn't like the idea of him hanging out with his low-life friends, boozing in the park, and now she had a very good reason to interrupt him.

She entered through the wrought-iron gates, and hurried past the children's area, where a few children were still playing, their shouts rising into the evening air. She squinted against the setting sun and searched the wider park, walking past couples and dog walkers.

She heard Finn's voice before she saw him. She honed in on the familiar sound and looked in his direction. He was a little way off, near a clump of trees with a small group of friends. She moved closer, intending to call out, but she heard him mention her name and froze beside a picnic table, where the only occupant was a drowsy bee looking for something sweet.

'No way Finn, you didn't! What was she like in bed? Vanilla right?'

'Yup,' Finn said, his words slightly slurred around the edges, sloppy. His hair was ruffled, blades of grass stuck to his back and he was clutching a can of cider; a number of empties littered the ground around him. 'It was boring. She was a good Catholic virgin, after all.'

Katerina flinched as though he had slapped her. The stupid laddish boasting in his voice made her heart sink and her knees gave way. She knelt on the grass, hidden by the table, and wished she could run away and pretend she had never overheard. She gripped the bench with both hands and breathed hard, listening, watching, as her foolish dreams were shattered.

'So, are you dating her?'

'Nah. Just messing around. Filling the time.'

'Till something better comes along?' Katerina heard a female voice this time, one she recognised from school. It was Carly – bright, perky, beautiful and curvy, not to mention unkind and gossipy.

'Why, are you making an offer?' Finn said flirtatiously.

Katerina couldn't believe this was her Finn. She had encouraged him, believed in him, given him everything, trusted him. This flirtation, this betrayal, this mockery at her expense, it all felt so cheap and degrading.

She raised her head slightly, her vision mainly obscured by the bench, but she could see Carly sidle up to him and stroke his hair. She didn't wait to see what happened next. She felt sick and cold despite the Indian summer heat. Whatever she had to speak about to Finn would go unsaid. He didn't deserve any more of her time. She ran home, her lungs burning and her eyes blurred with tears, taking no notice of the cars as she crossed the road, nor the pedestrians who gave her funny looks.

Katerina

She watched Finn's eyes as she recounted what had happened in the park the night before she left, the night he crushed her heart.

He dropped his head into his hands. 'Shit. Oh no, I never knew you saw that.'

She nodded. 'I know I didn't exactly behave the right way, but I was devastated,' she said, crisply.

'Kat, listen, you need to know something,' Finn started, but she held up a hand. 'I really don't want to hear excuses and explanations,' she said. 'The time for that has passed.'

'But you never gave me a chance to explain all those years ago,' he said. 'Please. I was saying stupid things, because I wanted to look like a big man in front of my mates. But I never did anything with Carly. Honestly. I never cheated on you.'

'Okay great, good to know,' Katerina said, sarcastically. She still remembered so clearly how it felt to not just have her heart broken, but also her trust in people, her ability to put faith in someone. She had really needed him that day and he hadn't been there for her.

Finn looked at her and his eyes were glimmering with tears. 'Kat, you don't understand. I was …' He swallowed hard, his voice choked. 'I was so in love with you. Completely. I didn't want my friends knowing, I didn't want to tell people how I really felt, because it seemed too precious, too good to be true, and I thought if I let the secret out then the world would try to interfere and tear us apart.'

Kat stared at him, and the "what-ifs" that she had agonised over for years screamed so loudly in her soul that she almost covered her ears with her hands.

'You should have talked to me. We could have worked it out. I could have explained.' Finn's expression was one of abject misery, his eyes dark with sorrow. 'I'm so sorry that I hurt you,' he said softly. 'That's the last thing I would ever want to do.'

Katerina felt a stab of shame at his apology, and at her actions, taken so rashly, fuelled by hurt and anger and pride. Things could have been so different if she had given him a chance to explain, and the years of wondering would have been filled instead with the possibility of Finn's love and their joint happiness.

'I should have talked to you,' she whispered.

'It was my fault for being an idiot in the park. I ruined everything.' He groaned, putting his head in his hands in despair.

The dogs looked up at his distress, staring at him quizzically.

She sighed. 'It was a mess.' She spoke more to herself than to Finn. 'Teenagers shouldn't be allowed to date, much less fall in love.'

'So, you were definitely in love with me then?' Finn looked up hopefully.

'You know I was,' she said sombrely.

'That makes it worse somehow. That I messed up something so good. What might have happened if I hadn't done that? Maybe you would have stayed. Maybe we would still be together now, with a house and kids and stuff.'

Katerina shook her head. 'We were very young, Finn. And no one has a crystal ball.'

He nodded. 'Right. I get why you don't want to meet up romantically after the show is over,' he said. 'But perhaps as friends? And then maybe we can see what happens?' There was a hopeful lilt in his voice.

'Maybe,' murmured Katerina. 'As friends.' Even as she said it, she knew she could never see Finn again after the show was over. It was better for everyone.

Chapter Thirteen

Finn

Finn could hear the happy chatter of the group in the living room, still on a high from the dog sledding earlier in the day. His fellow survivalists had been energised by the high-octane activity, but his and Katerina's sombre mood when they returned had provoked more than a few bemused looks. Katerina was sitting on her own in the kitchen, nursing a cup of tea. He could see the back of her head from where he stood looking out of the window.

His head throbbed from the intensity of their earlier conversation, his chest tight from words unsaid. He was desperate to go over to her, wishing he had the words to persuade her that they should give things another try, but they had had to return to the cabin to avoid the encroaching storm.

Finn turned back to the window, staring glumly out at the snow that whirled outside. The thick white flakes were whipped viciously in the air by a violent wind. The weather matched the way he felt inside, battered by emotions that he couldn't express because of the cameras' unflinching gaze. He had no choice but to keep it together and stay silent, haunted by thoughts of the future he and Kat had lost.

He couldn't believe that a stupid teenage drinking session led to him losing the girl he loved, putting him in limbo for years as he wondered why she left him the way she did. He had no one to blame but himself. No wonder she had been reluctant to spend time with him here. She must think he was a total scumbag.

Finn's only hope was to ask her again, when the show finished, if she wanted to meet up to try to rekindle their friendship. That would have to be enough. If that's all Katerina wanted to give him, he would accept it like a dog accepts scraps from the table.

Willow sidled up to him. 'What are you up to?' she asked, looking out of the window at the blizzard.

'Nothing.'

She smiled up at him. 'You know, I was thinking it would be nice to meet up after we leave here in a few days,' she said.

He looked down at the stunning woman who was clearly interested in him. Finn knew that if he was in his right mind he would just enjoy her attraction and her attention, but his spirit and his heart felt so broken by today's conversation that he could scarcely raise a smile right now, let alone think about another romantic relationship.

Willow's eyes flickered with hurt at his stony silence and Finn cleared his throat. He didn't want to be rude, especially as she was asking him publicly, risking humiliation.

'Sure,' he said, forcing the best smile he could muster. 'We can meet up for a drink or something.' She looked delighted.

'Guys, the TV is coming on!' Maz called out to them, and they hurried over. Finn nudged Darryl to make space on the sofa for Willow and him to perch on the edge. She leaned into him, looking at him with a sweet smile, and he hoped his lukewarm response hadn't given her the wrong idea. He would hate to mislead her.

'First of all, you're on the home straight, folks. Only a few days left,' Phineas began. Finn smiled at the thought of being able to go home soon.

'Unfortunately, we've had reports that the storm outside is set to turn into a raging blizzard and we have been advised that none of you should leave the cabin at present as it's too dangerous. Hopefully it'll pass by tomorrow morning but if not, we'll make arrangements for your food and wood to be delivered to you.' Phineas spoke gravely, weaving his fingers together.

Michael let out a large sigh of relief. Finn thought it was a shame to have to rely on the producers in those final days when they had been starting to fend for themselves, catching food and fish and keeping the fire stoked, but it was better than being caught in a blizzard.

Phineas' expression brightened. 'I know how hard it can be to survive in a harsh environment like this one, and sometimes it's the thought of friends and family that keeps you going. Well, we have a treat to share with you tonight. To help you make it through the next few days, your families pre-recorded these messages for you.'

Phineas smiled, knowing what the messages would mean to the group, who had been away from their loved ones for over a week. It didn't sound like a long time, but it felt like an age to Finn, and he didn't even have anyone he particularly missed.

The screen went blank for a moment and then an elderly Asian couple appeared, seated on a red sofa, smiling broadly.

‘Ashif, we hope you enjoy this message. We are so proud of you for trying this new challenge, of making it to the end. We are sure you will have used your medical training and helped others, we would expect nothing less. We can’t wait to see you when you get back. We know it must be very hard out there, but when you get back we will make sure you eat a whole month’s worth of food in one go!’ The couple laughed.

Finn looked across at Ashif and was surprised to see him dabbing away tears. He was a reserved man, but the sight of his parents was enough to make him cry. It struck Finn that he had no family to leave him a message and he wondered if he would get one at all. He tried to brush away his sadness, but it was only heightened as Maz’s mother and sister loomed on screen. Maz leapt up with her hands to her mouth, and watched, laughing, delighted by the sight of her family.

He caught Katerina looking at him and he wondered if she knew what he was thinking, as she looked tense and pale. It was nice of her to be worried about him, he thought. The messages continued, leaving only his and Katerina’s remaining.

He exhaled with relief as his two best mates came on the screen. One was a drinking buddy of his. The other was Todd, his band mate from 1Dream. Finn’s friends gave him a good shout-out, and he relaxed. He didn’t look like a complete loner. It wasn’t too bad after all.

Katerina

Katerina thought she had enough to deal with after today’s conversation with Finn. She wasn’t sure she could handle any more emotion after that, and the news of the video messages made her chest tighten and her heart palpitate. Surely the message would be from her mum? The videos were obviously recorded before the show, so her mum wouldn’t have known what was happening here, but even so, they wouldn’t have put Chris on camera? She buried the awful thought in a haze of anxiety and tried to focus on the screen, glancing nervously at Finn, who looked gloomy.

Her breath caught in her throat and she coughed, waiting nervously. She kneaded her fingers together, the skin roughened from the exposure of the past ten days, her palms starting to sweat. Hers was the final message.

Chris's face appeared on the screen, normally such a welcome sight that gave her such joy. But this time when she saw his easy grin and bright blue eyes her throat closed up and she thought she would faint.

'Hi Mum. I bet you're doing so well, and even if it's tough you've got to make it to the end.' He shook his head and smiled widely. 'Although me and Grandma obviously miss you loads and can't wait to see you!'

Please, don't say your age! Katerina wanted to beg him out loud but knew it was hopeless to speak back as the messages were pre-recorded.

'Oh, and I'm totally not angry at you missing my thirteenth birthday but you better get me a good present when you get back,' he said, laughing and rolling his eyes.

'Wow, you must have been a teenager when you had him,' she heard Michael mutter next to her.

She looked across at Finn, stricken, hoping he hadn't understood or hadn't heard, or that somehow he hadn't worked it out. The aghast expression on his face, his cheeks drained of colour, told her that he had. His eyes, just like her son's, stared at her, filled with shock.

Her secret was out.

Finn

Finn looked at Katerina, struck dumb, hoping he had heard wrong. Her son couldn't be thirteen. He just couldn't be, or that would mean … He wouldn't allow his mind to even stray close to the thought.

He took ragged gasps of air, his chest tight.

Willow turned to him. 'Oh, you look awful, are you okay?' she asked, putting a hand on his arm, but he stood up and brushed her away roughly.

'Hey!' Willow said, irritated at his dismissal, but he barely even heard her. He watched Katerina stand up and walk swiftly to the kitchen; he immediately followed her.

'Kat, tell me what the hell that was?' he asked. He was trying so hard not to shout that it hurt his throat with the effort of containing his rage. The group were watching with interest, but he didn't care who saw or heard.

'I don't know what you mean,' Katerina said, her hands trembling, fumbling over glasses, picking things up, wiping them, putting them down. He took a glass from her hand and slammed it on the counter and she finally stopped and looked at him directly.

'He's thirteen,' he said, and his voice choked with a sob. 'Please, *please* tell me I'm getting the wrong end of the stick.' He didn't want it to be true, he hoped desperately she would correct him, laugh off his concerns, tell him he was being silly to even think such a thing.

She didn't. Instead, she bit her lip without saying a word, glancing anxiously at the cameras.

'Don't look at them, look at me!' he shouted, and Michael came over, his hands held up placatingly.

'Now there, this probably isn't the time or the place,' he said in a hushed voice, and Finn knew that he had worked it out as well.

Finn shook his head and ignored him. 'Kat, I need to know,' he demanded, pounding his fist down on the counter so hard that his arm ached.

Her eyes were wide with panic, and she stuttered uncomfortably under his angry gaze. 'Finn, I was young. I didn't know what to do, and it all just happened,' she said miserably, tears tracking down her cheeks.

Finn put his head in his hands and groaned, wanting to be sick, wanting to shake her, wanting to sink to the floor. The truth was so awful that it overwhelmed him. In that moment, robbed of his reason and overcome by emotion, he could have screamed out loud. Instead, he opened his mouth to speak, although Michael began talking before he could.

'Oh dear, perhaps you both should—'

Finn snapped at him before he could finish. 'This is none of your business!'

Michael nodded and rejoined the group to watch from the side lines, realising he couldn't do anything useful in this situation.

Finn was perspiring with rage, angry waves of adrenalin making his heart pound and his hands shake. 'How the hell could you keep this from me for thirteen years?! Does he know?'

'No, he doesn't know,' she said miserably.

'What the hell did you tell him about who his dad was then?' he hissed, wanting to cry as he said the word "dad".

'I told him his father wasn't around, and he accepted it,' she said.

'Katerina, I told you how much I wanted to be around if I ever had children and you stole that from me, you took that chance away, and I didn't even know he existed!' Finn cried then, bitter tears rolling down his cheeks, hanging his head and sobbing at the thought of his boy not even knowing who he was.

It was the cruellest thing anyone could have ever done and it had been done to him by the only person he had ever loved. If he thought Katerina had broken his heart before, she had now well and truly shattered it.

Katerina

Katerina stared at Finn, furious and broken before her, and heard the shocked gasps from the group behind her. She glanced wildly at the cameras, thinking of all those people watching, and the fact that Chris would see this too. The guilt and the shame tore into her like knives and she bent her head down to catch her breath, before crying out.

'I want to leave! I want to leave now!' she screamed, surprising Finn and making him flinch with the force of her words.

'No!' he yelled out. 'You can't just run away again and avoid this!'

A voice crackled over a hidden loudspeaker. 'Katerina, we can't get transport to you in this blizzard today. You will have to wait until tomorrow at the earliest.'

Katerina gasped, thinking about spending another night under this roof with her secret exposed, having to look at Finn's agonised face, and she knew she couldn't take another minute. She ran blindly towards the front door, ignoring the shouts of Darryl and Maz, and wrenched it open, throwing herself outside into the blizzard.

Then – Katerina

Katerina couldn't take her eyes away from the white plastic stick that she clutched with anxious hands. She needed to see the result form before her eyes, so she could know there was no trickery, no mistake. Surely, she had got it wrong. Surely her period was just a bit late. Surely, she wasn't feeling nauseous and hungry and tired and swollen? *It's all in your head*, she said, a calming mantra, repeated as she watched one line appear, then another to accompany it. Pregnant.

She laid the test down with a shaky hand, the nerves burning up her insides. Three tests lay together, thrice confirmed. Pregnant, pregnant, pregnant. She sat on the toilet and looked at them for twenty minutes, her mind blank, until her dad banged on the door.

She secreted the tests in her room, wrapped in toilet paper, and looked at her diary. She was trying to be calm and practical as she counted the dates. A few weeks late. Maybe a bit more, or a bit less, she wasn't quite sure.

She touched her stomach, thinking about the tiny being that had set up home without her even noticing. A baby. Her and Finn's baby.

She knew immediately she had to tell her parents. She had no desire to try to hide this overwhelming burden. She had no idea what to do, but she knew she needed their help. They had helped other young girls before, always happy to donate money or gifts, anything to avoid an abortion, which they were vehemently opposed to. She knew that as early as six weeks pregnant could mean a heartbeat pulsing away already, no bigger than a lentil. It wouldn't look like a baby now, but it would pretty soon. She wondered what their baby might look like. Would it have her hair? His eyes?

She stood up, her knees weak as water, took the tests, and went downstairs. Her parents were bustling around, preparing to go to her aunt's party. She hated to drop this on them now, but she couldn't hold this secret with her all day, the weight of it would crush her.

'Hello love, we'll be ready to go in about thirty minutes,' her mum said, snapping the lid shut on her home-made coleslaw. Katerina felt a yearning for last Sunday when they were eating coleslaw and everything was normal. Now everything was going to change.

'Mum,' she said, her voice barely a whisper.

'Yes,' her mum said, not looking at her, still busy, still happily ignorant of the impending bombshell about to fall.

'Mum,' Katerina said more urgently, and she held the tests out in her hand, palm flat.

Her mum's face whitened and her mouth became thin as she took a long terrible moment to regard the tests in her daughter's hand. She regarded Katerina with a gaze that made her stomach turn to ice, then she turned her head towards the garden. 'Keith, come here, please. NOW!' she shouted.

Looking back at Katerina, she pointed to the living room. 'Go sit down. We'll be there in a minute.' Her voice was calm and cold, her eyes like stone.

Katerina nodded and went to the living room, sitting on the sofa, running her fingers over the tests she still clutched in her hand. She could hear hushed voices behind the kitchen door. Her dad's voice grew louder and she shoved her fingers in her ears, so the only sound she could hear was the swooshing of her blood round her body, pumped by her racing heart. She didn't want to hear his reaction.

She didn't know how long they took to come, but the minutes stretched cruelly as she curled over her knees, telling herself to breathe, trying not to be sick on the carpet.

She wasn't aware her parents had come into the room until her mum roughly pulled her hands away from her head from where she still had her fingers in her ears.

'Sit up straight,' she demanded. 'You are not a child.' Katerina knew her mum was seething but was trying to keep her voice under control.

Her dad sat on the sofa. 'Katerina, you've been incredibly stupid,' he said. His expression was grim, but his voice was soft. Somehow that made it worse and Katerina bit back a sob.

'You have all these opportunities, a glittering future, so much talent. Why would you want to throw it all away on a feckless teenage romance with that boy, who I am assuming is the father?'

'Dad, I'm sorry,' she said, her eyes filled with tears. 'We were careful.'

Her mum put out a hand to stop her. 'I don't want to hear any details,' she said. 'All we need to know is that you're pregnant. Three tests can't be wrong.'

Keith gripped his knees, his emotions tightly constrained under his veneer of practicality. 'Katerina, we can help you with this.'

She interrupted him before he could continue. 'I want to keep the baby,' she said determinedly. Her decision was not one made to please her parents, or God. It was made because she loved Finn, he loved her, and they would both love this baby. She knew it in her heart. She couldn't get rid of something that was forged in love.

Keith nodded. 'Well, you know our thoughts on matters such as these. Here is what you will do, Katerina.' He stood up, his hands tucked behind his back, looking down at his daughter, his voice leaving no room for arguments.

'You'll go to your Aunt Theresa's house. She's a paediatric nurse, and you know she's never been able to have children. You'll stay with her, have the baby, and she will help you look after it. No one has to know about the pregnancy. You can then finish your exams and take the drama school scholarship that you've been offered. I'm sure they will understand if you put it off for a little while. We will give them a reasonable excuse.'

He folded his arms, resolute in what he had decided should happen.

Katerina nodded along, his plan making sense to her. Her aunt seemed like a lovely, if slightly odd, woman. She had plenty of room in her house and Katerina knew she could be safe there. Her baby could be safe there. Only one vital detail was missing in her dad's plan.

'What about Finn?' she asked, and her dad's face hardened.

'You will never see him again,' he said. 'That is non-negotiable. If you want our help, then you'll leave that boy behind.'

'Shouldn't I at least tell him?' Katerina said, her mouth open in shock at her dad's callousness towards Finn.

'No. If you tell him he will want to be involved. It's best that he doesn't know, and he can move on with his life,' Keith said.

Pauline looked perturbed, her eyes wide. 'Well, Katerina has a point,' she said, putting a hand on Keith's arm.

'No. Absolutely not. Katerina, this is a condition of our help. Otherwise, go tell him, and you can sleep on his sofa and live off the dole while he pisses your money away down the pub.'

Pauline looked at Katerina with an almost imperceptible shrug. She had tried, albeit not very hard, but Keith's mind was made up.

Katerina shook her head. 'You're wrong about Finn and I'll prove it to you,' she said. She knew Finn's gentleness and his kindness, she knew he would be a good dad, with or without money.

She stood up and walked to the front door. Her parents made no attempt to stop her. As she shut the door behind her, she heard her mother's sobbing, and she quickly moved away. She had to find Finn, and fortunately she knew where to find him. She headed confidently in the direction of the park, half-walking half-running, breathing hard, energised by her need for him.

An hour later she returned home, her heart torn in two by what she had overheard. She was so heartbroken that she could barely raise her arm to open the front door. She stumbled in, still blinded by tears, and didn't bother to take her shoes off. Her parents were waiting expectantly on the sofa, exactly where she had left them. Pauline took one look at her daughter's agonised face and opened her arms to her. Katerina lay on her lap and sobbed while her mum stroked her hair, something she hadn't done since Katerina was a child.

Pauline murmured words of comfort, but all Katerina could hear were Finn's cruel jibes over and over again. Clearly, this man she thought she knew, and the father of her baby, was a teenage idiot, a cheater, a liar, and a user.

As she lay on her mother's lap her anguish hardened into rage. Her dad was right and she had to do what they suggested. Finn Drayson could go to hell.

Finn

Finn shouted out into the wind, his words stolen and snatched away, swirling with the snow. 'Katerina!' he called out, peering into the gloom.

'This is really dangerous!' Ashif bellowed next to him. 'None of us should be outside.'

'I have to find her,' Finn said urgently. He ignored Ashif's warnings and leant into the wind, stumbling with the force of it. He couldn't see more than a metre in front of him, and the clumps of snow fell into his eyes and mouth, clogging his eyelashes. He rubbed his face and squinted, trying to see where Katerina had gone.

He staggered forwards and felt the solidity of the hot-tub shed under his left hand. He moved forward slowly, grasping against the wall of the building, trying to shelter from the full force of the wind. His outstretched hand clasped at fabric, a lone figure hunched over, disoriented by the assault from the heavens.

'Katerina!' he said. 'Kat!' She looked towards him and began to move away.

'You need to come back inside,' he yelled at her, his fingers clasping only the slightest amount of her coat. If she moved again the material would slide right through his fingers.

'I'm sorry!' she screamed back.

He didn't want to hear apologies from her. He didn't even want to look at her or talk to her right now, but he knew he had to get her back into the cabin's safety. He didn't want either of them to die out here. Where would that leave their son?

'Finn, believe me, I went to tell you that day in the park. That's why I went to see you,' she babbled, the words jumbling together, the volume of them being drowned by the roar of the wind. 'I wanted to tell you everything so we could decide what to do together, but I heard those awful things and I just couldn't. My trust in you was broken. That doesn't make it right, but I was heartbroken and angry and sixteen years old and pregnant and completely terrified!' She screamed the last word at him.

'I may have said those things in the park, but what you did is … unforgiveable!' he roared back. 'I was stupid and trying to look cool in front of my mates, so I said some bad things, but *you*,' he spat out the word. 'You took my son away from me and kept him from me for thirteen years!'

She sobbed, crumpled against the shed. Finn wanted to see her cry, he wanted to see his own pain echoed in her, but her tears did nothing to ease his sadness and rage.

'I was going to tell you. I tried to, but then years went by. And then I got married, and then it was too long, too long, too much time to take back what I had done,' she shouted out. 'I regret it every day. But I don't regret loving you because it gave me my son and he is the light in my whole life,' she cried.

'He should have been that for me too!' Finn yelled.

He felt an arm on his shoulder, pulling him back gently, and he didn't have the strength to fight it. Michael led him towards the cabin, and Darryl guided Katerina. Neither of them protested. They stepped inside the cabin, shutting the door, still hearing the wind howl outside, the snow dropping from them onto the floor. Breathing hard, they faced each other, and both of them were crying.

Katerina

Katerina sat stiffly before the flames. Finn was at her side, in silence. The rest of the group had gone to bed, leaving them alone with the cameras.

They were both wrung out from the emotional turmoil of what had passed between them. Katerina was so shaken by the events and the shock of the blizzard that she could barely say a word, and Finn hadn't pressed her. They had sat in front of the fire the entire night, his stare burning like the embers in the fireplace. Katerina knew there would be many conversations to be had, apologies to be pleaded, but not now. The cameras had had way too much from them already.

A message came up on the screen. *Your transport will be with you at 9 a.m.*

She blinked at the screen, her eyes dry and woozy from lack of sleep. Her mind grappled with the words, her mind fogged from emotion and exhaustion.

Finn looked at her. 'You know I'm leaving too, right?' he said.

She nodded, unsurprised. She should be happy that she was going home, and she would get to see Chris, but all she could think about was him finding out about Finn. She hoped her mum could keep him from using the internet, watching TV, or listening to the radio, but she knew it was hopeless. The news was pervasive, and he wouldn't be able to escape it. Katerina hoped he wouldn't hate her too much for what she did, unlike Finn, whose fury was etched into his features.

The group was sombre and muted as they both prepared to leave, standing by the front door. Branches from the trees were scattered everywhere, their pieces jagged and torn, marring the peaceful whiteness of the snow that had piled up during the blizzard.

Cressida gave them both a hug. 'See you guys,' she whispered.

Willow wrapped her arms around Finn in a tight embrace. 'See you soon,' she said. She looked at Katerina coldly. 'Bye,' she said curtly.

Katerina flinched at the judgement in her voice. She knew that others would think the same, that columnists would say the sorts of things that Willow was thinking. But she couldn't think about that right now. She just wanted to talk to Chris.

She could hear the quad bikes crunch over the snow outside, the purring of their engines, ready to take her away. She walked out of the cabin and got on the bike, nodding to the driver to go, and didn't look back as she roared away. Although she was glad to leave, she knew that the storm she was about to step into, both professional and personal, would be far worse than the blizzard yesterday. She had survived Alaska, but that was just the beginning.

Chapter Fourteen

Finn

Finn tried to relax into his first-class seat as the plane accelerated and left the runway. He scrolled blankly through the film options, uninterested in everything but desperate to distract his mind from running over the events of the past few days.

He was grateful Katerina was on a different flight back to London. He had no desire to be in her company right now, and knew it would probably only lead to an argument. He felt distracted and restless, but above all he was angry. Every heartbeat felt like it pumped fresh waves of rage into his bloodstream at the extent of Katerina's deception. He couldn't believe he had a son, and that he had missed out on all the nappies, the bottles, the first words, the first steps. And not only that, it was Katerina who had inflicted this pain on him. The one person he had truly loved, and wasted years thinking about, had thought so little of him that she had kept his son from him. He squeezed his eyes shut and told himself not to cry.

A young woman on her way back from the bathroom, stylishly clad in jeans so tight he couldn't understand how she got them on, brushed past him and murmured, 'What she did to you was criminal.'

She walked away with a knowing glance back at him, and he cringed. He was holding off checking the headlines till he got home but he knew his and Kat's fight would be everywhere. He hadn't even checked his phone or email. He knew his agent would be going crazy and trying to get in touch, but he didn't want to talk to anyone. He just needed some time to think, away from Katerina, and away from the cameras.

When he arrived back at Heathrow, he jammed a baseball cap on his head. The crowds of tourists and foreigners was strangely comforting, and he felt a little anonymous in the swirling mass of humanity, although every now and then he caught someone staring at him. He collected his luggage from the First Class concierge and walked to arrivals. For a moment he could have been anyone arriving home, lost in the sea of people being greeted by family members, ignored in favour of those happier reunions, but then one photographer spotted him and a pack of them appeared from nowhere. He hadn't been paparazzi fodder for a while and certainly didn't expect to be upon his return home, so he was hopelessly unprepared for it. He regretted not talking to his agent and being ready for it.

He ran to the taxi rank and threw himself in the first cab he saw, ignoring the queue and hoping the people waiting would understand when they saw that he was being pursued by photographers.

'Wandsworth,' he said. The cabbie glanced at him twice, opened his mouth as if to say something, then put the car in gear and drove off.

'Welcome back,' he said, glancing in his rear-view mirror.

'Thanks,' Finn muttered, his arms crossed and his chin sinking onto his chest. He was exhausted, physically and mentally. He didn't manage any sleep waiting the blizzard out and for transport to arrive at the cabin and certainly couldn't sleep on the plane. He was desperate to get home to his bed, put a pillow over his head and pretend Alaska had never happened.

They pulled up outside his block of flats. It was a new-build block, nothing luxurious, but comfortable and modern. He hadn't been particularly flush with cash before the Alaska programme, and had earned surprisingly little from his boy-band days. He was grateful that he had at least invested in buying a place to live.

The cabbie took his card and swiped it. 'It's been declined mate,' he said. Finn tried all of his cards, with no success. Flustered, he sat in the back of the cab, feeling overwhelmed and confused.

'It's on me,' the driver said, eventually, taking pity on him. 'After what that woman did to you …'

Finn nodded, embarrassed at the charitable gesture. 'Thanks,' he said.

'Good luck,' the driver called out to him as he got out of the cab. Finn hurried to the front door. Of all the problems he had to sort out right now, cash was a priority. He had to call the bank and find out why all his cards were blocked. Then he could think about what on earth he was going to do next about Katerina and arranging to meet his son for the first time.

Katerina

'You've ruined my life.'

Katerina winced at the stony, cold resentment behind her son's eyes. He stood in the doorway to his bedroom, his arms folded, glaring at her. His hair was ruffled, and she felt a yearning to reach out and tousle it, but he hadn't let her do that since he was ten years old. It had taken her an hour of pleading to get him just to open the door to her.

'Chris, we need to talk. And not behind a door either,' she said, trying to be gentle but firm.

'I don't want to talk,' he said sullenly. 'You had thirteen years to talk to me about my dad and I had to find out on a TV show? Seriously Mum, what the hell?!' He looked at her, his eyes wide with disbelief at the secrets and lies that had been revealed to him and the rest of the world at the same time.

Katerina shuddered at what he had gone through, at how all his friends would know, at how his life had suddenly become headline fodder.

She held up her hands. 'You know what? You're right. Everything I have done is wrong and unforgiveable. You're right to be angry. And I am so so so sorry. But please know …' She clasped her hands together, begging. 'Please know that I love you more than anything and would never want to hurt you in any way.'

'But you did,' he interjected, 'with all the lies.' His disgusted expression hurt her more than any angry words he could throw her way.

She flinched and nodded, swallowing hard. 'I know. My only excuse, not that it's a great one, is that I was sixteen and afraid and stupid. I was only three years older than you are now. I know it's not an excuse but it's the best explanation I have.'

He looked down and rubbed his foot against the floorboard. 'You know what really hurts? When I spoke to Grandma I found out that both her and Grandad were in on this as well. They made sure that I didn't know my dad. You're all liars as far as I'm concerned.' He stepped back into the gloom of his bedroom and slammed the door shut, the sound reverberating around the house.

Katerina rested her fingertips on the door frame and sighed, tears coursing down her face. The worst part was that her indignant, angry teenage son was completely right. They had all let him down, but most especially her. She should have known better.

She went downstairs, the stairs creaking and protesting with every step. This house was their sanctuary, set down a country lane where it stood, proud and alone, away from any neighbours. She bought it after her divorce from Wyatt, and had made it their home. She loved the way the walls were slightly warped and the dark floorboards moaned in the night, thick with history and stories to tell of the footsteps that had fallen upon them. She loved the brick walls that always felt rough and cool to the touch, and she wondered about the many hands that had brushed against them in the years the cottage had stood firm, against war and turmoil, severe winters and fierce summers.

She made herself a cup of tea and looked around her. At that moment she would have exchanged all her wealth, her fame and her career for one kind word or one forgiving glance from Chris. Everything she had, meant nothing to her if her relationship with Chris was broken.

Her phone vibrated in the pocket of the long, green cardigan she was wearing. It was the message she had been expecting.

It's Finn. Need to make arrangements to see MY SON. Tell me date, time and place.

The message contained no overtly hateful words, but she could almost feel the rage emanating from the stark black characters on the screen. Finn had no need for pleasantries now. There was no winsome charm, no harking back to their romance, no trying to win her over. His affection, like her son's, was also lost to her lies.

She checked her calendar for free days in the last few weeks of May and into June. There was no point in putting this off. She had to start correcting the wrongs she had inflicted on the two people she loved the most.

Finn

Finn twisted his hands together anxiously underneath the gleaming walnut desk, tapping his foot with nervous energy that he couldn't quite get under control. His agent sat beside him. She gave him a look, her eyes flashing with annoyance.

'Stop fidgeting,' she hissed at him. 'What are you, eight years old?'

Finn had always rather liked Josephine's hard-nosed, bluntly honest approach, but right now he would have liked her to be a bit gentler with him.

His accountant paused, his glasses sliding slightly down his face. William Gurney had a pinched, worn look to him, like a book with faded pages, a fatigue that probably came from years of advising celebrities who couldn't manage their money.

'Mr Drayson, I'm sorry to tell you this, but while you were in Alaska, the Government ruled on the film investment scheme you decided to put your money in.'

He shuffled through some papers, shaking his head. 'The outcome for the investors wasn't good. The Government has decided that you need to pay tax on the scheme.'

Finn frowned with confusion. 'But I thought it was a way to pay less tax, not more.'

William paused. 'The ruling is final. It's been declared as a tax evasion scheme, and the bill is going to be big.'

Finn swallowed nervously, his throat dry. 'How big?'

'Well, everything you own. Pretty much.'

Finn glanced at Josephine, who averted her eyes.

'Everything,' he repeated, dumbly.

'Finn, you are close to bankruptcy,' Josephine said quietly, looking downcast. She rarely showed sympathy, but Finn guessed he deserved it in this case. Fooled by the woman he loved, humiliated on TV, and now facing financial ruin. It couldn't really get much worse than that.

He shook his head. 'Surely there must be something I can do,' he said, hating the pleading note in his voice.

Josephine nodded. 'Look, there has been much more interest in you since the Alaska programme, and I think the public really are on your side when it comes to the whole Katerina situation. But this tax evasion issue reflects so badly on you. You know how the public view celebrities who avoid tax.' She paused, looking at Finn's agonised expression with pity.

'I have some offers you can take up, some appearances, a cameo on the soap *Fairview Park* at the beginning of June, but not enough for this type of bill. You need to find a way to get back in the public's good books, get lots of publicity, get lots of money.' She leaned forward and touched him on the arm. 'Do you understand me, Finn? You've got to do something, anything,' she said urgently.

He rubbed his head, where a dull ache threatened behind his eyes. 'Get me signed up for any offers you have Jo. And I'll think of anything I can.'

Chapter Fifteen

Katerina

Katerina hovered in the kitchen, feeling like an intruder in her own home. She could hear the low murmurs of Chris and Finn talking, but she couldn't make out distinct words. She wanted to listen in, but at the same time didn't want to invade their conversation. They had both made it very clear that she wasn't welcome in their first meeting.

She washed up a coffee mug, even though she could have popped it in the dishwasher. She rinsed it again, standing at the sink with her hands under the warm running water, staring out into the garden. She had spent a few years cultivating it, nurturing the wisteria that now climbed up the outside of the stone walls. She had tried her best to nurture her son too, emotionally and physically, despite her aunt's best efforts to take over, control her and manipulate her. Marrying Wyatt had been her way out of her aunt's clutches, her ticket to a stable home for Christopher. She wondered what Wyatt would think now, seeing the headlines, and she was thankful that they weren't in touch since his remarriage and relocation to Hawaii.

Finn and Chris had been talking for well over an hour when Chris popped into the kitchen and grabbed two glasses.

'Can I get you guys anything?' she asked, hopefully thinking that he might throw her a small crumb of civility.

'Nope. I got it,' he said curtly, filling both glasses with lemonade and leaving.

She floated around the kitchen, straightening the tea towels, rearranging the mugs, refilling the coffee and tea jars. Time seemed to suspend and hang heavy in the summer afternoon heat. She could have sworn the kitchen clock actually stopped marking off the minutes, though when she peered more closely at it, the familiar faint ticking could be detected.

The front door creaked and closed with a familiar thud. It was slightly wonky on its hinge and always closed too fast.

'He's gone,' Chris said, barely turning his head to look at her as she poked her head around the living room door.

She walked swiftly to the front door and opened it, seeing Finn's back disappearing down the front path.

'Finn!' she called, dashing out before realising she was still in her socks, the sharpness of the gravel stabbing into her toes. Still she carried on walking, brushing past the fuchsia that bent onto the garden path, pregnant with blooms.

Finn stopped just before he reached his car and turned to face her with a slight frown.

'How did it go?' she asked quietly.

Finn shrugged. 'He's a great lad. I'll be seeing him regularly,' he said shortly.

She nodded. 'Yes, of course.'

He made to leave and she touched him on the arm. 'Look, perhaps you and I should talk as well?' She had seen reports in the paper about some celebrities caught up in a tax evasion scheme with large bills and bankruptcy threatened. Finn was one of those mentioned, and she was genuinely worried about him.

He shook his head. 'As far as I'm concerned Katerina, I have nothing to say to you.'

He jabbed the key in the car door and swung it open.

'Great car!' Finn and Katerina looked back to see Chris lounging in the front doorway, giving Finn a thumbs up. Finn gave him one back and waved with a grin, then reversed his way back down the country lane, the car bumping along the potholed road.

Katerina walked back up the path but by the time she got into the house, Chris had already ensconced himself in his room, and she was left alone in the kitchen, again.

Finn

Finn looked over his shoulder, guiding his car back down the narrow pathway to the main road.

He tried to focus on driving, but his head was swimming, running over the conversation he had had with Chris. His heart was full of both the sorrow and the joy of their first meeting, discovering that they liked the same things, had the same allergies, held the same opinions. He was so proud to hear about how well Chris was doing in school, especially in science. Finn didn't want him to end up a former boy-band singer on the verge of bankruptcy, like him.

Katerina had raised Chris well, he had to admit it. He was polite, smart, and self-aware. Finn found himself already looking forward to seeing him again, to getting to know his son better. It was just a shame he had to see Katerina too, which had dampened his good mood. He didn't want anything to do with her and wasn't sad to see the disappointment in her eyes at his refusal to talk to her. As far as he was concerned, she could go to hell.

He changed gears and felt a burst of pride that Chris liked his car. It was another item he was likely to be forced to sell in order to avoid bankruptcy. He hadn't told Chris about any of his money issues, and hoped his son hadn't bothered to read the news reports about it. Instead, Finn had boasted about the offers of work he was getting and had told Chris to look out for him on *Fairview Park,* enjoying seeing the look of admiration on his son's face. Finn wanted Chris to be able to show off about him to his mates. He wanted his son to have a life he wasn't ashamed of, unlike Finn, who had spent his childhood racked with shame about his mum's problems and their crappy life. Finn needed to make sure that he could afford to buy Chris the things he wanted, that he could treat him, take him on holiday, whatever he desired. He knew Katerina could do that for him too, but he wanted to provide for his son as well.

Now he just needed to find a way to solve his money worries, he thought, his mind racing as he grasped for solutions, but kept coming up with nothing.

Katerina

'I thought this would blow up terribly in our faces.' Pauline sighed, gripping her mug. 'I told your dad it was a bad idea. It didn't seem moral,' she said, shaking her head. 'I was right.'

'Yes Mum, well, here we are.' Katerina spread her hands, feeling a snap of irritation at her mum for not saying so thirteen years ago. 'Now Chris hates me, Finn hates me, the public think I'm terrible, and I don't know how to make any of it right.'

Katerina took a mouthful of black coffee, feeling shuddery from exhaustion. She had barely slept since coming home, lying awake most of the night, her anxious worries churning around and around in her head. If she did sleep it was fitful and, more than once, she had awoken in the midst of a nightmare in which she was trapped in Alaska with Finn discovering the truth again and again. She occasionally looked at her phone or her computer only to see stories or comments online that were judging her and full of spite. She couldn't read more than one or two without feeling like there was a pillow being held over her face, suffocating her. Her agent told her not to look at the reports and to focus on her upcoming work. Katerina was thankful she was already signed up for a few projects, as she was sure that they wouldn't have offered her the roles now, given her unpopularity.

Every day she tried to speak to Chris, but he was having none of it. He was stubborn and moody at the best of times, let alone after finding out his mum and his beloved grandparents had lied to him for his whole life.

'Just give him time,' Pauline said, looking out of the window. The sun reflected off her hair, pure white without a single strand of colour remaining. The original rich chestnut tone had started to leach away when Keith was unwell. The stress of seeing her husband waste away with cancer had sucked the life out of her too, leaving her an older, frailer shell of who she used to be. Katerina felt such sadness when she looked at her that she didn't have the heart for angry recriminations. After all, Katerina was the one who chose to go along with their plan. The responsibility rested with her.

'Give who time?' Katerina said. 'Finn or Chris?'

'Both of them. They'll come round eventually.'

Katerina shook her head. 'I don't think so, Mum. Finn looks like he wants to murder me every time I see him.' She smiled weakly, but it was true. He had come to see Chris a few times, or to pick him up to take him out, and he had glared at her darkly when she tried to greet him at the door. She wondered what awful punishments he must want to inflict on her that spun in his imagination behind his dark gazes.

She sipped her coffee and hoped one day they could at least be civil, but for now, she was better off staying out of Finn's way.

'What more can I do?' Finn asked helplessly, as his accountant raked over the paperwork before him. William paused, resting his fingertips on the sheaf of papers splayed across his desk.

'Your car …' he began, but Finn held up his hand to stop him.

'My son loves that car,' he said, shaking his head.

William raised an eyebrow. 'Be that as it may, it costs a lot in monthly payments and fuel, and the insurance is sky high. It's a money drain,' he said, grimly.

'Find something else,' Finn said. He knew he was teetering on the edge of financial ruin, but he didn't want to get rid of something Chris had expressed such admiration for. He was getting some work, but the tax bill was hanging over him like a dark cloud, and he wasn't making enough to pay for his daily life and meet the huge costs of the bill. He had to find a solution, and soon.

He left the meeting feeling downcast, walking outside the plush offices into a cool mist of rain. He barely looked where he was going, and got out his phone, dialling his agent while he walked. 'Hi Jo.'

'How's my favourite singer?' she said.

'Not so good. Any big offers?' he asked hopefully. He glanced around furtively to make sure no one was listening, but he was in central London, where the crowds ebbed and flowed like the tide. He was anonymous in the midst of the tourists and the sightseers, his conversation drowned out by the heavy drone of the traffic and the buses grinding past.

'Hmm.' He could picture Jo frowning at her computer screen, and heard the faint clicking of her mouse as she browsed her emails.

'Look, Finn, not much has come in that's going to pay loads, although there are lots of smaller offers and interview requests. I'll send you a list of the latest ones, okay?' she said, and Finn could hear the pity in her voice.

'Thanks,' he said morosely, and hung up.

Just as he did, his phone beeped with a new message. He saw it was from Willow, and the pleasant memory of her friendliness in Alaska chased away his worries for a small moment.

How are you? Are you free for drinks tonight? I'll be at Avenue.

He had heard of Avenue – currently the coolest club for young celebrities in London. There were always paparazzi waiting outside, presenting a good photo opportunity. It wasn't his scene at all, although he had spent a lot of time at clubs like that when he was in 1Dream, enjoying the attention from scantily-clad clubbers. He was about to decline but the thought of another night in his apartment stewing over his problems filled him with despair. In truth, he was lonely, still hurting from Katerina's deception, and a night out with a friendly face would probably do him good.

He texted her back before he had a chance to change his mind. *Love to.*

You're on the guest list. See you there! she replied.

Finn hurried home, and stood in front of his wardrobe that evening, struggling to decide what to wear. In the end he settled for dark blue jeans and a maroon shirt. It used to be a bit too tight on him, but he had lost weight in Alaska and still hadn't put it all back on. His appetite had been a little off since coming back – the anxiety about his financial woes and his anger and hurt about Katerina had suppressed his hunger.

He jumped out of the cab outside the entrance to the club. It looked unremarkable, just a doorway in a brick wall, a plain black sign above it with "Avenue" written in sparse white lettering. There was a crowd of hopeful people queuing behind velvet ropes, all wanting to enter and be part of this life where the beautiful partied the night away, even if it meant £30 a drink and nowhere to sit down unless you were spending a lot more than that. He approached the towering doorman and breathed a sigh of relief when there was no quibbling about his entry.

He walked down the narrow stairs, feeling the throb of the music waiting for him. Despite the shabby exterior, the club was gorgeous. It smelled of incense and roses, the walls covered with artistic black and white photographs of world cities. He passed New York, Istanbul, and Tokyo before he saw Willow. She was laughing on the dance floor, throwing her arms in the air, her hair loose, her figure wrapped in a one-shouldered black dress. She waved excitedly when she saw him, trotting off the dance floor in her heels and beaming a huge smile, the plump redness of her lips shining in the low light.

'Finn, I'm am so glad you came,' she shrieked in his ear, throwing her arms around him and pressing him close. She was slightly damp from both the heat and the dancing, and her perfume floated up to him and lingered on his shirt.

'Drink?' he said in her ear, and she nodded and took his arm, walking with him to a small table in an alcove. She was swaying slightly in her heels and Finn realised that she was already quite tipsy. They sat down and a waitress swiftly appeared.

'Rum and coke,' Finn said. 'I'll have a Long Island Iced Tea,' Willow said. She turned to Finn with a smile. 'The club asked me and some of the girls to come, so the table is free, as long as we put at least one photo each on Instagram and we get photographed outside for the magazines. Easy,' she said, shrugging her shoulders.

'Who are you here with?' Finn asked, looking around. The lighting was dim and he wasn't sure who Willow meant by "the girls".

'Andrea, Justine, Maddison.' She gestured to a cluster of beautiful women on the dance floor. They saw her looking and blew her kisses, which she returned with a smile. Finn recognised them now she had pointed them out. One of them was a fellow soap actress, the other two were models. Finn waved at them and they waved back, giggling.

'So, how have you been?' she asked him, leaning in closer so he could hear her. Her arm pressed up against his, and if he looked down his eyes would have travelled straight to her cleavage, which was barely contained by her dress. He maintained eye contact.

'Not too bad,' he said, not wanting to talk about his bankruptcy dilemma.

She smiled down at the table. 'I missed you these past few weeks,' she said, holding a hand to her chin and running a manicured finger gently over her lips.

He smiled, flattered that she would have thought of him. 'Is that so?'

She nodded, and their drinks arrived. She took a few large sips of hers, when the latest track by Dua Lipa boomed over the speakers. 'Wanna dance?' she said eagerly, her eyes wide.

'I'm a bad dancer,' Finn said, eyeing the dance floor nervously.

She laughed and shook her head. 'No matter. I'll dance around you.' She took a few more gulps of her drink, draining the glass. 'Come on,' she said, extending her hand to his. He followed her slightly reluctantly, wishing he'd had more to drink first.

The tempo of the music wasn't reflected in the way she danced. She stood close and swayed in front of him, sashaying her hips against his. Willow was making her attraction to him obvious and Finn couldn't deny that she was alluring, and that the attention was a boost to his fractured ego. But he kept his hands to himself, no matter how hard Willow tried to entice him that evening.

As the night wore on, she became increasingly drunk, hanging onto his shoulder and giggling helplessly. Although Finn was trying his best to enjoy himself, even the thumping music, alcohol, and a beautiful woman hanging on his arm couldn't lift his spirits. The stress of the past few weeks had made his mood so low he wondered if anything could make him feel happy again. He was sure that no woman would be able to piece back together his broken heart, not right now, and perhaps not ever, not after what Kat had done to him.

As he prepared to leave, Willow pouted at him. 'I wish you didn't have to go,' she said. 'Now I'll be all alone.'

'What about your friends?' he said, glancing around, realising he couldn't see them any more.

'They already left without me,' Willow said, sounding mournful and slurry.

Finn glanced at her. She could take care of herself, no doubt, but she was very drunk and Finn wasn't comfortable with the idea of leaving her alone in the club. It didn't seem right to him.

'Let's get you home,' he said, and ushered her out of the club. The paparazzi bulbs lit their way to a waiting cab, where Willow promptly fell asleep and Finn had no choice but to take her back to his flat.

Chapter Sixteen

Katerina

'I still don't understand why you did it,' Chris muttered, glaring moodily at the people swirling around them as they walked through the shopping centre. He poked the straw angrily in his large chocolate frapuccino. Katerina hated the amount of sugar in those drinks, but she was trying to get Chris back on side, and if he wanted a day's sugar in one sitting, he may as well have it.

'It's not something I'm proud of,' Katerina said in a hushed voice.

They passed through the brightly-lit rows of shops, attracting the occasional stare or murmur of recognition. Katerina had never quite got used to being recognised, although the number of people who actually came up to her to ask for a selfie was usually low. People liked to stare, or even point, but not interact. Sometimes she felt a bit like an exhibit in a zoo.

'Everyone else in the world found out the same time I did,' Chris said bitterly. She could see the hurt shining in his eyes, which were the same shade of blue as Finn's. She had spent years looking into Chris's eyes and being reminded every single time of her deception to both him and Finn.

'Chris, I've been trying to talk to you about this for weeks, but I'd really rather not do it here,' she said, glancing around uncomfortably as they walked and Chris took long quick gulps of his drink.

He sighed. 'Oh, so it doesn't suit you here and now? It didn't suit me hearing about it all on TV but I didn't have a choice, did I?' he said, narrowing his eyes angrily.

'Okay, fine, you're right,' she said, holding up her hands placatingly. She had been desperate to have a proper talk with him, and if this was the moment he chose, then she had to take it, regardless of where they were. 'Listen Chris, I made mistakes. Big ones.'

Chris snorted at the understatement. Katerina tried to put a hand on his shoulder, but he shook it off angrily.

'Would you even have told me if you hadn't been forced to come clean on the show?' he said.

Katerina shrugged. She knew she could lie to make herself look and feel better, but she wanted to be completely honest. She couldn't stand to have any more lies between them. 'I don't know,' she sighed. 'I really don't know.'

He tutted and shook his head in disapproval, and Katerina felt as though he was the parent and she was the child who needed to be corrected.

'Listen,' she said, wanting to make him understand. 'I want to explain it properly.'

'Not sure I want to hear it.' He looked away, staring at the shoppers swirling in and out of the doorways, juggling shopping bags, laughing in groups.

'Well, please do anyway,' she said. 'I was sixteen and pregnant and completely freaked out. I went to Finn, I really intended to tell him. I was so sure that we could make a go of things. I was …' She paused. 'I was so in love with him.'

Chris glanced at her, an eyebrow slightly raised. A classic Finn expression, she thought.

She continued. 'When I went to the park that day, I was horrified by what I overheard. Of course, I accept now that Finn was just boasting and being stupid, but at the time it really felt like my heart had been ripped in two. I was devastated, and I was furious. And I suddenly felt that I didn't really know him at all, and my trust in him was shattered. It all came screaming into my head that we were … just kids.'

He nodded slowly. She took his silence as a signal to carry on.

'Dad, your grandad, he offered to make arrangements. At the time they seemed like my only option, so I took them.' She shrugged helplessly, remembering how both her fear and her heartbreak had led her to desperation. 'I just didn't know what else to do.'

'What about Wyatt?' Chris interjected. 'Where did he come into all this? He was a good stepdad, most of the time.'

'I was twenty-one when I met Wyatt. I was totally upfront that I already had a child, and he was fine with it. He was, is, a very good man,' Katerina said. Wyatt had been an excellent father figure to Chris, though she had never encouraged Chris to call him "Dad". She had never been comfortable with that.

'Why get divorced then?' Chris asked, sounding exasperated.

'Because I didn't love him,' Katerina said. 'I was just looking for a stable home for you and for me, and a way to get out of Aunt Theresa's house. She was …' Katerina paused, not wanting to speak ill of her aunt. 'She was a very difficult woman to live with.'

'I remember,' Chris said, rolling his eyes. 'She was potty.'

Katerina tried and failed to suppress a smile. 'Yes, well, she had her issues.'

'She was pretty mean to you. I remember that.' He played with the straw in his near-empty cup.

'I didn't know that you picked up on that.' Katerina was surprised. She had hoped that Chris wasn't aware of the meanness of her aunt. Her aunt had never been able to have children, and she seemed furious that her silly teenage niece had been given the blessing that she was herself denied. She took that anger and bitterness out on Katerina, with constant corrections and nasty comments, and Katerina had always felt on edge in her presence, dreading the next criticism.

'Yeah well, I was little, but I wasn't stupid,' he said with a shrug. He fiddled with a napkin, wiping the drink from his fingers as he dumped the cup in a bin. 'You know Finn really hates you for what you did.'

She flinched at his harsh honesty. 'I know.'

They walked in silence for a moment.

'I'd like to talk to him properly. We haven't really spoken since the show ended,' Katerina said.

Chris pressed his mouth into a line. 'I'll drop a hint, but I can't do any more than that,' he said.

Katerina felt a warm glow of joy at her son's support. She felt that perhaps he had softened towards her, that maybe he couldn't ever understand what she did but could at least see things from her perspective a bit more.

'Did you see Finn in the news this morning?' Chris asked curiously.

'Nope. What do you mean?' she asked, frowning with concern, hoping it wasn't bad news about Finn's tax evasion scandal.

'He was with that actress, the fit one from Alaska. I think maybe they're dating. It certainly looks like it.'

He showed her the headlines on his phone, with a photo of Finn and Willow holding hands, leaving what looked like a club or bar. His hair was swept back, the shirt he wore was unbuttoned at the top, a grin on his face. He looked slightly dishevelled but happy. Willow did too.

Katerina felt a niggle in her gut from an emotion she couldn't even name. Envy? Relief? Regret? She wasn't quite sure.

'Well, good for him,' she said.

'You don't care?' Chris asked, his eyebrows raised.

'Why should I? He can do what he wants,' Katerina said with a dismissive shrug.

'You two seemed to be good friends, you could tell on that show, especially the way he gave you his bread, and you saved him from that bear. I thought that maybe you liked him,' he said, frowning at her.

Her cheeks felt slightly warm. 'Finn and I were very close, and I'll always be fond of him,' she said. The bland statement did nothing to express all the emotions that Finn stirred up in her, but she couldn't share those with Chris.

'So, you're happy he's dating this soap actress girl?' he asked incredulously.

'Woman,' she corrected him. 'And yes, of course I'm happy for him, if they are dating.'

He shrugged, checked his watch and stood up to leave. 'Okay, well, I'll see you back at home. I'm meeting some people at the cinema.'

She nodded and watched him walk away. So full of bravado, and so terribly hurt by what she had done. She would count herself lucky indeed if he chose to forgive her. She idled in front of Marks and Spencer and pulled out her phone, scrolling through the news, flicking through the gossip headlines which she usually ignored. She paused momentarily on the photo of Finn and Willow outside the club, then forced herself to scroll on. She wanted him to be happy, and maybe it was fate that Willow was there with them in Alaska, to help him heal from the pain she had caused him.

Finn

Finn squinted against the sun filtering through his window. He had forgotten to close the blinds last night and the beams of light were shining brightly on his face as he lay stiff and uncomfortable on the sofa. He groaned as he sat up and shrugged his shoulders, trying to release some of the tension from sleeping at an odd angle.

He heard a rustle from the bedroom and Willow appeared in the doorway, her hair tousled, still in her dress from last night. Despite how much she had drunk, she seemed remarkably fresh-faced, whereas Finn felt terrible. She smiled as she walked over and perched on the sofa next to him.

'Morning,' she said brightly.

'Hey, how are you feeling?' he asked, his voice raspy from tiredness.

'Thirsty.' She grinned.

Finn stood up and fetched her a glass of water, which she drained in one go.

'Thank you,' she said appreciatively. She set the glass down on the coffee table. 'And not just for the water. Thanks for taking care of me last night.'

Finn shook his head, running his hands through his dishevelled hair. At least he wasn't in last night's clothes, having changed into grey joggers and a T-shirt before he put Willow to bed. 'It was nothing, really.' He headed back to the kitchen and put the kettle on. 'Do you want a tea or coffee?'

'Tea thanks,' Willow said. She spied her bag on the floor near the sofa and picked it up, rummaging for her phone, then leaned back on the sofa cushions, extending one long, tanned leg out onto the coffee table. 'I can't believe my friends abandoned me last night,' she sighed dramatically. Her chagrined expression fell away as she scrolled through her phone, and she looked up at Finn, beaming.

'What?' he asked.

'Have you seen the photos of us from last night?' she asked.

Finn stifled a yawn. 'Nope.' He checked his phone, finding several missed calls and a voicemail from Jo.

'Finn, you're in a couple of newspapers today. Good job with the photos at the club. People loved it – great gossip, beautiful couple, a nice outcome to the Alaska show,' she gabbled in her message. He checked the links she had sent and smiled. They were great photos, and Jo was right, he and Willow looked good together, although Jo didn't seem to realise that he and Willow weren't actually a couple.

Finn took Willow her tea. 'Aren't those photos fabulous?' she chirped. She set her mug down on the table and nudged aside a pile of papers that were stacked precariously there. They fluttered down around the side of the sofa. Finn flinched at the final notices, the demands from HMRC, the bills piling up.

'Just ignore those,' he said, desperately, and hopped around to clear them away, not wanting Willow to see his financial mess.

'I know you've had some trouble with that whole tax thing,' she said sympathetically. 'That's awful.'

'Yes, well, it'll all work out,' he said, feeling embarrassed.

'You know Finn, my agent said to me that people love it when two celebrities they've seen on a show get together.' She leaned towards him and arched an eyebrow. 'Remember Katie Saunders and Jamie Welsh from that skating show? Their wedding was huge news. And Katie Price and Peter Andre met on *I'm a Celebrity ... Get Me Out of Here!* and they made an absolute fortune off their marriage.'

'I remember,' he said, not really interested. He had never kept up with much of the celebrity gossip, knowing most of it to be made-up anyway.

Willow stared at him intently, her expression serious. 'You and I could really make a go of things, Finn,' she purred at him. 'We got on so well in Alaska. My agent said people are always asking if we will get together.' She looked at him hopefully. 'We could you know. The world is our oyster.'

Finn looked into her beautiful, hopeful eyes, which gleamed like gold in the morning sunshine. His tired mind grasped for the right words, the tactful way to say no to her offer. As attractive as she was, Finn just couldn't imagine himself in a relationship right now. He felt wounded in the heart, messed up in the head, and he was still trying to process all the emotions he had about Katerina, all the hurt and anger and sorrow and years of longing for her which had come to such a devastating conclusion.

'Listen, Willow.' He cleared his throat awkwardly. 'You're a lovely girl, but ...'

He stopped as she raised her eyebrows in surprise. 'You're not interested?' she said, a slight note of incredulity in her voice. 'But Finn, think about it, think about the magazine deals, the headlines ...' She indicated the bills on the floor with a manicured finger. 'Us getting work together could really help you out right now.' She shuffled closer to him and curled her hand around his arm. 'So maybe you don't want a relationship right now. I understand that, given what *she* did to you.' Her upper lip curled in disgust at the mention of Katerina. 'We could just look like we're in a relationship. Bag the work while interest is high and hey, if you change your mind, then I'll be open to suggestions.' She smiled archly, and Finn gazed at her, amazed by her willingness to pretend and impressed by her media savvy.

'I'll think about it,' he said, and Willow smiled, seemingly satisfied by his lacklustre response, perhaps knowing that her plan was, at this point, looking like the best option he had.

He promised Willow he would think about her business proposal, and it played on the edges of his mind all day, long after she left his flat to go home. Although the idea seemed ridiculous at first, he could see the merit in what she was suggesting, and his agent was more than enthusiastic about the prospect of them flaunting their new "love affair".

Finn was pondering the idea when his phone rang that afternoon, the ringtone piercing through his thoughts. He sighed when he saw Kat's name pop up.

'Hi,' he said curtly as he answered.

'Hi Finn, how are you?' Katerina's voice sounded soft and tentative.

'What do you want?' He ignored her question. He was in no mood to make small talk with her and had no time for pleasantries. He was annoyed that even the sound of her voice could still stir something in him, could still cut to his heart.

'I just wanted to check what time you're coming to see Chris tomorrow?' she asked. He could hear a note of sadness in her tone at his manner, but Finn couldn't allow himself to feel sympathy for her.

'12.00. I'm taking him out for lunch,' he replied.

'Okay, great,' Katerina said.

Finn was about to hang up when he heard her speak again, the words tumbling out quickly, as though she were nervous.

'I saw the photos of you and Willow,' she said.

Finn scowled. 'So?'

She coughed awkwardly. 'Are you two ...?' She left the rest of the question hanging in the air and Finn wondered why she was asking. Finn wasn't one for playing games, but he wanted Katerina to know that he wasn't just sitting around moping after her, that he was in demand, that she hadn't left him wounded, even though of course she had.

'Yes. Willow and I are dating.' He said it firmly, his resolve hardening.

'Great, um, good for you,' Katerina said, but Finn was already ending the call, cutting her off. He paused a moment, then messaged Willow. He wasn't over Kat, but he was determined to move on, and the fake relationship Willow had suggested was the perfect way to start.

Katerina

Katerina looked up at the apartment building from the driver's seat, wondering which flat was Finn's. The building was sleek and modern, peppered by glass balconies. It was a far cry from the charm and cosiness of her cottage, which she knew Chris hated. He always complained that they were living in a house straight out of a Beatrix Potter book. He missed their London townhouse where they used to live with Wyatt before the divorce, where the walls and floors were straight and the Tube was just a short walk away. She was sure Chris must love Finn's apartment, with its clean modern lines and central London location.

'Perhaps I'll pop up and say hello,' she said, speaking more to herself than to Chris, who was fumbling with his bag in the back seat, trying to slide out quickly.

'Erm, no need,' he said. He looked disappointed as she turned the engine off and got out, checking the parking restrictions. She just wanted to be civil and say hello while she dropped Chris off. It was nothing to do with being nosy about where Finn lived, she told herself.

'I'll be quick,' she said. Chris looked embarrassed and walked ahead of her with his head down. They entered the lobby, warmed by the July sun filtering through the glass doors, and took the lift. Katerina didn't even know what button to press, as she had never been invited inside. Finn had been keeping her at arm's length, avoiding her at all costs. They had barely exchanged two words since returning from Alaska.

The lift doors pinged and she followed Chris down the plushly carpeted corridor to flat eighteen. He knocked and Finn shouted out: 'Come in, it's open!'

Chris pushed open the door. 'Hey, my mum insisted on coming up too,' he called to Finn, then dumped his bag by the sofa, slumping down and grabbing the TV remote. He was so at home there already, Katerina thought.

There was an awkward silence as Finn walked towards her from the open-plan kitchen, wiping his hands on a tea towel. He gave Katerina a cool nod.

'I just thought I would come up and say hello,' she said, hopefully.

She knew she wasn't invited, but she felt increasingly shut out of her son's life, and out of Finn's. She knew she didn't have any right to be involved in his life at all, but she wanted to be there, to exist, to be seen, and to be welcome in his presence again. The smallest crumb – a polite hello or a handshake from Finn – would make her feel that way and that would be enough, she thought.

'Your flat is lovely,' Katerina said softly, glancing around. It was tastefully decorated, shades of grey with the occasional burst of teal adding a little colour. As she expected, everything was high-spec and modern. It was a far cry from the flat Finn used to invite her to, embarrassed by its shabbiness but desperate for her company.

'Thanks,' he said stonily.

Katerina was wracking her brain to think of something else to add to the conversation when Willow emerged from the bedroom door. She stopped short when she saw Katerina.

'Hello,' she said, her tone unwelcoming. She gave Katerina a cold stare and walked to the kitchen, taking a bowl from a cupboard.

'Oh, hi Willow, I didn't know you would be here too,' Katerina said, surprised to see her in Finn's flat. She knew they were dating, but she hadn't expected her to be there at that moment.

'Why wouldn't I be here?' Willow said, taking a bowl of crisps across to Chris, who nodded his thanks and munched on them happily, seemingly unaware of, or deciding to ignore, the tensions between the adults behind him. 'This is my apartment too,' she said.

'I didn't know you two had moved in together,' she said, directing the statement to Finn and forcing a weak smile.

Finn shrugged, looking nonplussed. 'It's on our Instagram,' he said.

Katerina bit her lip. She had checked out their joint feed a few weeks ago when it went live. She had scoured through the posts, and then forced herself to delete the app from her phone. She had felt both intrusive and jealous, and she didn't want to feel either of those things when it came to Finn. She just wanted to be happy for him.

'That's great news,' she said, forcing her smile wider, but it felt tightly stretched and insincere.

'Any exciting developments with your music plans?' she asked, spotting Finn's guitar, the same one he used to play for her.

'Nope,' Finn said. Katerina thought she saw a flicker of disappointment cross his face, but it could have just been her imagination.

'We've been busy with loads of other projects. In fact, they are planning to do a TV show about us,' Willow said, standing next to him and looping an arm around his shoulder.

Katerina looked at Finn questioningly and he shrugged. *What are you playing at?* she wanted to ask him, knowing that he was highly unlikely to want to do a reality show about his and Willow's relationship. She was sure that music was the only thing he really wanted to do. He had told her so when he was a teenager, and she could see when he sang for them in Alaska that his dream was still very much alive.

'Well, that's very exciting,' Katerina said politely, still looking at Finn, but he had turned his head to face Willow.

'Okay, have a great afternoon,' Willow said, pointedly. Katerina turned to go and waved at Chris. 'Bye' she called out and was rewarded with a nod of his head. She suppressed a sigh and left the flat, berating herself for going up there uninvited and wasting her time.

Finn

Finn watched Katerina leave, gently shutting the door behind her. She had looked tired and seemed a little deflated, but what did it matter to him? He was irritated by her presumption that she could come to his flat uninvited and poke around his life, and he hoped that she wouldn't come back again. He joined Chris on the sofa and took a handful of crisps.

'So, what's new?' he asked.

'Not much,' Chris said.

'How's the drumming going?'

Finn was chuffed to discover that Chris loved music, just like him. He played the drums, well from what Finn had heard, and he was keen to encourage him. He still couldn't quite believe this awkward, slightly lanky, smart, witty thirteen-year-old was his own flesh and blood. Finn hoped Chris would get used to it and feel less stilted around him. He knew he was going to have to work hard to develop the bond that should have been established naturally when Chris was born, he thought, with a prickle of anger at Katerina.

'Really well.' Chris perked up, his eyes finally turning from the TV screen. 'We're getting a band together at school. You should come and see us perform at the talent show,' he said eagerly.

'That's brilliant – I'd love to,' said Finn, feeling a swell of pride that his son was in a band. He glanced wistfully at his guitar, which was unused and out of tune. He wanted to do more musical projects and had hoped taking part in *Celebrity SOS* would help to raise his profile. Before the show he had been stuck doing appearances at night clubs and student union gigs, plus a few TV quiz shows. Now he was back in the public eye but there wasn't much time for his music around his and Willow's work. Aside from when she had scenes to film, they were busy with promotions, appearances, endorsements, events, discussions with the TV channel. Finn felt a slight emptiness about it all – the work just didn't enthuse him. He didn't feel passionate about it, and hated the time spent posing for Instagram pictures, or giving inane answers to magazine interviewers. He found it boring and uncreative, but Willow was totally absorbed in it. She was a savvy businesswoman and knew what she was doing.

Despite the fact that he wasn't enjoying the pretence, he was grateful to Willow and her plans. Their agents were happy, work was steady, and he was managing to pay off his bills. Willow seemed content that their relationship was just for show, and although she always offered for him to share the bed with her every night, he always slept on the air bed on the floor instead. No one knew about their arrangement, not even Chris.

He tried to shake off the yearning he felt to get back in the recording studio and asked: 'When is the talent show?'

'It's in a couple of months, on October the twentieth,' Chris replied, looking pleased at Finn's enthusiasm. 'We've got lots of time to get ready.'

'Oh, what a shame,' Willow said, strolling over from the kitchen and leaning over the sofa. 'We're at the Inside Soap Awards ceremony that night.'

Chris looked crestfallen.

'Couldn't I make it to both?' Finn asked her.

Willow shook her head. 'We'll take ages to get ready. There won't be time for anything else.'

Finn sighed. 'Sorry mate.' He spread his hands helplessly, wondering if he could get out of the Awards night. He knew it was unlikely – it was a big night for Willow and she would need him there by her side.

'That's okay. The awards ceremony sounds better than some crap talent show anyway,' Chris said, shrugging and turning back to the TV. He sounded nonchalant but his tone was more muted and Finn knew he was probably disappointed.

Willow walked to the bedroom to finish doing her nails.

'Katerina, your mum I mean, looked a bit tired,' Finn said carefully.

Chris nodded. 'I think she's a bit stressed out. She's been filming that new drama for the BBC, but the last one got bad reviews. She was pretty upset about them.'

Finn had seen the reviews for Katerina's latest period drama. It had only recently aired, although it was filmed long before she went to Alaska. Critics had called Katerina's performance stilted, stiff, uninspired, and the whole drama had been roundly criticised for mumbling. It was rare for Katerina's work to have bad reviews, and Finn knew how much that must have distressed her. He couldn't help but wonder if what had happened in Alaska, almost two months ago, had tarnished her reputation.

'Guys, lean in,' Willow instructed, appearing from the bedroom with her phone. She stood in front of them, silhouetted against the bright sunshine filtering through the balcony doors. She angled the phone. 'Smile!' she chirped, and Chris and Finn both grinned on demand for the picture.

Katerina

Katerina scrolled through Instagram. Willow and Finn. Finn and Willow. Always close, always kissing, smiling, wearing complementary outfits, laughing in unison – the perfect couple with the perfect life. She shouldn't have reopened the app, but there it was, as Finn had said, their moving in together announcement, so soon after they had started dating.

Moving day! Can't wait to wake up together every single day!

Only two months had passed since they had returned from Alaska but so much had changed already. Chris was spending more time with Finn, and Willow and Finn were living together. Katerina felt like her life had stalled while everyone else's moved forward. Her new drama hadn't been well received, and although she had lots of offers for interviews, they all wanted to focus on the one thing she wanted to forget: her secret teenage pregnancy scandal.

She was about to close the app when she took a look at the latest photo, posted only a few minutes before.

Hanging out with these cool guys! #family

It was a selfie, the three heads in the photo squeezed together to fit in. Willow and her perfect complexion, Finn and Chris, with identical eyes and similar smiles. Willow didn't have to spell it out in the post or the hashtags – it was obvious from their resemblance that this was Finn and his son – the first time they had been photographed together.

Katerina put her hand to her mouth in shock to see Chris's face staring back at her on the post. She knew she shouldn't read the comments underneath but she looked at them anyway, torturing herself.

Cute family!

OMG is that your son? Gorg just like you

Glad you finally got to meet your boy! Take him away from that stuck-up cow

I bet you're a great parent unlike your ex

She jabbed at the phone to close the app, squeezed her eyes shut and tried to compose herself. The comments horrified her, but more than that she was furious that Chris was featured on Finn and Willow's Instagram, for all their hundreds of thousands of followers to see.

She thought about phoning Finn immediately but decided to wait, as she was too angry to have a reasonable conversation right now. Finn would be dropping Chris back tomorrow. She would have to talk to him about this then.

Chapter Seventeen

Finn

Finn pulled up outside Katerina's house and turned to Chris in the passenger seat. He had been able to keep his beloved car, thanks to Willow. Her decisions meant that his money situation was still precarious, but it was getting better.

'Ready to go?' he asked.

'Sure. Thanks for a great weekend,' Chris said. He got out and shut the door behind him with a quick wave goodbye to Finn. As he moved away from the car, Finn could see Katerina walking swiftly down the path towards them both.

My cue to leave, he thought, putting the car into reverse and hoping he could drive off before she reached him, but she got there before he could move off. She rapped on the window.

'Finn, could you come inside please? I'd like to talk to you about something,' she said tersely.

He sighed. 'Can it wait? Willow and I—'

'No, it can't wait,' she snapped, not giving him a chance to finish.

He turned the engine off and followed her unwillingly up the pathway, ducking to avoid the honeysuckle hanging low above his head.

He sat on the sofa in the living room, where she perched stiffly on a chair opposite. She didn't offer him a drink or ask how he was, like she usually did, and Finn felt tense, wondering what she had done, or he had done, or Chris had done, to make her look so strained. She took out her phone and turned it around to show him his Instagram feed.

He eyed the phone and looked at her questioningly. 'What am I supposed to be looking at?'

'This.' She pointed at the picture Willow had taken of them all the other day. It was a good photo, he thought admiringly as he looked at their three faces bunched together. Willow had taken quite a few until they had gotten one in which no one was blinking and they all looked happy.

'What about it?' he said, frowning in confusion.

'Why are you putting my, *our*, son up on public display?' she said, the sinews in her neck starting to stand out.

'It's just an Instagram picture,' he said wearily. 'There's no need to get uptight.'

She shook her head. 'I have always tried to keep him out of magazines, newspapers, social media, all of that stuff. He's just a kid, he doesn't need that kind of exposure. Now people know what he looks like. If they find out where he goes to school or where he lives …' She trailed off. 'The internet is full of dangerous and strange people.'

'I think you're being a bit paranoid,' Finn said, feeling scornful of the anxiety etched on her face over nothing. 'It's one picture, and besides, he is old enough to give consent for that.'

She ground her teeth. 'I can't believe you're being so blasé about it. He's only thirteen! I want him to stay grounded and do his schoolwork, not be put all over your Instagram feed for people to comment on.'

Finn gave her a tight smile. 'Well, I'm sorry but what's done is done. Is that all?' he asked, standing up to leave.

She clenched her fists in annoyance. 'No, Finn, that's not all. What's this I hear about you and Willow taking him to the Drake concert in November?'

'What's the big deal with that?' Finn snapped.

'It's a school night. He needs to be in, do his homework and have a decent night's sleep.'

'Let the kid live a little. It's just one night,' Finn said, rolling his eyes, feeling frustrated at Katerina's petty attempts to curtail his fun with Chris. He knew Chris was thrilled with the idea of going to the gig, and Willow had great tickets. There was no way he would cancel just because Katerina didn't want him to bond with his son.

'You have no idea what's best for him!' Katerina shouted.

'Thanks to you!' Finn yelled back, his fury stoked by her unreasonableness. 'You made bloody sure of that, didn't you!'

'I've said I'm sorry a thousand times!' Katerina shrieked at him. 'All I want now is for things to work best for Chris.'

'You mean best for you?' said Finn, his stomach churning with annoyance and frustration.

'Don't you dare accuse me of not putting him first. I'm the one who went through pregnancy and birth alone, and had to deal with a newborn, and school exams, and trying to make a career. I know what sacrifice is!' she cried out.

'I would have helped you if you'd let me!' Finn shot back, the images in his head of the things he missed out on hurting him more than Katerina could ever imagine.

He couldn't bear to stay and continue the argument, especially as he knew Chris would hear them. He turned and walked away without another word, unable to look at her any more, leaving her fuming behind him.

Katerina

Katerina stared at Finn's back as he walked resolutely down the path, refusing to turn his head and acknowledge her, even though she shouted after him to come back.

Her heart thumped with rage, the beats reverberating around her chest and her neck. She put a hand to her forehead and tried not to crumple into tears as she drew deep shuddering breaths.

'Mum?'

She looked up to see Chris hovering in the doorway. A crushing guilt swept through her to see his face etched with worry.

'Chris, oh, I'm so sorry,' she mumbled, swiping underneath her eyes so he wouldn't see the tears that were starting to gather.

'I heard,' he said, his mouth a thin line, frown lines gathering around his forehead.

She sank onto the sofa, the adrenalin from her anger dissipating, leaving only a feeling of weakness and fatigue, and a sadness that she and Finn still couldn't find a way to be civil.

'Finn and I are trying to sort through some things. It's taking some time to adjust,' she said carefully, not wanting to speak ill of him in front of his son. She owed Finn that, at the very least. And much more besides, she knew.

Chris nodded. 'Do you have any painkillers?' he asked. 'I'm feeling a bit weird.'

Katerina touched his forehead, concerned. It wasn't like Chris to feel ill. 'I'll get you some paracetamol,' she said. 'Are you okay?' she looked anxiously into his eyes, but all she saw was tiredness.

He shrugged. 'I think I'm getting a cold,' he said. 'I might go to sleep for a bit.'

She nodded. 'Good idea.'

She imagined he had been up late and eating junk food at Finn's all weekend. No wonder he didn't feel too well, she thought.

'Dinner at six-thirty? I'll make your favourite pasta if you like,' she said, knowing how futile it was to make up for her terrible parenting even with a lovingly made carbonara.

He nodded. 'Okay.'

She watched him leave, her heart aching, her arms longing to hug him even though she knew he would hate it. He had never been a cuddly or needy child. She had always admired his independence, but sometimes she just wanted a way to show him how much she loved him, besides the usual practical things like giving him paracetamol and pasta.

She sighed and hung her head, rubbing her temples to ease the dull pain that was starting to throb there. The situation between Finn and her was so broken, she didn't think it could ever be right again. It was pretty obvious that he would never, ever forgive her.

Finn

Finn was still energised by annoyance when he arrived home, so he ignored the lift and dashed up the stairs to burn off some of his frustration. He needed to go to the gym and work off some of the irritation that Katerina had made him feel. He bounded into the flat, ready to search for his gym bag.

'Finn!' Willow called out from the bedroom.

'Yeah, I'm just off to the gym,' he yelled back, sticking his head in the hallway cupboard to look for his gym gear.

'What?'

'The gym!' he called out.

He heard Willow's heels tapping behind him. He stood up straight and turned to see her, arms folded, looking stunning in an emerald dress, the Grecian-style folds draped over her curves.

'No, you can't. Don't you remember?' she said, looking exasperated and pursing her lips.

'What? Remember what?' he said. 'Why are you all dressed up?' He wracked his brains to remember if they had an event to go to, but his mind was full of Katerina's face and her angry words, and he was having trouble thinking of anything else.

'Have you forgotten about the photo shoot?' she said incredulously. 'It's in thirty minutes, and you're not even ready! Why were you delayed coming back?' She narrowed her eyes in suspicion.

'Oh, I got into a fight with Kat when I dropped Chris off.' He rolled his eyes.

She raised an eyebrow, a slight smile playing on the corners of her glossy lips. 'Oh yeah? What about?'

'Nothing major, just a disagreement,' he said, not wanting to go into too much detail, knowing his feelings of aggravation would resurface, and he certainly didn't want those bubbling under his skin while he was at the photo shoot.

'Okay, well come on,' she snapped her fingers at him. 'Time to get ready. I've got your outfit all picked out.'

Finn tried to suppress a sigh. He wasn't really in the mood for this shoot today, but he knew it was an important one. The gym would have to wait, and he would have to put his anger at Katerina aside, for now.

Katerina

Katerina tried Finn's number and could have screamed in exasperation as she got his voicemail greeting once again. She wished desperately that he picked up the phone.

Hey, this is Finn, leave a message.

'Finn, *please* pick up, *please* answer, *please* listen to your messages,' she begged down the phone, her voice shaking with sobs. She hung up, wanting to throw her phone against the starch-white walls of the hospital room that contained their son.

He looked so thin, suddenly seeming so much younger than thirteen. He lay pale and waxy against the scratchy hospital pillow, his face partially obscured by the oxygen mask. A deep purple bruise marred his hand where the cannula joined to the IV drip. She gently linked her fingers with his and prayed silently.

Please, Finn get here soon.

Chapter Eighteen

Finn

Finn sipped his champagne, enjoying the crisp fresh taste, hoping it would ease his tension about the argument with Katerina earlier that day.

He held Willow's hand as they looked through the results of the shoot, the photographer looking at them with a smile, as if they were like any other loving couple. Willow was a great actress and it would be hard to guess that their relationship was merely a business deal.

'These are amazing,' she cooed. 'What do you think, honey? Which ones shall we choose?'

He stared at the beautiful photos of them, laughing, joyous, on the brink of their future, and it was like he was looking at someone else's life. He felt like these were images of a different version of himself, his more successful twin, living a glamorous lifestyle he had never particularly desired with a woman he could never have imagined ending up with.

'Finn?' Willow waved a hand in front of his face. 'Hello?'

'Oh, sorry,' he said, realising he hadn't responded to her question. He smiled at her. 'They are all so good, it's really tough to choose. You look amazing in all of them.' He wasn't lying. Willow looked fantastic, and she smiled triumphantly at his compliment.

He was content to let her choose. He zoned out again while she spoke to the photographer, and replayed the argument with Katerina in his head. He didn't know how they were going to find a way around this mess, how they could be peaceful with each other when their emotions always seemed so heightened by each other's presence. Everything that had happened between them had left them with broken, sharp edges, so that when they were together someone always ended up damaged and hurting.

Willow finished selecting the photos, giving a final nod of approval, satisfied with her choices.

'This is going live ASAP,' she said to Finn confidently. 'It's all planned, and I've let Jo and my agent know too. All we have to do is wait for the offers to come flooding in.' She was practically dancing with excitement as they prepared to leave.

Finn collected his jacket from the studio cloakroom and fished his phone from his pocket. He frowned at the slew of notifications that greeted him as he turned it on.

'What the hell?' he murmured, flicking through them. A cold fist of panic seized his chest as he listened to his voicemails. He started to tremble, breathing hard.

'Willow, I have to go right now,' he said, letting go of her hand, and grabbing his car keys. 'You can get a cab back to the flat.'

'What? Why?' she said, her eyes wide with indignation.

'Chris is in hospital,' he said, his voice choking on the words. He sprinted out of the studio to his car. His mind was almost frozen with fear and he didn't dare let himself think – he simply ran through the motions of getting in his car, programming the satnav and driving as fast as he could. He had to get to his son.

Katerina

Katerina watched the polystyrene cup fill up slowly with a dull brown trickle from the machine. It smelled like a mixture of coffee and tea, a murky medley of all the drinks that had flowed through that one outlet.

She grasped at the cup and took a sip, instantly burning her tongue. She felt faint from lack of food and water, her chest and stomach aching, but she couldn't leave, she wouldn't go further than this hot drinks machine. Not while Chris was here and he needed her, more than ever.

She heard a door slam and looked up, seeing Finn racing down the corridor towards her, his footsteps echoing. She felt her legs weaken with relief at seeing him.

'Finn!' she tried to cry out, but her voice rasped instead.

She could see he was in a panic, his eyes wide, his hands shaking. He grasped at her shoulders, looking into her face with urgency. 'I came as soon as I saw your messages. What happened? Where is Chris?'

She put a hand to her mouth, trying not to cry. 'Chris said he felt a bit poorly and he went for a sleep. When I went to wake him up he was curled in a ball, clutching at his head because the pain was so bad. He started being sick again and again and kept saying how the light was hurting his eyes.' She took a shuddery breath.

'At first I thought it could be a migraine, but he was crying out with the pain, his body was aching, and he passed out.'

She squeezed her eyes closed against the mental image of her precious son flopping onto the floor, sweaty and limp and not responding to her frantic cries.

'I dragged him to the car and rushed him here, as I thought it would be quicker than waiting for an ambulance,' she said. She couldn't remember much of the journey, her mind blinded by panic. She must have driven like a maniac.

'Do they know what's wrong?' Finn said, swallowing hard, grabbing her hands and holding onto them tightly.

'They're not sure but they said it's some kind of infection – maybe meningitis.'

She watched him inhale sharply and hold a trembling hand to his face. He took a moment to drag in a breath and compose himself before looking at her again. 'Can I see him?' he asked.

She nodded. 'Follow me.'

She took him to Chris's room, and paused before opening the door. 'Be prepared,' she said, softly, touching his arm, knowing that the sight of Chris in the bed would shock him to his core.

They entered quietly, and almost immediately Finn turned away, his shoulders shaking with barely suppressed sobs.

She put her arm around him and pressed her face into his upper arm till he was able to talk again. He wiped his cheeks and looked down at her, his eyes reflecting the agony she felt.

'What do we do?' he asked helplessly.

She had never seen Finn look afraid until now. Even when they faced the charging bear in Alaska it was nothing compared to the pure terror she saw in his expression now.

'We wait,' she whispered.

Finn

Finn shifted uncomfortably on the hard, plastic chair. His legs were aching but he didn't want to move too much. Katerina had slumped beside him and about fifteen minutes ago her head had rested lightly on his arm, and he had turned to her and realised she had fallen asleep. She hadn't slept in over twenty-four hours, so he let her rest now, even if it would only be for a little while.

Her hair fell across his arm and he found himself stroking it lightly, trying to comfort her, or himself, he wasn't sure. All he knew was that this was the worst possible place to be; it was the worst possible thing that could have happened. Dread churned in his stomach and he tried not to google anything to do with meningitis, fearful of what he might see, afraid of imagining it happening to Chris.

His phone vibrated with a message and he gently removed it from his pocket. It was Willow. He couldn't deal with her right now, so he ignored it. He wanted to stop the world and shut everything off, so he could focus completely on being here for Katerina and for Chris. They needed him now. He knew he had to try to be strong and keep it together.

Katerina stirred and sat up, blinking against the intrusive brightness of the hospital lights. 'Oh, I'm sorry,' she said, patting his arm where she had lay.

'Not to worry.'

'How long was I asleep?' she asked.

'Not long enough,' he said, tucking his phone away. 'Did you want something to eat?' he asked her.

She shook her head.

'You have to eat something,' he said gently.

She smiled wryly. 'You sound like my mother.'

He nodded. 'Well, she is very wise, like me.'

She managed a tiny thin smile, but it fell from her face when she saw the doctor approaching them. She leapt up from her seat and Finn did the same, waiting to hear the doctor's conclusions. He leafed through medical notes and looked about as weary as Katerina and Finn felt.

He cleared his throat. 'We've looked at the results of the tests we did on Chris, including the lumbar puncture. It is viral meningitis.'

Finn could feel Katerina trembling next to him. He put an arm around her, trying to hold her and himself together. 'What does that mean?'

'Well, the good news is viral meningitis is usually completely curable, nowhere near as bad as bacterial meningitis. He should make a complete recovery.'

Katerina gripped Finn's arm, her eyes filling with tears of relief, unable to speak.

‘Thank God,’ he muttered. He wasn’t a praying man but in the last few dark hours he had prayed over and over for his son’s life.

‘He will need some time to recover though,’ the doctor said. ‘I want to keep him in for a few days then he should be okay to go home, although it’s likely he will feel very weak for some time, possibly a few weeks.’

He caught sight of a nurse gesturing urgently to him down the corridor. ‘Excuse me, I think I’m needed,’ he said, walking off briskly.

Katerina turned to Finn and without saying a word they embraced tightly, clutching at each other with grateful and intense relief. After a few moments, Katerina leaned back slightly, wiping her eyes.

‘I’m going to stay here, but you can go home and eat or sleep if you want to,’ she offered. Finn knew by the way she gripped his arm and looked up at him hopefully that she wanted him to stay with her, and there was nowhere else he was going to be other than here.

‘Let me get you a tea,’ he said, and she nodded gratefully. Even though they were both exhausted, he already felt energised from the doctor’s optimistic outlook, and he could see from Katerina’s brightened expression that she felt the same.

He grabbed two hot cups of insipid tea, and two bags of salt and vinegar crisps from the vending machine. He didn’t have to ask her what flavour to get – after sharing so many bags with her in the park he already knew her preference.

She took them from him eagerly. ‘Thank you,’ she said.

‘Hey, it’s just crisps and tea.’ He shrugged.

‘No, I mean thank you for being here, for staying all night,’ she said.

‘Where else would I be?’ he said, running his thumbs round the edge of the cup.

They ate in silence and Katerina drained her tea, the first time Finn had seen her eat or drink for hours.

‘I’m going to go in and see him for a bit,’ she said, checking her watch. ‘You can go in after me if you like? The doctor said it might be a bit much if we all go in at once.’

Finn watched her walk down the corridor. Chris was lucky enough to have his own room in a private hospital, paid for by Katerina’s many successful TV dramas. Finn stood up to stretch his legs and peered in the doorway as he walked past. He watched as Katerina leaned over Chris, stroking his hand. Chris lay slumped on the pillows, too ill to sit up, but his eyes were open. Finn could see the look of devotion on Katerina's face as she brushed a strand of hair away from Chris's forehead. She had always been a loving and caring person, but Finn could see how motherhood had magnified those qualities in her. He swallowed hard and wished he had been there with her from the start of Chris's life.

'Finn?' He heard a hushed voice and turned to find Pauline standing behind him. It had been many years since he had last seen her, but she had changed remarkably in that time. She looked aged beyond her years and worn out from worry. He guessed that she hadn't been able to sleep much that night. Despite feeling a nudge of pity for her, he couldn't help but be reminded of when he went searching for Katerina, and Keith had shut the door in his face. Pauline had been there, and she could have told him where Katerina was. The familiar sense of bitterness and injustice rose in his chest and stole any pity he might feel for her, knowing she was partly responsible for cutting him out of his son's life.

'Hi Pauline,' he said, coldly.

'How is he?' she asked, inclining her head in Chris's direction.

'He's coming out of it, but he's still very weak,' Finn said quietly.

She sighed and put her hand over her heart. 'What a terrible scare.' A tear ran down her cheek. 'Is Katerina with him?' she asked, peering around Finn.

Finn nodded. 'She's there.' He turned and walked down the hallway to take a seat once again. She followed him and sat beside him.

'I'm glad to see you,' she said.

'Really?' he said incredulously. 'I can't believe that's true.'

She raised her eyebrows. 'Finn,' she began, but he held up a hand to stop her, not wanting to hear what she had to say.

'You took them away from me,' he said, the softness of his tone a reflection of where they were rather than his anger abating.

'Yes, we did. And it was wrong,' she said, and looked at the floor. Her admission took him by surprise. 'I wasn't really happy with the idea of it all to begin with, but Keith was adamant. He was stubborn and he was so mad at you. After all, his only daughter was pregnant at sixteen, out of wedlock. She had opportunities, and we wanted to try to help her.'

'By persuading her to leave,' he said bitterly.

She nodded. 'But I want you to know something. Every day, for years after she left, every day after she had Chris, she spoke of nothing but you.'

He frowned. 'Really?'

'Yes. Every single day without fail, Finn. She told me she wanted to tell you. And I would say the same thing again and again. *It's too late. That boy is no good. Remember what he said in the park.*' Finn scowled at her as she said it, but she held his gaze. 'Eventually she stopped talking about you, but it took her a long time to lose her love for you.'

'It was so wrong of you to do that. I would give anything to claw back those years that you stole from me,' Finn said furiously. His heart ached to think of Katerina crying over him, torn by what she did, guided by people who didn't think he was worthy. She had been young and impressionable, but the adults around her should have known better.

Pauline put a hand on his arm. Finn turned from her and stared stubbornly ahead. 'I am truly sorry. But do you understand what I am trying to tell you?' She paused when he didn't respond. 'It wasn't Katerina's fault. You're blaming the wrong person,' she said insistently.

They both stared at the wall in silence until Katerina left the room. She walked over, wiping away tears, and gave her mum a hug.

'I'm so glad you're here,' Katerina said, in a voice barely above a whisper.

'How's he doing?' Pauline asked her, smoothing away a tear from Katerina's cheek.

'Better. He might still be here for a few days though,' Katerina said.

'I'd like to see him now, if that's okay?' Finn asked, getting to his feet. He couldn't think about the past any more when the present was so fleeting and so precious. Every moment with his son counted, and he was more determined than ever to be there for him. And for Katerina too, if and when she needed him.

Katerina

Katerina stared out at the dark roads slipping past. They looked oily and slick, the streetlights reflecting off their wet surface. She didn't even know that it had rained, as she hadn't set foot outside of the hospital for the past thirty-six hours.

'Thank you for driving me back,' she said, glancing at Finn. She was in no fit state to drive and was grateful Finn offered, even though she knew he was utterly spent too. He was unshaven and red-eyed, and drove carefully while stifling multiple yawns.

'No problem,' he said, the slight gruffness to his voice belying the dehydration and hunger they were both feeling after many hours of hospital tea and no proper meals.

'Have you got any food in the house?' he asked, as if reading her mind.

Katerina shook her head. 'I'm not sure to be honest. I don't remember what I have in, and either way, it's a bit late to cook.'

'Do you want to grab something on the way?' Finn asked, and she nodded gratefully, spotting the drive-through signs glowing warmly through the misty rain.

They sat in the car, eating their chips. Neither of them spoke for a few moments while they ate, and Katerina felt that the atmosphere had changed. There was a companionable softness to the silence between them that hinted at forgiveness. The rage and frustration that had marred their last conversation had entirely dissipated, erased by the fear and uncertainty of the past few days, when they needed each other more than they had ever done.

'It's just like old times,' Katerina said, with a smile. 'Chips for dinner. Just not in the park.'

Finn grinned. 'We ate junk all the time then. I'm surprised I didn't get ill more often.'

She laughed and took a sip of her coke, feeling revived by its cold sweetness.

'Your mum said something to me in the hospital,' Finn said, not looking in her direction.

Katerina raised an eyebrow. 'What did she say?' she asked, hoping her mum hadn't tried to interfere. She was pretty sure there was nothing her mum could do to help matters between her and Finn – that was up to them to resolve.

'She said that you wanted to tell me about Chris for years. And they persuaded you not to.' He paused, then glanced at her, looking troubled. 'She said that it took you a long time to stop talking about me.'

Katerina nodded and chewed slowly on a chip, remembering how painfully bittersweet that time had been for her. She had her beautiful, healthy son, but she also clearly recalled the broken nights, the aching loneliness, the machinations and moods of her overbearing aunt, and missing Finn to the point where she felt that she might go mad.

It took her a moment to respond, trying to think of the right words. 'I missed you every day. I was trying to deal with Chris and it felt like everything I knew had come to an end. And I was still completely heartbroken over you. It was a difficult time to say the least,' she murmured.

'I want to know how long,' Finn asked insistently. 'How long did it take for you to stop loving me?'

Katerina looked at him, surprised at the question and the desperation in his voice. 'I left because I was angry at you, Finn. Not because I stopped loving you.'

She wouldn't say it to him now but there was a part of her that had never lost her love for him. The memories of him and the result of their love had always been with her, so a piece of her heart was always reserved for him. It was taken territory, a piece she could never fully reclaim. She had always wondered what could have been, and always regretted the choice she made, and she was reminded of her decision every time she looked into Chris's eyes and saw Finn's reflected back at her.

She opened her mouth to say something, but Finn spoke first. 'I better drop you off, and get back to Willow,' he said, his voice rough from lack of sleep.

He left her at the gate and waited in the car till she got in the front door. She told herself not to watch him drive away and made herself a tea, sitting on the sofa to check her messages. She knew she should sleep but though her body felt deflated from exhaustion, her mind was still racing. She let her agent know what was happening, caught up on emails, checked her social media. She was beginning to switch off, feeling sleep approaching, when she idly browsed through Instagram. Her drooping eyes widened as she saw Willow's recent post of her and Finn, looking stunning and dazed with joy in their latest photos.

They looked at each other, laughing and carefree, holding hands in a blooming rose garden. It was an engagement photo shoot. Katerina's heart sank as she read the caption and realised that Finn and Willow were getting married.

It had all been carefully staged. The photos were culled, filtered, captioned, and released at the optimum time for public interest. Finn had never intended for his and Willow's sham relationship to go this far, but an engagement, a wedding, those were the big-ticket items with regards to headlines and magazine deals. Finn went along with it all, knowing he should stop it. But he didn't, and it was because part of him had started to like the pretence. He was nearly thirty and he genuinely wanted to settle down. He wanted a marriage and a wife who loved him, to create the happy family that he never had when he was growing up. So he went along with it, enjoying the idea of it, even though it wasn't real, even though he didn't love Willow and never let her believe that he did.

The engagement news had gone live the evening he arrived at the hospital. He wished he could have stopped it, but it had been scheduled and done before he knew what had happened with Chris. Willow had been texting him incessantly for the past two days, but he had only sent her minimal replies and mainly kept his phone turned off, barely able to cope with the emotions from recent events, which buffeted him like waves. He felt overcome by confusion, exhaustion, and sheer relief that it looked like Chris would be okay. He didn't feel capable of handling anything else at that moment.

He walked in the front door of his flat, closing it gently.

'Willow!' he called out.

'Finn!' she shrieked. She came running to him, her arms outstretched. 'How is Chris?' She enveloped him in a tight embrace.

'Chris is going to be okay,' he said. His adrenalin had gone and the tiredness suddenly slammed into him, leaving him breathless and shaky. He broke off the hug and slumped on the sofa. 'I'm just so exhausted,' he said, rubbing his hands over his face.

She nodded and sat beside him. 'I'm glad Chris is recovering. How scary,' she murmured.

He smiled, too tired to speak.

She looked up at him with a wide smile. 'The engagement announcement went live – I didn't get your message about Chris till way after. I'm sorry about the timing,' she said. Finn knew she was trying to look contrite, but he could practically feel the excitement bubbling from her. 'It's been massive. I've been fielding calls and messages all day from people wishing us well, and there's been a lot of interest. Media, sponsors, magazine deals.' She listed on her fingers the potential coverage, the money they could make, burbling happily, and Finn wondered how she could switch from desperate concern for Chris to wedding plans in a matter of seconds.

He nodded along as she spoke, feeling slightly blank, bothered by how much Katerina kept coming into his mind. He cringed as he thought of her looking at the announcement. He'd been planning on telling her about the engagement on the way home, but the timing didn't seem right, and he had left her to discover the news herself. He knew Katerina would never want her life to be on public display in the way that Willow did. Katerina relied on her talent rather than photo shoots and magazine deals and Instagram follower counts. Finn's eyes flickered to his guitar, wishing he could do the same. Bankruptcy had forced him down this surreal path and it didn't leave much time for dabbling in his unfulfilled teenage dreams of singing stardom.

'Finn? Hello? Did you hear what I just said?' Willow said, peering at him, a glimmer of annoyance crossing her perfect features.

He shook himself. 'Oh, erm, no sorry, I can't quite focus on anything right now,' he said.

'Poor thing, you really need to rest, don't you?' she said sympathetically.

He nodded. 'Sleep would be good.'

She stroked his arm. 'You go and relax,' she said. 'Leave everything else with me.'

Finn nodded and walked to the bedroom. He flopped onto the air bed, a symbol of his sham relationship, and closed his eyes, both Chris and Kat playing on his mind.

Chapter Nineteen

Katerina

Katerina stared at the invitation in her hands. It was a beautifully-designed, delicate ivory card, with spring green embellishments and gold cursive writing.

"We are delighted to invite you to celebrate our special day with us …"

Katerina sighed, unsure what to do. She didn't expect an invitation, nor for the wedding to be in October, just months away, but here it was, lying in her hand, a tastefully decorated dilemma. How could she go? How could she not go?

Chris walked in and brightened at the sight of the card in her hands.

'Hey, you got your invitation!' he said, snatching it from her excitedly. 'I can't wait to be a groomsman,' he said, waving the card in the air. 'There will be loads of celebrities there – it's going to be an amazing party.'

Katerina nodded and forced a smile. 'I'm sure it will be,' she said. 'Although it's a wedding, not just a party.'

Chris raised an eyebrow at her. 'You don't look that enthusiastic,' he said, suspiciously.

'Of course I am. I am very happy and excited for Finn,' she said brightly, forcing each insincere word from her throat.

Finn had been avoiding her since Chris's illness. He had visited regularly while Chris recovered at home, but every time she tried to talk to him, he ducked away hastily, making excuses of having to rush to another event or appointment. His wedding plans were progressing at speed and she felt as though the gap between them had grown once again, a Willow-sized chasm sitting awkwardly between them.

'Mum,' Chris said, sitting down next to her, his hands on his knees. 'You are going to the wedding, aren't you?' he asked hopefully.

She nodded, unable to think of a decent excuse. She cleared her throat. 'Yes, of course, absolutely.'

He sat still for a moment, picking awkwardly at a thread on the sofa. 'Willow is nice you know. Though I wish …' He paused. 'I wish you and Finn could have worked it out. That would have been pretty cool.'

She pressed her lips together. 'I think when two people have been through a lot together and there's a lot of history between them, it can be hard to overcome that, even if there is still mutual affection,' she said.

'So, you still have feelings for him then?' He flushed slightly, embarrassed at the question.

Katerina was surprised at Chris's forwardness in asking such a personal question. She couldn't quite find the words to express the muddle of emotions she felt when she thought of Finn. She had so many clashing feelings about him it was hard for her to even understand what she felt, let alone find a way to suitably express that to her teenage son. It took her a moment to reply.

'I just meant that Finn and I have been through a lot, we'll always share a past, and I'm very fond of him, but that doesn't mean we could be together.'

Chris frowned. 'I don't get it,' he said, throwing up his hands. 'I think it's a shame.'

Katerina smiled and ruffled his hair. Chris ducked and swatted her hand away playfully. 'Well, you're only thirteen. Give it time,' she said, with a laugh.

He walked away to the kitchen and his question burned in her heart as she turned the invitation over again and again in her hands.

Finn

Finn's intercom buzzed, making him jump and interrupting his lunch. He put down his sandwich and pressed the button on the wall.

'Hello?'

He was surprised to hear Chris's voice crackle back, tinny and anxious over the speaker.

'It's Chris. Can I come up?'

Finn buzzed him in and opened the front door. 'Hey mate, I wasn't expecting you today,' Finn said.

'Um yeah, can I come in?' Chris was slightly pink and out of breath, and dressed in his football gear.

'Sure.' Finn gestured for him to come inside.

'Is Willow here?' Chris asked, peering around. He was shifting nervously from one leg to another and Finn looked at him curiously, wondering why he didn't take his trainers off and make himself at home like he usually did.

'Nope, she's filming today so it's just me,' Finn said. 'Want a drink or something to eat?' he asked, heading to the kitchen.

Chris leant on the kitchen counter. 'No thanks,' he said. 'It's only a passing visit.'

'How's football going?' Finn asked, grabbing himself a glass of water and continuing to eat his sandwich.

Chris nodded. 'Good. I'm getting my energy back now, but I'm not quite back to normal yet. The doctor said that's pretty standard though.' He rummaged in his bag. 'Listen, I know I shouldn't do this, but …' He slapped a bunch of crumpled papers down on the kitchen counter. 'I found these and I wanted you to see them. Mum is going to kill me,' he said, grimacing. He nudged them towards Finn across the counter.

'What are they?' Finn said, confused, picking up a piece of paper from the stack.

'Umm, you'll see. I better go. Mum will worry if I'm late.' He walked quickly towards the door.

'Wait, I can give you a lift if you want?' Finn called out, but Chris shook his head and pulled the front door shut behind him, clearly keen to leave.

Finn frowned at his odd behaviour and sifted through the papers in front of him. It was a bunch of handwritten letters, starting from shortly after Katerina had left. All the letters were marked with crossed-out words, smudges and scribbles. His heart stuttered to see his name on every single page.

He carried them to the living room and gently laid them out in order on the coffee table. Then he read through them all, his eyes blurring to read the sorrow and the fear that poured out from Katerina's neat hand. The letters spanned years, the last one was dated the year before she married Wyatt, trying to tell him the truth. He didn't know why she never sent them. He wondered if writing it all down was just her way of dealing with her emotions or if she planned to send them but was prevented from doing so, but that didn't really matter to him right now. He put the last one down on the table, hardly able to breathe.

Why was Chris giving him these letters? What was the point? Finn sat looking at them, his mind whirling. He heard the door open and swiftly swept the letters into a drawer, unsure what to do with this record of Katerina's secret emotions, uncertain how to feel.

Willow swept in, still glowing from her heavy filming make-up. 'I'm just going to change,' she called out.

Finn nodded. He looked at the drawer that contained the letters and felt a desperate urge to read them again, but he restrained himself. He knew it would only mess with his head.

Katerina

Katerina dried the last dinner plate and stacked it neatly in the cupboard. She looked out at the sheeting rain that thudded against the window. Autumn had well and truly arrived – a new storm to start a new month. The wind and the rain had been relentless for two days and she felt trapped by it, pacing up and down restlessly, unsure why her nerves were so frayed, unable to discern why she felt such a need for change.

'Mum, it's starting!' Chris yelled out from the living room. She took her time making her way from the kitchen, stopping to neaten the shoes in the hallway and straighten the coats, hers still slick with dampness from her afternoon walk.

'Hurry up or you'll miss it!' Chris called urgently.

'Okay, I'm here,' she said, sitting next to him on the sofa and stealing one of his crisps. He mock-glared at her then picked up the remote and turned the volume up as Finn and Willow appeared on the screen. In truth, Katerina had no desire to watch Finn and Willow's interview on *The Ian O'Donaghue Show*, but Chris was desperate to see it and she couldn't think of a way to avoid it, without seeming churlish, so she pretended to be excited along with him.

'I like Dad's suit,' Chris said, and Katerina felt a pinch in her heart at him using the word "dad" when it came to Finn. He had only just started saying it, casually dropping it into conversation, and every time he did it made her feel guilty and sad all over again. If it weren't for her deceitful actions, Finn would have been "Dad" a long time ago.

Katerina felt a stab of jealousy at how Willow and Finn sat closely, their legs pressed together, and the way that Willow was so tactile and affectionate with him, stroking him on the arm. They were obviously very much in love and Katerina hated the way that it made her ache, reminding her starkly of what was lacking in her life. She hadn't experienced affection like that for a long time, and her marriage to Wyatt had been practical rather than romantic. She wanted to feel love and desire again, but for some reason she just couldn't imagine it with anyone else other than Finn, so she tried not to think about it at all.

Willow chatted animatedly about their upcoming wedding plans and Finn chimed in with the occasional witty comment. Inevitably, Ian turned to the subject of how Finn and Willow met, and Katerina winced, knowing that she was an unwanted part of their story.

'Of course, we were all so shocked by the revelations on the Alaska survival show,' Ian said, leaning forward with a shark-like smile. 'I don't think anyone could have seen that coming.'

Willow nodded sagely and Katerina could see Finn's hands tighten together in his lap. Tension flickered across his jaw, and his charming and engaged smile faltered slightly.

'It was just so surprising,' Willow said, her eyes wide. She opened her mouth to continue, but Finn interrupted her.

'Obviously, it's a very private matter now, between Katerina and myself,' Finn said shortly. Katerina felt a surge of gratitude that he was trying to close down the conversation, that he wouldn't use what happened between them for publicity.

Ian nodded. 'So, are you and Katerina on civil terms, or is there no love lost between you two after what she did? And we're all keen to know if you're a part of your son's life now.'

Finn's eyes narrowed. Katerina couldn't quite tell what he was thinking, but she glanced across at Chris to see how he reacted to being mentioned. He looked at her and shrugged.

'Come on Mum, it was bound to come up. It probably always will,' Chris muttered. 'It was huge news.'

He turned his attention resolutely to the TV and Katerina wondered if the burden of guilt she felt about it would ever ease. She doubted it. It was a just punishment, she supposed, for all the lies she had told and the mistakes she made.

'Yes,' Finn said curtly. 'My son is a great kid, and I'm very happy to be part of his life. That's all I have to say about that.'

Katerina could have sighed with relief as talk turned to their potential reality TV deal and she wasn't mentioned again.

'I'm not a kid,' Chris said indignantly, and she had to laugh.

'You always will be to me, little man,' she cooed, and he threw a crisp at her in disgust.

'You never watched the Alaska show, did you?' Chris asked her after Finn and Willow's interview was over.

She shook her head with a grimace. 'Oh no. I've no desire to see it.'

'It's on catch-up,' Chris said. 'Maybe you should check it out sometime? It's great TV.' He flashed her a cheeky smile, just like Finn's, and she laughed at his suggestion.

'Thanks for the tip,' she said sarcastically.

He grinned. 'I'm off to bed.' He stood up with a stretch.

'Goodnight love,' she said, watching him leave.

She curled up on the sofa, flicking idly through the channels, bored. It was at times like these when she missed having someone to share the evenings with. She loved spending time with Chris, but she had no one to put an arm around her, no one to share a bottle of wine with or to make future plans with. She was turning thirty soon and most women her age were out having fun, but she had never felt very connected to them, having had a child at such a young age. She felt older than her years, and lonely. She imagined Finn and Willow out for a drink, celebrating their interview, and tried to shake the image from her mind.

She browsed through catch-up, and inevitably, *Celebrity SOS* popped up on the feed. Her finger paused over the select button. She didn't really want to watch the programme but a part of her felt compelled to. It was like driving slowly past a car crash – she knew she shouldn't, but she wanted to see, to make sense of it all.

She clicked on the first episode, her heart jumping as the opening sequence started.

Phineas stood proudly on Mount Denali, frost in his beard, sweeping his arms wide. 'Welcome to Alaska,' he announced grandly, as the camera panned over him and zoomed over the wilderness.

'We've put ten celebrities here, in the middle of the Gates of the Arctic National Park and Preserve, the northernmost national park in America, where there are no roads, no trails, and virtually no people. Stuck out here in the wild, can they stay safe, stay fed, and stay sane? They'll face hunger, dangerous animals, unpredictable weather, and they'll have to work as a team to survive the two weeks.'

Katerina caught her breath as the camera soared over the scenery. It reminded her of why she had signed up for the programme in the first place. She wanted to experience something completely different, something completely unknown, to challenge herself. Since she was a teenager she had been busy looking after Chris, trying to create a career, trying to make a marriage of convenience work. It had been hard and exhausting, and after her divorce was finalised she had wanted to do something, anything, that was a change of scene.

She watched the episode, her cheeks burning. She never normally watched herself in her work as an actress, she couldn't bear to, and that was when she was playing a role. This was worse because she was watching herself with no script and no costume to hide behind.

She shuddered as she watched the moment when Finn entered the cabin and the cameras captured the look of pure surprise and delight on his face when he noticed her. She remembered her horror at that time and jabbed at the remote to forward through the episode.

The show contained clips of some of the individual interviews with participants that they had filmed in the little outhouse. They showed Finn's. He looked giddy with excitement as he settled in the chair in front of the camera.

'It's, um, it's really nice to see an old friend here,' he said with a smile. 'I'm really pleased to see Katerina again.'

Katerina felt tears prick her eyes at Finn's boyish enthusiasm, before he had found out about her lies. All he knew at this moment was that the girl he once loved, the one who left without a word, was there with him, and he showed nothing but joy at seeing her again. She cringed and switched the TV off. It was too hard to watch any more. She wondered if Finn had watched it too, but she doubted she would ask him. It might just lead to another awkward conversation between them, and they had had enough of those already. She couldn't keep going over old ground, thinking about the love they had lost. She had to move forwards, just like Finn was doing.

She pondered for a moment, the searing views of Alaska still burned into her mind. She realised that the desire to go there hadn't left her. She hadn't seen enough and the experience had been overshadowed by the mess that she had created with her personal dramas.

She checked her diary. She was scheduled for filming for a few weeks, and then … her finger hovered over the next available date she could go.

She hesitated, then switched on her laptop to look at the flights.

Chapter Twenty

Finn

'What are these?' Willow said, her eyebrows raised as she slapped the letters from Katerina down on the coffee table in front of Finn.

He winced, feeling slightly woozy from the champagne they had drunk at dinner to celebrate their interview. 'Ah nothing, they're just, um …' he muttered as Willow gazed at him incredulously.

'Just what? Years of love letters from Katerina? Why are these here? Why were they in the drawer? Why do you even have these?' She crossed her arms and fired the questions at him.

'Listen,' Finn said, trying to clear his mind. 'Chris gave them to me, I honestly don't know why. I shoved them in a drawer because I didn't know what to do with them.'

Willow tutted, shaking her head. 'Don't you think Katerina used Chris to ferry these to you as some sort of message? As some way of messing with your head?' She paced around, her patent stilettos clacking manically on the wooden flooring. 'You know, she just can't stand it that you've moved on, that she doesn't have that control over you any more. I wouldn't be surprised if she gave them to Chris. How manipulative.'

Finn shook his head with a frown. 'I think you're reading too much into this,' he said. 'I'm pretty sure Katerina wouldn't want me to see the letters at all.'

'You don't still have feelings for her, do you?' Willow stood still and stared at him intensely. 'Because you were like a lovesick puppy in Alaska and it wasn't that long ago, Finn!'

He stood up, feeling hot with irritation. 'I don't have feelings for her,' he snapped.

'Good.' Willow huffed. 'You know, I would really prefer it if she didn't come to the wedding.' She looked at him to gauge his reaction. 'I mean, I don't like her, and neither do you. So why does she have to be there? There are other people we can invite in her place.'

'You can't uninvite someone to the wedding,' Finn protested. 'Plus, she's Chris's mum. Like it or not, we're going to have to see her sometimes.'

Willow folded her arms and pouted. 'Fine,' she said gloomily. She turned to go to the bedroom and then spun back to face Finn, her expression softening. 'You know I care about you Finn, don't you?'

He nodded. He knew that was true. Willow had given up trying to win him over, as he'd been clear that he wasn't going to enter a romantic relationship with her, but he knew she cared about him and he saw her as a friend.

'Well then, believe me when I say that Katerina is no good for you,' she said earnestly, her eyes wide. 'She hurt you, and you need to break free from whatever hold she has over you. Including returning those letters.' She indicated the pile of pages with a disdainful look.

Finn looked at the letters, then back at Willow. 'You're right,' he said, and Willow nodded, vindicated, walking away to the bedroom.

Finn stood still, staring at the pages littering the table, wondering what to do with them. He knew what Willow was saying made sense, even if her words were potentially motivated by jealousy. But the logic inherent in what she said simply bounced off his heart. It wouldn't listen to logic or persuasion or reason. He looked at the heart-rending sentiments that Katerina had poured out on those pages, the times she had written his name and cried over it, and all he wanted to do was go to her. It was enough to drive him mad and he almost wished Chris had never brought them to him.

Katerina

Katerina studied her reflection in the bathroom mirror. She reapplied her lipstick and tamed a few stray hairs. She didn't look bad for thirty, she thought. Her hair tumbled in loose waves over her shoulders, the slightest hint of auburn hidden among the dark tendrils, her slender figure wrapped in a simple off-the-shoulder black dress. Her red lipstick added a pop of colour, both classic and a little bit sexy, she thought, admiring the smoky eyeshadow the make-up artist had applied.

She headed back into the bar. She hadn't wanted a fuss for her birthday, but her agent had insisted on upscaling her modest plans, scolding her for not wanting to mark the big occasion and saying she must let her hair down for once.

Katerina smiled at the group of people milling around her. She didn't have many close friends, but she did have lots of good acquaintances from her years of working on dramas, many friendly co-stars whom she was delighted to see there tonight. She flitted from one person to another, thanking them for coming, enjoying the drinks that flowed freely. Her agent had been right – it felt good to have a night out for once and not feel weighed down by problems and worries.

She felt a hesitant tap on her shoulder, and swung round, feeling a warm wave of happiness to see Finn standing there.

'Oh hi,' she said. She had invited him and Willow out of politeness, not expecting them to turn up. He leaned in and gave her a kiss on the cheek. She tried not to breathe him in too deeply, or stare too longingly at him in his navy suit. His hair was tousled with gel, and he looked trim and toned. She guessed he'd been working out, probably in preparation for his wedding.

'Thanks for coming,' she said, smiling. 'Where's Willow?' She looked around.

'Ah, she's in LA, partly for work and partly for her hen do,' Finn said, shrugging. Katerina tried not to feel too pleased. It would be nice to see Finn on his own for a change. She hadn't seen much of him recently, and whenever he was around, Willow was there too, staring suspiciously at her and making comments which were thinly disguised snipes.

'Can I get you a drink?' Finn asked and she held up her champagne glass, still half-full.

'I'm good thanks.'

'Happy birthday!' he said. 'The big three–oh.'

She rolled her eyes. 'I'm so old!'

He laughed. 'Well, you look amazing.' She beamed at the compliment. Her cheeks were flushed but she was sure it was the champagne she'd been drinking all evening, not Finn's presence, that was making her feel a little too warm.

'It was your big birthday just two weeks ago, too,' she said. 'I saw your Instagram pictures of the trip to Vegas. It looked like you had a great time.' Katerina had wanted to see Finn on his thirtieth but he'd been away. She had helped Chris pick out a present for his dad, but she hadn't known what to get him from herself, and she wasn't sure he would want anything from her anyway.

Finn nodded. 'It was a surprise gift from Willow. And speaking of gifts, I got you something.' He was looking pleased with himself. He took a slender gift-wrapped present from the inside pocket of his suit jacket.

'Oh, you didn't have to,' she murmured, turning it over in her hands, admiring the delicately embossed silver wrapping paper, the carefully curled ribbon. She felt guilty that she hadn't got him anything.

'Are you going to open it?' he asked, nodding at the present.

She delicately removed the paper. '*Breakfast at Tiffany's*,' she said, clutching the novella and looking up at him.

'It's a first edition,' he said proudly. 'It was hard to find, but, well, you know, it's a special birthday.'

She smoothed her fingers over the cover. She knew a first edition in this pristine condition would have been difficult to track down, and expensive. It meant all the more to her because this book was the reason they were thrown together all those years ago at school. In her mind she still saw every scene and heard every word as spoken by her and Finn.

'Thank you,' she said, unsure what to say. 'That really means a lot, Finn.' What she left unsaid was that the best present he had given her was simply the gift of his time that evening. The fact that he had shown up, and wished her happy birthday, was more than she could have asked, more than she could have expected, given how bad their relationship was just months ago.

He smiled. 'I'm glad you like it.'

'How's wedding planning going?' she asked, trying to keep her voice level. 'It seems to be happening so quickly. I can't quite believe you've managed to plan a wedding in just a few short months.'

She thought his face darkened a little at the question, a slight frown flitting momentarily between his eyebrows. 'It's going well. There's a lot to do in the next two weeks. It'll be a really good day, although I don't think I've seen your RSVP yet,' he said, a little flatly, she thought.

'Ah, that's something I kind of need to talk to you about,' she said, shifting uncomfortably in her heels. 'I can't make the wedding.'

He nodded sombrely, not seeming too surprised or even disappointed by what she said. 'That's a shame. How come?' he asked.

'Well, you may not believe this, but now that I've finished filming my current series, I'm going on holiday next week. To Alaska,' she said. He raised his eyebrows, and then let out a laugh.

'You're joking, right?' he said incredulously.

'No, I'm being totally serious. I really want to go, although this time I'm going to a nice lodge where the food will be caught for me and I won't have to fight with any bears.' She smiled. 'I'll be gone for a few weeks. Chris will be staying with my mum, so don't worry, he can still be your groomsman and see you as usual, although I guess you'll be away for a few weeks on your honeymoon in ...'

'... the Maldives.' He shook his head. 'Well, you have surprised me. It's a shame you can't come to the wedding though.'

She gave him a sad smile. 'How can I possibly go to your wedding, Finn?' She spoke, not quite thinking, her words sliding out quickly.

He frowned. 'What do you mean?'

She stared at him for a moment, knowing she couldn't really elaborate. 'Oh nothing, really. Just that I can't go of course, I'll be thousands of miles away!' she said brightly, forcing a ridiculous smile, and they looked at each other, and both of them knew she wasn't being sincere.

Finn opened his mouth to say something but Katerina caught sight of a broad-shouldered man just over his shoulder and waved him over. As much as she wanted to talk to Finn, this was important.

'James, so good to see you, thank you for coming.' She kissed James on the cheek and turned to Finn. 'Finn, this is James Boldwood.'

James reached out and shook Finn's hand. 'Nice to meet you,' he said. 'Katerina has been raving about you to me for a few weeks now, so I'm glad we finally have the chance to meet.'

Finn looked at Katerina and raised his eyebrow, a look that Katerina had always loved and found irresistible. She tried to ignore the way it made butterflies swirl in her stomach and took a breath. 'James is a record producer,' she explained. 'He's interested to talk to you more about your songwriting, like the song you sang on *Celebrity SOS*.'

Her cheeks burned at the mention of the show and of their song, but there was no point pretending it hadn't happened. What mattered now was that she wanted Finn's talent to be recognised. She had seen it, long ago, and she wanted others to see it too. She wanted Finn to be happy and successful. He deserved it, and if she could help in some way then she was determined to do so. It wouldn't rectify the harm and the hurt she'd caused him, nothing ever could, but she hoped it would help a little. She had been hoping to introduce him to James and tonight presented her with the perfect opportunity, quite unexpectedly.

Finn looked at her, his eyes gleaming in the low light of the bar. She couldn't quite read his expression, but she thought he looked pleased.

'I'll leave you two to chat,' she said, walking away to leave Finn and James to talk, hoping for good things for her friend.

Finn

Finn spent a long time in conversation with James. It was the most he had talked about music for a long time. His recent conversations were always about photo shoots and magazine deals and the wedding. He rarely had a chance to explore other opportunities, so this was a welcome change, and the night slid by quickly.

James checked his watch. 'I'd better be going now,' he said. 'I'm so glad we finally had the chance to meet. Katerina has been singing your praises to me for weeks and I would have been in touch sooner, but I was working with Kiara Jacobs on her new album in New York.' He took out a business card from his pocket. 'Call me. We'll arrange a meeting and we'll get you in the studio, okay?' He handed Finn his business card and walked away, and Finn couldn't help the delighted smile that spread across his face as he looked at the record producer's contact information.

Finn glanced around. A few of the guests were starting to leave, and he couldn't see Katerina anywhere. He walked through the bar, scanning people's faces, searching for her. His mind replayed over and over her words about the wedding and he couldn't help but feel a sense of relief that she wasn't coming.

The truth was that he didn't want her to come. He didn't want to stand at the top of the aisle and watch Willow walk down it, only for his eyes to drift to Katerina, which they always did, no matter where he was or who he was with. It was as though she were the only woman he could see, and nothing could stop his gaze from seeking her out.

Despite his relief he was also confused by what she said. *What did she mean?* There was something about the way she said it that made her comment seem about so much more than just the diary clash she was referring to.

Finn spotted the door to the roof terrace. He could do with clearing his mind. He walked out into the night, the air pleasantly fresh from the recent rain, the terrace surface spattered with droplets. It was deserted but for one lone figure, the glow from the decorative lanterns illuminating her hair with a halo of warm light. She stood with her back to him, looking out over the Thames, which flowed before the riverside bar, dark and swollen from the rain.

Finn walked up beside her, his hands in his pockets. 'Hey, you shouldn't be out here alone on your birthday.'

She turned to face him with a warm smile on her lips. 'I just needed some fresh air. How did it go with James?' She looked at him eagerly.

'He's very interested in working with me,' Finn said. 'I guess you pulled a few strings huh?'

A frown flitted between her eyebrows, darkening her expression. 'No, I didn't Finn. I just wanted to introduce you. James wanting to work with you has nothing to do with me, it has everything to do with your talent. I sent him the clip of you singing in Alaska and he was genuinely interested. He would have contacted you anyway, but I'm glad I got to introduce you two tonight.'

Finn saw the sincerity shining in her eyes as she leaned forward and rested a gentle hand on his arm.

'You're so talented,' she said. 'Believe in yourself a bit more.'

Finn could hardly speak. The touch of her hand sent sparks up and down his arm, the quiet words she spoke went deep into his heart. Katerina believed in him when he was a teenager in a grotty flat, strumming songs on an out-of-tune guitar. She still believed in him now, even after all they'd been through.

Finn once thought that his anger at her would never abate. But the fury which once consumed him had burnt off, extinguished by the realisation that Katerina also suffered with the decision foisted upon her to leave and to keep him from Chris. Chris's illness united them again, the letters he'd seen showed Kat's heart remained his for a long time after she left. After all his anger and all the drama, the emotions he previously had for Kat remained intact. And were perhaps even stronger for having survived what they'd been through.

Finn studied her expression. He thought if he spoke his voice would shake but it didn't. His voice was low, but steady. 'Kat, what did you mean when you said you couldn't possibly come to my wedding?'

She looked out over the river, unable or unwilling to meet his gaze. The eager smile on her mouth fell away. 'I can't watch you get married,' she said softly. 'It's too hard.'

'Why?' Finn pressed her. 'Because of the way you felt about me in the past? Or because of the way you feel about me in the present?'

Her gaze flickered back to him and he could see the tears that shimmered in her eyes, reflecting the light of the lanterns. 'What does it matter?' she said wearily.

He reached out and took her hand, holding it firmly, savouring the feel of her skin on his. 'It matters,' he said insistently.

She didn't speak, but her fingers curled around his and a tear rolled down her cheek as she stared at their entwined hands.

'Kat, if there's any reason I shouldn't marry Willow, then you should say so,' he said. He waited, almost holding his breath. Mere seconds passed before her response, but they moved at a glacial pace and Finn was both desperate for her reply and fearful of it.

She met his eyes and held them as she opened her mouth to reply. 'I just want you to be happy,' she said simply, giving him no clues.

'You made me happier than anyone else ever could,' Finn said. He stepped forward and put his hands on the side of her face, tilting her head up to him. All he wanted to know was if there was a chance for them. The tiniest indication of hope would be enough.

She leaned towards him as if to kiss him on the cheek, but as he turned his head to speak her mouth met his, just fleetingly. He felt the softness of her lips, tasted the salt from the tears that dampened her cheeks. She moved away quickly, the lights from the lanterns flickering in her eyes, and Finn felt flooded with disappointment at how the kiss had ended so swiftly, leaving every cell in his body burning for more.

Katerina ran her fingers over his cheek. 'Marry Willow and be happy,' she whispered, her lips grazing his ear. This was the response that Finn had dreaded, the words he didn't want to hear.

She smiled softly then began to walk away, and he stood rooted to the spot, unsure what to do. He wondered if he should tell her the truth about Willow, but that wouldn't matter if she'd moved on and was encouraging him to do the same. His indecision and emotional turmoil rendered him mute.

She reached the doors and turned back to him. 'Do you remember how we had to keep the fire always burning in Alaska?' There was a faraway look in her eyes.

Finn nodded, his jaw clenched, his throat knotted.

'Well, I always kept a little bit of our spark alight. There will always be part of me aflame for you, Finn Drayson.'

She left the terrace, the sound of her heels tapping swiftly away.

But there was hope. She'd given him hope. Now Finn needed to talk to Willow.

Katerina

Katerina walked away from the terrace, her head held high. The bar was largely empty now. She took her coat and bag, and left without a moment's hesitation. She followed the path beside the river, matching the pace of its steady flow with her footsteps. The tears were on her cheeks and she did nothing to wipe them away, letting them course down her face.

She'd told him to be happy, told him to marry Willow. He deserved a fresh start, not an old romance, sullied by sorrow and anger.

Her skin still tingled from where he'd touched her. The way he'd looked into her eyes had made her entire body tremble. She had intended to kiss him on the cheek, but instead her mouth had found his, like it had done all those years ago when they first kissed. She had wanted to kiss him again so badly, so intoxicated by his presence that it made her head swim. But she couldn't do that to Willow; she had enough on her conscience already. It took every ounce of self-control she had to wrest herself away from his lips and leave him on the terrace. Perhaps she shouldn't have said what she did before she left, but the words escaped her mouth, tumbling out into the night before she could stop them.

She followed the river, and made her way home. It was time to move on.

Finn shuffled uncomfortably as the tailor stared at him in surprise.

'You haven't tried it on yet?' he asked, looking at Finn over his spectacles, indicating to the suit that hung on the back of the door of the changing room.

'Not yet. I'm waiting for Willow,' Finn said.

The tailor walked away with an imperceptible tut, the sound of his shoes softened by the plush carpeting in the bridal boutique.

Finn turned to look at himself in the mirror. He was supposed to be trying on his wedding suit while Willow was having a dress fitting. He hadn't intended to be here at all. He had planned to collect Willow from the airport and take her home so they could talk, but her flight was delayed and she'd rung him from LA, babbling about meeting him directly at the boutique, then hanging up before he had a chance to respond. Since then he'd not been able to reach her. So here he was, staring at a suit he had no desire to wear, waiting for his fake fiancée to arrive.

The changing room door opened. 'Hey! I finally made it!' she said cheerfully. She gave him a brief hug then held him at arms' length. 'Why haven't you got your suit on?'

Finn cleared his throat. 'Willow, I think we should go home.'

She stared at him, one hand on her hip, eyeing him suspiciously. 'No, I think you should try on your suit.' She turned and shut the changing room door. 'What's going on?'

Finn didn't want to have this conversation here but in the event he didn't have to open his mouth. Willow was looking at him, and understanding filled her eyes. 'You're not with me on this, are you?' she asked. 'Your heart's not in it.' She stated it quietly, matter of factly.

Finn shook his head. 'I'm sorry Willow.'

Willow huffed with exasperation. 'Come on Finn, you can do this. I've had wonderful meetings in LA about a series focusing on us. There are so many offers on the table. Think of all the work, and the money that we'll lose if we back out now.'

Finn sat down on one of the plump, luxurious couches and gestured for Willow to join him. She sat next to him and folded her long legs, her skin golden from the LA sun.

'I know this isn't a good time, and I know I'm letting you down. I know our agents will be pissed off, and all the work we've secured will fall through.' Finn's financial situation remained precarious, but the money meant nothing to him when there was a chance to be with Kat again. 'But I can't have a fake wedding, a fake marriage, not when …'

'… not when you're actually in love with someone, for real,' Willow interjected. There was no bitterness or anger in her voice.

Finn nodded.

'I don't understand the hold she has on you,' Willow said sombrely. There was no need to say who she was.

Finn met her gaze. 'I can't explain it. Other than that I gave her my heart a long time ago, and she still has it. There's a chance. I have to take it.'

'Did she tell you there was?'

'Actually she told me to marry you,' Finn said.

Willow snorted. 'Finally something she and I can actually agree on.'

She sighed and gave him a weak smile. 'I guess we'd better talk to our agents, find the right way to announce this.'

Finn was taken aback at her cool, collected reaction, the way she whipped out her phone and began making a to-do list, the way that she just calmly accepted the break-up of their false relationship.

'I thought you would be more upset,' he said, raising an eyebrow.

Willow put down her phone with a pained expression. 'Honestly Finn, I saw this coming. Every time you spoke about her, or saw her, or saw Chris, I could see it in your eyes. I knew it was only a matter of time. That's why I was trying to rush the wedding!'

'It was that obvious?' Finn said.

She gave him a small smile. 'To me it was.' She turned to him and put her hands on his shoulders. 'I hope you'll be happy. Genuinely, I really do.'

Finn wrapped his arms around her. 'You deserve so much more than a fake marriage for magazine headlines. You deserve someone who really loves you and who wants to marry you for real. I hope you find them.'

She laughed out loud. 'Me too!' She gave him a gentle shove. 'Go get her Finn.'

Chapter Twenty-One

Katerina

Katerina took a deep breath of pure mountain air and stared in wonder at the sunset across the bay. The sun spread fire across the sky, suffusing the snowy peaks with red and gold, and setting the water aglow. She leaned on the rough wooden porch rail and wished she could press a pause button to enjoy this moment a little longer. The air was cold, but it felt a little warmer than when they had filmed there. Fortunately, this time she didn't have to make her own fire. She came here for the space and the solitude rather than for a survival challenge. There was no fishing, no foraging, and no Finn, she thought, with a tinge of sadness that she brushed away.

Chris had been disappointed about her not going to the wedding, but she got the sense that he understood why she couldn't go, although neither of them said it. He was wiser than his years, wiser than she'd been at his age.

She checked her watch and worked out the time difference, realising it would now be around 2.30 p.m. in England. The ceremony was due to begin. Finn would probably be waiting nervously for his bride, fiddling with his tie, trying to make a joke to diffuse the tension. Willow would be surrounded by giggling bridesmaids, sipping champagne, getting ready to walk down the aisle. Katerina imagined Chris in his suit, looking so grown-up, and she was sure he would be so proud and happy to be there.

She imagined Finn's face as he saw Willow walking down the aisle. She wondered if he would cry a little or feel choked up. Katerina thought back to when she was a teenager and she had imagined their own wedding in her head, walking down the aisle towards Finn, her dad beaming, Finn's mum frail but proud. She had picked out the music, imagined the details of the dress. Childish dreams, she thought now, shaking her head at their impossibility.

She walked back into the cabin, shutting the glass door quickly against the freezing air, and looked over the pile of books she'd brought with her to read. A slim volume nestled in the middle of the pile and she reached for it, toppling the rest of them over. She ignored them and ran her fingers over her birthday gift from Finn. *Breakfast at Tiffany's*. She hugged the book close to her chest and curled before the fire, a glass of wine beside her.

She opened to the first page and an envelope fell out. She frowned, scooping it off the floor, and opened it, instantly recognising the handwriting on the papers neatly folded inside. The envelope contained the letters she'd written to Finn after she left him. She turned them over in her hands, utterly baffled, wondering how Finn had got hold of them, wondering why they were tucked into the book.

'Our son thought it would be a good idea for me to see those,' a voice behind her said.

She jumped up and shrieked, throwing the letters on the floor and almost knocking over her wine glass. Gasping, she put her hand to her heart in shock.

'Finn! What the hell are you doing here?' she cried out, her heart pounding from the shock of seeing him standing in her cabin. She blinked hard, wondering how much wine she'd drunk, but it was definitely him. In the flesh. In Alaska.

'Wait, it's supposed to be your wedding day!' Had she got the date wrong?

'Um, yeah,' he said, looking sheepish. He tucked his hands into his jeans and nudged the thick rug with his shoe. 'I'm not getting married today.'

'I can see that,' Katerina said, breathing steadily to calm her pulse. 'Did you guys have to postpone for some reason?' She was already hating the way her heart had begun to beat erratically with hope.

He shook his head. 'I'm not marrying Willow.' He gazed at her, his eyes reflecting the leaping flames of the fire behind her. 'I can't.'

'Why?' she breathed out the word, barely a whisper, afraid of what he might say and what he might not say.

'Willow and I were never in a real relationship,' he said.

She frowned at him in confusion. 'But … But … I'm sorry, I don't understand. What do you mean you …?'

'It was all for show, for work, for headlines,' he said. 'I was so angry and broken-hearted that I entered into it without really thinking and I let it go too far.'

Katerina found the edge of the sofa and leaned on it, her mouth open and her knees weak with shock. 'I had no idea …' she murmured. *None of it had been real? All the Instagram posts, the moving in together? The engagement*?

'I guess you didn't see the headlines about the wedding being cancelled then?' Finn asked.

Katerina shook her head. 'I've been offline.'

Finn walked over and stood before her, his eyes searching hers.

'Wait, why *are* you here?' she asked, her voice shaking.

He reached out and gently brushed a strand of her hair away from her forehead. She closed her eyes and luxuriated in that brief touch and the tenderness with which he did it, bringing back a multitude of memories.

'Ever since you left me I've been like a puzzle put back together in the wrong order,' he said. 'With one Katerina-shaped piece missing from here.' He took her fingers and pressed them to his chest. Katerina shivered as he lifted her fingers to his mouth and pressed them to his lips.

'But what about all the lies I told, what about Chris, what about what I did?' she said eventually.

Finn sighed. 'I don't want what happened in the past to rob us of the future,' he said. 'We've both made lots of mistakes, and I want, *I need*, to start doing things right. And you, you're what I got right in the first place … I never lost the love I had for you. It's survived everything we've been through.'

Katerina couldn't speak. She was overwhelmed by the words Finn had spoken, by the expression in his eyes as he looked at her.

'I was going to wait till you got back, but I feel like I've waited long enough, lost enough time. I didn't want to wait anymore,' he said. 'I need to know Kat, can you love me again? The way that I love you, the way I've always loved you?'

Ever since she had left Finn at the age of sixteen, Kat had closed off her heart. All her love had been reserved for Chris, and the feelings she had for Finn were locked away. As she looked into the eyes of the boy, now man, she loved, she allowed herself to open up that part of her heart reserved for him.

'I'm yours Finn. I always was, and I always will be,' she said, without hesitation, without fear. There was nothing standing in their way now – no more lies, no more secrets, no one telling them to change their minds.

He wrapped his arms around her and drew her close, pressing his lips against hers. Katerina shivered despite the warmth of the cabin, and kissed him back, with all the fierce sweetness she remembered from when she had first fallen in love with him. It felt both new and familiar, utterly enthralling and completely comfortable, as though their two hearts had finally found their way back home.

Finn ran his hands through her hair as the kiss deepened, and the longing she felt for him flooded over her, stronger than anything she had felt for anyone. Only Finn could make her feel that way, and she hadn't felt that way in a long time.

He picked her up and took her to the bedroom. This time there was no cluttered apartment, no fear of being discovered by disapproving parents. It was as though time had simply stalled and they were back where they should always have been, in each other's arms.

Finn

Finn lay looking at Katerina for a long time after she had fallen asleep. He relished every second of watching her, so peaceful and quiet. He couldn't quite believe that he was lying by her side again, after all this time, after so much had occurred.

She stirred and opened her eyes, looking at him with affection, a look he had replayed over and over in his memories.

'Hey,' she said, leaning on one elbow, pressing her lips against his. 'What time is it?'

Finn checked his watch. 'Late. Are you hungry?'

She nodded. 'I'll order some room service.'

Katerina slid out of the sheets, grabbing his T-shirt and pulling it on over a pair of pyjama bottoms. The suite was warm from the fire and Finn was perfectly comfortable following her in just his boxers, guessing from her appreciative glances that she didn't mind either. She phoned in their order and they curled up on the sofa together. Katerina rested her head against his shoulder, running a finger over the scar on his chest, the tiny delicate movement making him shiver with a longing for her that was nowhere near satisfied.

'So, what do we do now?' he asked.

She raised her head. 'The food will be here soon.'

Finn laughed. 'No, I meant, you and me. Us. Where do we go from here?' He wrapped his arms around her and pulled her close, his mouth resting on her hair, breathing her in. 'You will always be part of my past Kat, but I want you to be my future too. You and Chris.' The idea of it seemed so perfect to him that he could hardly say the words, fearful that somehow the bubble might burst, or that he might wake to find it was all a dream.

Katerina ran a hand fondly over his cheek, lightly tracing his lips with her fingers. 'That's what I want too. You, me, and Chris. We could be …' She inhaled sharply and a tear swelled and spilled from her eye. 'We could be a family,' she said.

Finn swallowed against the tears that knotted in his throat and buried his face in her hair. 'A family,' he agreed, and then her mouth found his once again. Her hands pressed the back of his head, her fingers grasping his hair, until they were interrupted by a knock on the door with their food.

Katerina drew back and went to collect the food. As she returned, Katerina glanced at the terrace doors and gasped. 'The Northern Lights,' she said, pointing at them excitedly.

Finn joined her and they stood before the glass, as emerald and ruby mists danced their mysterious way across the darkened sky, the stars shining through beneath the veil of colour.

'I love Alaska,' she said, leaning back against Finn. He chuckled and tightened his arms around her, feeling complete for the first time since she had left him those years ago. 'And you, Finn. I love you. Always.'

Chapter Twenty-Two

One year later

'It's on the radio again,' Katerina said with delight, as she turned up the volume on the car stereo.

Finn chuckled and gave her a quick sideways glance before returning his eyes to the road ahead. 'You don't have to listen to it every time it comes on.'

She opened her window slightly and a cool breeze wafted over her, ruffling a few stray strands of hair. 'I love this song. You wrote it for me and I'm going to listen to it on repeat till I die,' she said, laughing. 'I'm so glad everyone else seems to love it as much as I do. It's been number one for ages now.'

Katerina looked at Finn as he drove and she felt so proud of him. His meeting with James the record producer had led him on the path he'd always wanted and his talent always merited – to be a singer-songwriter. He'd written the most beautiful album, inspired by their love, he said, and it was topping the charts in many countries.

He drove into the car park and pulled up, switching off the engine and turning to face her.

She never tired of looking at him, never ceased to be amazed that they were together after all they had been through. He was the most handsome she had ever seen him, his skin lightly tanned from the summer just ending, his eyes matching the deep blue of the suit he wore.

She checked her reflection in the car mirror one last time. Her hair was in a simple braid, and her eyes were shining. Happiness was the only filter she needed today.

'Are you ready for this?' he asked.

'I've been dreaming of this day for a long time,' she said.

'Is it how you imagined it would be?' Finn said, and his forehead creased with worry.

She squeezed his hand to reassure him. 'It's better than any of my dreams,' she said. 'Let's go.'

Finn got out of the car and opened her door for her, extending his hand. She smoothed down her vintage-style dress. The cream silk chiffon floated around her, the embroidered draped sleeves fluttered over her shoulders and upper arms. She carried a small bouquet of pink roses that Finn had picked for her from their garden. The empire line cut of the dress concealed the tiny bump which Finn rested his hand on for a moment, and they smiled conspiratorially at each other, their secret, for now.

Finn took her hand and they turned to walk towards the steps of the county hall, where Chris and her mum awaited them, beaming. Katerina's eyes dampened to see her son, standing tall and proud in his suit, the mirror image of his father. There was a time when she thought Chris would never even know Finn, let alone be at their wedding day.

Kat felt her heart soar with happiness. There were no photographers, no social media posts or magazine deals to worry about. There were no crowds, no fanfare. Just her and Finn, and their growing family, together, forever.

Thank You

Dear reader,

Thank you so much for choosing to read *Celebrity SOS: Love Survives*. I must admit that Finn and Kat's story is one of my favourites. I adored writing about the dramatic Alaskan scenery, and the dramatic scenes between the two teenage sweethearts.

I love survival shows and films about people who conquer challenging environments. I think it's partly because I know I wouldn't survive five minutes in the wild, and I can watch them with admiration from the comfort of my sofa, eating chocolate and feeling thankful that I'll never have to do such a thing.

If you've enjoyed *Celebrity SOS* I'd be so grateful if you could leave a review on Goodreads or the website where you bought the book. To find out more about me and for updates about my upcoming books, follow me on Twitter, Facebook and Instagram (details on the following 'About the Author' page). If you sign up to my newsletter, you'll get my free novellas to download as well as exclusive updates from me direct to your inbox: www.BookHip.com/RZSDFSW.

Thanks again and get in touch – I'd love to hear from you!

Love Helen

x

About the Author

Helen Buckley lives in Bedfordshire with her husband and two sons. After working in the charity sector in the UK and abroad, she turned her hand to writing stories of fame, romance, and happy ever afters.
Apart from being addicted to writing and enjoying soft play with her sons, she's an avid reader, action-movie fan, and chocolate addict.

Follow Helen on social media to find out more about her work or to get in touch:

www.twitter.com/HelenCBuckley
www.instagram.com/helencatherinebuckley
www.facebook.com/HelenBuckleyAuthor

More Choc Lit
from
Helen Buckley

Strictly on Ice

Book 1 – Spotlight Series

When falling in love comes with the risk of falling flat on your face ...

Former Olympic skating champion Katie Saunders is well known for her 'ice queen' persona in the press. On the face of it, perhaps Katie should have forgiven her former skating partner and ex-boyfriend, Alex Michaelson, for the accident that shattered both her ankle and their Olympic dreams – but she just can't seem to let it go.

When Katie reluctantly agrees to take part in a new TV skating show, it's only because she's desperate for cash. What she didn't count on is the drama – not only is she partnered up with infamous love rat rugby player Jamie Welsh, but one of the judges is none other than Alex Michaelson himself.

As the show progresses, will Katie be shown the hard way, once again, that romance on the ice should remain strictly off-limits?

Visit www.choc-lit.com for more details.

Introducing Choc Lit

We're an independent publisher creating a delicious selection of fiction. Quality stories with a romance at the heart.

See our selection here:

www.choc-lit.com

We'd love to hear how you enjoyed *Celebrity SOS: Love Survives.* Please leave a review on the eBook store where you purchased this novel or visit **www.choc-lit.com** and give your feedback.

Choc Lit novels are selected by genuine readers like yourself. We only publish stories our Tasting Panel want to see in print. Our reviews and awards speak for themselves.

Could you be a Star Selector
and join our Tasting Panel?

Would you like to play a role in choosing which novels we decide to publish? Do you enjoy reading women's fiction? Then you could be perfect for our Tasting Panel.

Visit here for more details:

www.choc-lit.com/join-the-choc-lit-tasting-panel

Keep in touch:

Sign up for our monthly newsletter Choc Lit Spread for all the latest news and offers: **www.spread.choc-lit.com.**

Follow us on:

Twitter: **@ChocLituk**

Facebook: **Choc Lit**

Instagram: **ChocLituk**

Where heroes are like chocolate – irresistible!

Printed in Great Britain
by Amazon

36213581R00126